Under an
Angry Sky

Penny Bill

ENBROOK

A catalogue record for this book is
available from the British Library

ISBN 978-0-9573988-0-1

Cover Design by John Oakey Design
Photography: © Hannah Durant / Flickr

ENBROOK

For Chris, Emma and Charlotte

With special thanks also to Danny Rhodes and
Luke Thompson for their time and expertise, and to
family and friends for their encouragement.

Under An Angry Sky

One

When Dad wasn't looking, I picked up the photograph on the mantelpiece – the one of Mum and me, sitting on her lap. I was only a baby then. I liked the way she'd tied my hair into a topknot with two plastic ladybirds, and the way it stuck up like a firework. I was wearing a lacy cardigan that had definitely been home-knitted, and I thought my mother could have made it herself. I'd looked at the photograph so many times, I could picture it with my eyes shut. Mum had brown, wavy hair touching her shoulders, and a kind smile. I'd always had trouble with that smile. She didn't look like the sort of mother who would abandon a baby, especially as she'd gone to all that trouble to make my hair so pretty. But that was exactly what she had done. Mrs Gayle said.

I asked Dad, and he said whatever Mrs Gayle said was usually right. The woman in the photograph, my mother, was wearing a charm bracelet with a bell, a lantern and a key, which must've tickled her hand. She had a white dress on, splattered with posies of leaves and blue daisies. Sprigs, Mrs Gayle called them. And she said the neckline of my mother's dress was called sweetheart, which I thought was just right, because she looked summery and easy to love. I spent ages trying to copy the pattern in my sketch pad. It was hard to see

1

how a mother who took that much care over her frock, and propped me up so smartly on her lap, with a hand around my side to stop me falling, would leave a child behind.

Dad had taken the photo away once. He said it was troubling me too much, but Mrs Gayle had fought my corner because she said I'd become depressed and not at all myself. So Dad relented and the photograph was returned to its place on the mantelpiece, but I wasn't to keep picking it up and taking it off to my room. It was to stay in its place and I wasn't to be *obsessed* with it. That's what Mrs Gayle said, and she had to explain what that meant. After that, I only took the photo down when Mrs Gayle had gone home in the evening and Dad was busy in his office.

The other strange thing about the photograph was that my mother's eyes were grey, as glassy grey as a winter sky, whereas mine were brown-cow dark. I loved Mum's eyes. They were smiling but sort of drifting at the same time, as if she had a dream going on. I often wondered about that dream. I imagined it was the thing that took her away, and I asked Mrs Gayle about it once, but she said there was no understanding why people did what people did sometimes, and I wasn't to brood about it, because I had a dad who loved me and a housekeeper who took care of me, and that was two people more than a lot of children in the world had. I'm glad she told me that my father loved me, because you'd never be able to tell otherwise.

Try as I might, I couldn't help watching my dad. He was pacing up and down the kitchen flags again, looking out of the window with a worried expression.

"Concentrate on the game, Imogen Wise. You'll miss a pair," Mrs Gayle scolded. She never could stand playing cards unless her partner was paying absolute attention. I was trying hard, but as soon as I'd put down my card, my gaze wandered back to my father. He was rubbing his chin now, leaning on the sill and peering out at the rain.

"Will you come and sit down, Andrew. It won't get any better with you staring out at it."

"The level's rising, Mrs Gayle. I don't like the look of it."

His words were making me anxious, although I couldn't tell exactly what I was supposed to be worrying about. Dad had already piled sandbags around the back door, three layers high. Mrs Gayle said it always did the trick. It had worked five years ago, when the river had flooded a third of the valley, and it would work now.

"King."

I paid her three cards, the last a Jack.

"One back."

"Good," Mrs Gayle said, but she laid another Jack.

"One card left," I replied, but my last was a King, and that gave me three more cards to get rid of. "It's not fair."

"Life never is, Imogen."

Dad opened the door, to check the rising water level in the back yard.

"We might bail it across. What do you think? We could pass the worst of it through to the front. That drain's clogged again."

I could tell Mrs Gayle wasn't best pleased with all Dad's fretting, but she went to fetch the stack of buckets, probably to shut him up. Sometimes Mrs Gayle and my dad had an understanding that passed between them, like the buckets we were handing from one to another, across the kitchen to the front door. They didn't use words, just looks. And I could tell the looks had words in them, but I didn't know what they meant because I was only nine.

Dad opened the door, moved the top two layers of bags to one side, and climbed over into the back yard, which by then was a dark green pool. You could hardly see gaps between the rods of rain, and it was making a deafening roar as it smacked down on everything. Dad's jacket turned black. He was standing in the water up to his calves, dragging his bucket low to collect as much as he dared, as much as I could carry. The rain was soaking his hair, running in a river from his nose to his jacket, and I thought he looked like a waterfall, which would've been funny if he was a different sort of dad.

"You stay in the dry, Imogen. Try not to slop too much on the floor."

He was shouting over the rain music. Mrs Gayle was taking each bucket from me, hurrying across the kitchen and chucking the water outside the front door in that purposeful way of hers. She likes a definite job to do.

The water in the yard never seemed to be going down and we must have done more than thirty loads, but I didn't dare argue. Dad's mouth was working away, the muscles tight around it like sprung wire, his eyes keen as a huntsman.

It was Mrs Gayle who put a stop to it all.

"That should do it, Andrew. My back won't take any more."

We all peered out of the back door, making our assessment of the new state of things. Sure enough, the water level had sunk to half way up the first step. Dad repositioned the bags and shut the door firmly in our faces, pulling the bolt across. Then he went to the front, where the gravel path slopes up towards the drive and the entrance gate. The land is slightly

4

higher at the front of the house, with less risk of a flood because it slopes away to one side, but you'd never know it if you looked at my dad's face.

"You ought to be getting home now, Mrs Gayle," he suggested. "Would you like a lift? The lane might be bad."

"No thank you, Andrew. You can't leave Imogen here by herself."

"I'd bring her with us."

"I'll be fine. If I can't get through, I'll turn around and come right back."

"Mind the bend at Three Boys. The water often collects there."

Mrs Gayle gave Dad a look as she did up the zip of her anorak, and I knew it meant she was perfectly able to look after herself. She pushed her curls inside the hood and pulled the toggles tight.

"Now you look after your dad, Imogen. You can show him that new card game I taught you. Bed at eight, mind."

"Yes, Mrs Gayle," I replied, knowing full well my dad wouldn't be playing a game with me, not now. Not anytime.

Dad helped her up the drive to her car, holding his umbrella over her head, even though she'd told him not to bother – her hair was past worrying about, and anyone born and bred in Yorkshire never minded a spot of rain. He climbed back over the sandbags and shut the door. The water made quick puddles around his boots. I was still watching him but he didn't look at me, so I pretended to be busy, clearing the clutter from the kitchen table.

He took off his boots and mopped the floor over and over, like he was rubbing out a stain that wouldn't go away. Then he dried his feet with the towel, which was supposed to be for cutlery but I wouldn't tell. Out of the corner of my eye, I could see he was summing up the situation, trying to decide what to do next. I put the cards away in their packet and pushed them into the drawer. Then I looked at my watch – quarter to seven. Still ages until bedtime.

Dad went to his office and shut the door behind him. I hated him doing that. It meant I shouldn't go in, even though he'd never exactly said as much. It was all right when he left it ajar a few inches. Then I could see the back of his checked shirt, his head bent forwards, one bony elbow sticking out as he scribbled away. Mrs Gayle said he was doing the books. She said it was about totting up numbers and I shouldn't disturb him, or he'd forget which one he'd got up to and have to start counting all over again. I always wondered how many numbers he had left to add up, and where they all came from. Why didn't he run out? I didn't know about infinity, when I was small. I always imagined everything had an ending, and every story would have a happy one.

I'd often heard Dad and Mrs Gayle discussing the mill, where to get the next penny from. Mrs Gayle didn't like me listening in, but Dad said it was the real world, I'd have to know about it sooner or later, and there was no time like the present. Then our housekeeper would sigh and press her lips inside her mouth, until all that was left was a straight line.

Sometimes Cedric joined in. Cedric helped in the shop on weekdays, when Mark Wheeler was at school. Cedric's real name was Mr Reeves, but he let me call him by his first name. Dad had said I shouldn't, it wasn't polite, me being only a child. That's why Mrs Gayle couldn't be plain Gayle. She refused point blank to be auntie anything, and when I was small I couldn't get my tongue around Mrs Stockington, so I

6

fixed on Mrs Gayle and it stuck. Now we all had it straight and there was no changing things. Even Dad called her that, until we could hardly remember she'd ever had any other name.

Cedric and Mrs Gayle would sit dreaming up ways Loraligh Mill could pay its way in the world, and Dad found a hundred reasons why each suggestion couldn't possibly work, which Mrs Gayle called being negative, and then he tried them anyway. And they did work, some of the time. He's a proud man, my dad. When Grandma had been alive, Loraligh Mill was a success, he said. A going concern. The family had plenty of money and had even bought extra acreage beyond the river, up into the hills. But Foot and Mouth had ruined things for everyone, and then Grandma died and left the farm and mill to Dad. He was her only child, so there was no one to share it with. Mrs Gayle said sometimes it was a millstone round his neck, which she thought was a bit of a joke, and Cedric would laugh, but I didn't get why it was funny. I get it now. I understand most things now.

Mrs Gayle hit on the idea that Loraligh didn't have to be only a farm and a mill. It could have a shop with ice-creams, and be a place for people to visit. A Tourist Attraction, she called it, and my eyes must've lit up because it all sounded exciting to a small child who lived in the back of beyond. Dad wasn't convinced. He sighed and rubbed his chin and stared at us. He'd never liked crowds much.

There had always been a small museum at Loraligh, inside the big gate that swings open when the visitors come. You could see how the mill used to work inside, and the next room was full of farm machinery from ancient times, covered in rust. I never went in there much, because of the spiders that

7

collected in the eaves. They were bigger by half than the ones we had indoors, and I'll swear they sat there waiting to drop on my head.

There was an old plough, the sort that needed two horses to pull it, back in the last century, and rows and rows of dead boring tools. It wasn't much to get excited about. Cedric suggested we spruced it up a bit, found a few more objects of interest to pad it out from some of the neighbouring farms. He'd ask around, see what people would give away. I couldn't get excited about that, and didn't think other visitors would either. That's when I had the idea of filling the place with chickens and, for once, Dad thought that was a good suggestion. Animals would bring in the visitors, because youngsters would always be interested in anything that moved. We already had deer, scores of them. They'd been at Loraligh since Grandma was small.

If ever I was ill and staying at home, school children would flock in from time to time, banging their clipboards on their knees and asking lots of questions. They were noisy and spent all their time in the shop, asking what there was to buy for twenty pence. It was a good thing Cedric had said we needed pencils and rubbers inscribed with the name *Loraligh Mill*. There were coloured plastic sharpeners too, and for the rich children, there were china mugs which cost nearly two pounds. Mrs Gayle said it was daylight robbery, but we sold the whole box in a month and Cedric had to order more. Mrs Gayle said children had too much money for their own good these days, and Cedric said they had the manners of a housefly.

I liked the children coming, and then I didn't. They were something to watch, something new. But they had the knack of staring at you as if you were foreign or daft – as if you were something to write about on their clipboard. They would rush over to the wheel, attracted by the noise of the water thundering round, and their teacher would yell at them not to go near the edge. Not that there was any chance of that. My dad had put up fences so strong and high, with only thin gaps to look through, that you had to stand on tiptoe, or crouch down low and then peer through the slits, to catch a glimpse of the waterwheel. Cedric said it was a bloomin' barricade and Mrs Gayle said small wonder to that, and they had shared a look, but it was one of those grown up looks that I couldn't read. As a child, I spent half my time trying to work out what grown-ups meant by the way of their frowns and smiles and winks.

The trouble with Dad leaving the office door shut, was that I was left to worry about the flood by myself, and I had to keep going over to the window. Across the back yard, I could just make out the shiny surface of the dark water against the brickwork, because the light was fading. And light fades fast when it's raining. I counted the number of bricks from the water to the guttering under the eaves of the outhouses. That way, I could check for any alarming changes to things. Twenty eight: I made a mental note. Cedric had taught me about mental notes, because you didn't always have time to find a piece of paper. You had to have different compartments in your brain for different things: one at the back for memories, another for facts, and one at the front you have to keep handy, for mental notes. I liked the way he described it, like his toolbox – all neat and organised. I wished my head felt as tidy as that.

I put back the photo of Mum and me, and scanned the mantelpiece. There was a separate one of Dad when he was much younger, about in his twenties. Before he had me, anyway. He was sitting on a huge rock out on the moor, hugging his knees and grinning. I liked that photo, because he didn't smile much. Then there were two of my school photographs. One of me when I was six and had lost my two front teeth; the other one was taken a year later. I was wearing a stupid jumper I had to borrow from lost property, because I'd forgotten to take one to school that day. It was all the wrong size and made me look sloppy. Mrs Gayle said you didn't look at the clothes on a person, but at their smile and their eyes. She always said the eyes were a way to a person's soul, and mine was a treasure. That was the nicest thing Mrs Gayle had ever said to me, so I let her put the photograph on show, but I made sure my baby picture overlapped it. I didn't want anyone forgetting about my mother. Mrs Gayle must have noticed, because a smile crept out from one corner of her mouth when she saw me fiddling.

The rain was calming down, which was a relief because it was getting darker and darker in the kitchen, and I wasn't sure whether or not I was allowed the light on. I walked over to the office door and stood staring at the black door knob. I'd stared at that door so many times, I knew all its faults: where the paint had dripped before it dried, and the way the knots swirled around like the water in the mill. I couldn't hear a sound from the other side. I wanted to go in, but decided against it, so I fetched a glass of milk and went upstairs to get myself ready for bed.

When nights were too early for sleep, there were things I could do. I had a whole system going, which involved a complicated list of activities from filling in my diary, to arranging my books and ornaments and rearranging them, in case there was a better way of doing things, to changing my bear into his nightclothes and then brushing out Amber Jane's hair for the night. I neglected her for about six months once, because Mark Wheeler, who worked in our shop, said girls my age shouldn't be playing with dolls, but when Mrs Gayle noticed the dust on my doll's head, she asked how I'd like it if someone thought I was too old to have my hair brushed, and I could see her point.

First, I would change into my pyjamas, because they were easy to move around in. Then I would tiptoe through to Dad's room, because he never came upstairs until eight on the dot. I'd climb into his bed and lie there for a few minutes, to smell his smell on the sheets. I liked wrapping his quilt round me, imagining it was really his arms. If I rolled round twice, I could actually trap myself in a cocoon, like a moth. Once, I was so warm and comfy, I dropped off to sleep and when I woke up, I thought it was my mother lying there. I could even smell her perfume, and it was lily of the valley like our bath cubes. Her arms were so tight around me that I couldn't break free and I started to sweat and fight with the covers, because I realised I was in the wrong bed and Dad might find me.

It wasn't exactly that he would shout – he wasn't a shouting sort of man. Not like Nicola Coleman's dad, who yelled so loud you would need a place to hide once he got going. Mr Coleman never waited patiently at the school gates like other mums and dads. He'd march across the playground, yelling at Nicola to hurry up and what was she keeping him for? Didn't she know he'd got things to do? And he never had a smile for her. Most of the class wouldn't go to Nicola's

11

house, for fear of Mr Coleman's bark. Not that I was allowed to go in the first place.

With my dad, it was more what he *didn't* say that would unsettle you. I asked questions, the way children do, and you could tell that he didn't want to be bothered. The answers always took such a long time coming, as if it had been hard work in his brain trying to find them. Not like Mrs Gayle – ask her a question and she could shoot the answers back at you, more or less as fast as a rifle could spit bullets. Cedric put it like that and I agreed.

With Dad, there were things you weren't allowed to bring up. Like whether or not you could go and play round Nicola's house, or anyone else's, boy or girl. You weren't to ask about Mum, about where she was or whether she had any other children now. That was a pity, because I'd cottoned on to the idea that I might have a brother or sister out there somewhere.

Mrs Gayle said my dad had a tendency not to *trust* anyone anymore. I asked why she said *anymore*, because that implied that he had been able to, once. But she said implied was a big word for a girl of nine to know and to use in the right context, which made me proud of myself, and then later I realised she hadn't exactly answered my question, but Mrs Gayle was wily like that. *Wily* was another of my words that impressed her. Cedric told her I got all my big words from listening to her for much of my childhood, and Mrs Gayle said if that was true, then all her grand words would've rubbed off on him too, which didn't seem to be the case. Cedric could've taken offence to that remark, but he pretended to make a hurt face and winked at me, so I knew he didn't mind.

The situation worked the other way round too. Dad couldn't see why I would want friends over to play, when I

12

spent all day at school. He told Mrs Gayle that I needed time to be quiet and independent. He thought it was a good thing for children to get bored once in a while, because they would become more reliant on their own resources. Mrs Gayle said it sounded like a good argument, the way he put it, but from my point of view the evenings were long and the weekends deadly. Or at least, they would've been, if it hadn't been for Mark Wheeler.

Two

Up to our Ankles

Mark worked in our museum shop on Saturdays and Sundays. He said he needed the money to pad out his newspaper round. Dad thought he worked hard, holding down two jobs as well as going to school, but Cedric thought he was lazy because the shop was always in a mess on Monday mornings, and the bins hadn't been emptied. I didn't think Mark was lazy, but he did get distracted easily when I kept him talking. Sundays would've been unbearable without Mark to talk to, and he was nearly always in a mood to chat. Sometimes the shop was empty, especially when it was raining, and then other days the visitors came in a relentless stream, as Cedric described it, and then you couldn't get a word in edgeways.

Mark and I would talk about anything – camping, fishing, what to do if you came across an adder, because I'd always thought you had to run like hell. We even talked about football. He supported The Arsenal, so I did too. He had an Arsenal scarf which he tucked into his parka every day, and an Arsenal shirt which was his favourite thing to wear. Mark would explain all the rules of the game to me until I had a pretty good understanding of things. I could even grasp the offside rule by the time he'd finished, and would proudly pass on my knowledge to Mrs Gayle, and Cedric, and anyone else who would listen. Mrs Gayle wasn't that interested and wondered why I would want to fill up my head with such things, particularly as we didn't have a television, and why was Mark Wheeler supporting a London team anyway, instead of somewhere in Yorkshire?

I didn't know the answer to that, but I suspected it was something to do with pressure from all his school friends. The sixth form had an Arsenal craze at the time, and Mark wasn't one to stand out in a crowd. I'd watch them sometimes, streaming out of the school gate from St Simon's High, which was right next door to my school, red and white scarves flashing boldly down the street, because St Simon's colour was supposed to be bottle green. Cedric said it was a rebellion and Mrs Gayle said it was all quite normal, to which he replied he was glad he'd never had any. Kids, he meant.

The other thing Mark liked to talk about was Maths. He was good with numbers, which came in handy, Dad said, working in a shop. You could rely on Mark not to give the wrong change, because he was canny with figures. Mentally, he could add up long lists of hundreds, tens and units, and if you checked them later with a calculator, more often than not he'd got them right. I told Cedric about how clever Mark was with numbers, but he wasn't impressed. He said it wouldn't be that useful in his future employment, because we were moving into the computer age, and perhaps he should concentrate on his organisational skills instead, like learning to tidy up after himself or washing his shirt once in a while.

I suspected Cedric was jealous, because he took that bit longer to work out the change, and he didn't know his tables as well as he should for an old man. I tested Cedric on his sevens and eights once, when I'd been learning them in the juniors, and he fluffed the difficult ones in the middle. I reported that bit of information to Mrs Gayle, and she said it was odd for a person of Cedric's generation, because mainly they prided themselves on their arithmetic, and because Cedric seemed to be a well-educated man in other ways. But she told me to keep quiet about it and definitely not to test Cedric out again, because men had their pride and it wasn't our job to knock it down.

Sometimes I would set Mark challenges. I would collect a pile of things off the shelves, merchandise, and give him a set time to work out the total in his head. Then, when he'd finished, I would ask him to work out the change from different amounts, like a hundred pounds, which was far too easy, so I'd pick harder amounts like ninety eight pounds forty seven pence. I always checked his working with the shop calculator. Even in the top juniors, I had to write hard sums down, because you had to carry and borrow and put something on the doorstep, and it was all a bit of a mystery to me.

Once, Dad came in when we were right in the middle, and all the objects were spread out on the floor in front of us. Dad didn't approve one bit, it was easy to see. I was told to scram and stop leading Mark astray, which wasn't fair, because why was it all my fault? I was always worrying about what was or wasn't fair, at that age. I don't mind so much now, because I'm fifteen and practically finished growing up. I've learnt a hard lesson, Mrs Gayle says.

Mark had to do stock-taking all the rest of that day, because there weren't any more visitors. I knew, because I kept my eye on the gate from my bedroom window, right through until five when I saw Mark lock up. I rubbed the glass clean with my sleeve, and gave him a wave, but he didn't see me.

When it was time for Mark's lunch break, my dad would take over the shop for a while, or Mrs Gayle would help out if he was busy. Then Mark and I would run, literally, through the back field, scattering the deer because they weren't used to anything moving very fast at Loraligh, right down to the river at the bottom. This was our absolutely favourite place. I made sure to prepare a pack-up for us during the morning, because time was short and we didn't want to be wasting any of it buttering bread.

The river curved like a bracelet round our land, from the mill, past the western fringe of the back field, and then carved its way along the valley floor like a lazy snake. This meant there was a lovely, wide, shallow section of river for several hundred yards at the bottom of the field. It was a brilliant place to play. Dad had created shelves, so the water flowed slow and flat in sections, gently tipping over each level in several small waterfalls. It was shallow enough to paddle, which was the general intention, since Cedric and Dad had devised the whole thing. It was to be a crowd-puller in the hot weather and it worked.

Families would come from Easter to September, even October if the summer stretched on. It was especially beautiful then, because the sun made the whole scene golden, like an old film. They would set up their aluminium chairs with the stripy plastic seats, and spread out a travel rug, and that was the grown-ups happy. The children would be contented near enough all day, wading through the clear water, getting excited over anything living and new. I didn't like it when they poked the minnows with their sticks, or stirred up the mud on purpose, because it would be hours before you could see your feet again. I'd stand there scowling at them, until I couldn't stand it any longer, and then I'd have to say something – like how would they like it if someone came along and bashed them with a big stick? – because their mothers clearly weren't intending to bother.

But apart from that, I didn't mind them coming. At least visitors meant money, and money meant we could stay at Loraligh forever. So I tried hard not to mind too much.

The best days, which I called *blissful*, were the ones when Mark and I had the river to ourselves. It was our kingdom and Mark was my king. We called it Shallow Falls. The stones under clear water looked like jewels, so we pretended we owned them all and we were rich. Every part of Loraligh had a name. Apart from Shallow Falls, there was The Beach – which was actually just a crescent of pebbles running around the edge of the water, but it was good enough to put down a towel and pretend. Then there was Murderer's Wood. Nobody had actually been killed there, not as far as we knew, but they might've been because it was that sort of place. In springtime, the wood floor was filled with anemones and violets, and I was careful not to tread on them because of the fairies. The field we called Deer Meadow, which wasn't exactly original, but at least it wouldn't be confused with anywhere else. We used to spend ages hiding in the long grass, when it was warm enough. I liked making daisy chains while Mark was talking, and I taught him the song about daisies and buttercups, that Mrs Gayle taught me.

'*Daisies are our silver, buttercups our gold.*
All the little treasures we can have and hold.'

18

She said it came from Sunday School and it was a pity I didn't go, but she supposed it couldn't be helped. Mark liked the words, and I was surprised that a boy would like a girl's poem. We named each colour of stone after a jewel, like a topaz or an emerald, and we'd line them up along the grassy bank, counting our treasure. Which was a funny thing for a boy to do, and he was six years older than me. But he didn't care when we were out on the land like that. He knew it was only between the two of us.

The Slopes were on the other side of the river. They marked the end of the valley, and climbed hard and fast to the sky, but because they were to the north, you didn't have to worry about losing the sun in the afternoon. Dad often worked up there, mending the dry-stone walls that were always collapsing. I had no idea how many walls there could be on our land, or what they were for, since all the sheep had long gone. The Slopes were a NO GO area as far as I was concerned, unless I had a grown-up with me, on account of it being too far for anyone to call me in for tea. At least, that was their excuse, but secretly I thought it was all part of Dad's neurosis. That's a word for people who are tense and anxious and work themselves up over nothing. Mrs Blunt, my teacher, taught us that word when she was trying to think up something really hard for our spelling challenge – something that would fox even the best spellers in the class. I was never one of those, but I would keep quiet and secretly add her difficult words to my brain bank. So we learned *neurosis* and *neurotic*, and I held onto those, because I could see how relevant they were, even to my short life.

Mark and I had sandwich-spread in between two slices of Sunblest, or fish paste or chocolate spread. Sunblest was the

19

only bread I would eat, which Mrs Gayle moaned about non-stop, because she said it didn't have an ounce of goodness in it. Mark complained sometimes, because there was never any meat or cheese, which is what a man ought to eat, and I would worry that my careful preparations hadn't come up to scratch.

Occasionally, Mrs Gayle would sneak in a couple of her shortbreads or marmalade cakes, because she'd had a baking morning, and then Mark's face would light up. I'd glow inside, because I'd been satisfactory. That was the trouble with being the youngest; someone else always had power over you.

The river was crystal clear, the day of the attack. The day Mark got into trouble. You could see the patterns on the stones that day, and the minnows darting between them. We were standing on the stepping stones, and I was trying to flick weed off the long stick I'd found. I kept this stick because it was a useful size, and I always put it in the same hiding place, buried under a pile of debris beneath the old larch tree.

"How many brothers and sisters did you say you had?"

"Two of each. I told you."

"I know, I forgot. So there's five of you?"

"Five."

I tried to imagine a house with five children, all vying for attention, all fighting over the lavatory after tea.

"And where did you come, out of the five?"

"Bang in the middle. Two girls above me, two boys below."

I contemplated how that must have panned out, having two little girls in a family, and then three baby boys following on in a row behind.

20

"It was a good thing your mum had the girls first, or she might have gone mad."

Mark laughed.

"I doubt if she sees it like that. She says they'll drive her into the ground one day."

"Why? Are they bad?"

"They're a pain in the neck."

I wondered about that. I wondered if Mrs Gayle, or Cedric, or Dad would call *me* a pain in the neck.

"Why did she have them then, if she didn't like children?"

Mark stared at me for a moment, and joshed my elbow.

"Blowed if I know," he said. Then he changed the subject, so I could tell he was bored with that conversation.

"Come on, Immie. Let's paddle across and see if we can get to the top of The Slopes today. I want to see what's over the summit." He started taking off his trainers, so I copied him. I had to hold my skirt up, and try not to drop my shoes in the water. It wasn't easy.

I knew I wasn't allowed, but I liked Mark calling me by that nickname. To everyone else, I was always Imogen. I chased on up the hill after him, leaving my shoes behind because he didn't give me time to put them back on.

"I'm not really allowed. Dad'll kill me if he finds out."

"He won't."

Mark was wearing his red shirt and you could see him a mile off. I stopped and looked back at the house over the trees, to check no one was looking, but it was so far away you could barely tell.

Mark had much longer legs than mine, so he reached the top long before me. When I eventually caught up with him, I was gasping for air. That familiar smell of chemicals was filling my lungs, because I had a weakness in there, but it wasn't Mark's fault. I hadn't told him.

I had to sit down on the grass and I was wheezing noisily, which was embarrassing, but you can't hide it when it takes over you like that.

"You all right? You've gone a funny colour."

"I'll…be all right…in a minute."

But it was a long time before the smell and the taste went away. A long time before I could speak properly again.

When I finally cooled down and the oxygen found its way back in, I wanted to ask Mark something else.

"You're fifteen, right?"

"Nearly sixteen."

"And your sisters are older than you, right?"

"You ought to go on Mastermind."

Mark laughed and tickled my nose with the stem of grass he was chewing. I told him to leave off, and grabbed the stalk and poked him back.

"So they must be…what, at least seventeen or something?"

"Coleen is eighteen next month, and Denise is nearly twenty."

"Wow!"

"Why?"

"Well, you'd think they'd be really grown-up by now. You'd think they couldn't possibly be pains in the neck. You'd think they'd be…civilised."

Mark fell back onto the grass when I said that. I didn't know if it was my choice of vocabulary, or the distance between my word and the truth of things, but I loved it when he laughed like that and I started to laugh too. We both laughed until it hurt and we'd long forgotten what was supposed to be so funny, but it was just the laughing that was funny. Then Mark decided it would be hilarious to roll me down the hill, so he gave me a push-off and set me in motion, and because I was laughing so much, I couldn't control how my descent was going.

As I rolled down and down, I could feel the dry grass brushing against my face and into my clothes. I could smell its strong scent. When I reached the bottom, I was going so fast I only just managed to stop myself before the water. By now, my chance of breathing with any success was fast disappearing. My whole windpipe was closing up, the way it had when I was five and Dad had bundled me into the Land Rover and rushed me off to the District, because he said my face was turning blue. I'd never seen my dad drive so fast, and he kept looking across at me and then back at the road again, because the journey to the hospital is five miles of bends and hills, and all the way he was looking scared.

I stood up, to get as far away from the grass as possible, but it was no good because I was choking and wheezing and could hardly balance properly, so I fell onto my knees again, my head bent over.

"Immie! Immie, are you all right? What's the matter?"

But it was more than I could do to answer in words. I grabbed Mark's sleeves and stared him right in the eyes, trying to communicate the seriousness of things. The wheezing was changing from a rattle to a low whooping noise, and the combination of signs must've alarmed him because he picked me up, my knees hanging over his arm, and carried me right across the river, back to The Beach. I could tell he found me heavy, because he was getting breathless too.

"Bloody hell, Immie! Why didn't you tell me you get asthma?"

But he didn't expect an answer. He carried me across the pebbles, through the strip of trees into Deer Meadow, and then he stopped, in an effort to get his breath back. I could tell he was contemplating putting me down at that point, because I was making his face red and sweaty, but one look at me must've changed his mind because he kept on running up the track, trying not to drop me, until we reached the back gate. Then he couldn't go on, and lowered me to the ground, calling and calling for help.

Mrs Gayle came running from one path, while Dad appeared from another, more or less at the same moment. Mark was sent to the shop without another word, even though I could tell he didn't want to go, because he was worried about me. Dad said he would be talking to him later, and I knew that was bad.

Then Mrs Gayle carried me into the kitchen on her shoulder, like a baby, smoothing my back and talking gently to me all the time. Dad followed on behind us, a frown set deep into his forehead. They put me up on the kitchen top and both looked at me.

"What do you think? How bad is she, do you think?"

"Let her get her breath back, Andrew. Then we'll see."

"But if she can't? What if she can't, like last time?"

Mrs Gayle was holding my chin up, to keep me from closing my throat. She was looking deep into my eyes, telling me to breathe nice and slow, that's it, count with me, slowly Imogen, five...six...seven...good girl.

All the time she was counting and I was wheezing, I was worrying about what was going to happen to Mark.

24

"It…it wasn't his…"

"Be quiet, Imogen. Don't try to talk, child. Now concentrate on each breath and do as you're told."

It wasn't the worst attack I'd ever had, but it was the one I remember, because of Mark carrying me right across that river and all the way up the meadow, and the expression on his face. Before he went home that day, he was sent to fetch my shoes from the foot of The Slopes. He'd had to take his trainers off for the second time, and wade through the cold water again, to reach them.

I was terrified he'd lose his job, but in the end Dad thought it was more my fault than Mark's that we'd gone that far. I was forced to explain about rolling down the hill and stirring up all the grass, so Dad knew I'd broken one of his golden rules. Mrs Gayle said she was disappointed in me, because she'd always had me down as a responsible girl, and I felt ashamed inside because this meant Dad wouldn't trust me ever again. I realised how much it had mattered to me, to be that person, that special person, and I'd ruined my chance for ever.

At a quarter to eight on the night of the buckets, when it rained so hard it made you scared, I crept downstairs to check on the state of things out in the yard. I wouldn't be able to sleep if the water was rising, and I hadn't heard Dad come out of his office all evening. It was dark outside, but the kitchen light was picking out flecks of brightness on the water's surface. It was impossible to count bricks, so there was nothing I could do until morning.

Dad came into my room as I was putting my book down.

"Time for lights-out, Imogen."

He pulled my blanket up and I thought for a minute he was going to sit down on the bed next to me, but then he changed his mind.

"Dad?"

"What is it?"

"Is the water going to come up any higher?"

"No I don't think so. The rain's eased off."

"How do you know?"

"Because I can hear it. Stop worrying. You go to sleep now."

And I thought, you're a fine one to talk about worrying, but I said goodnight Dad, and he switched off my lamp. He didn't leave my bedroom straight away and I could sense him hesitating, as if he was about to say something else, but my eyes were shut so I couldn't be sure. Eventually, he must have given up trying, because I heard the boards creak, and when I looked back he was gone.

Three

Stranger at the Gate

I woke with first light and listened hard for the sound of rain. It was eerily quiet and not one bird had bothered to sing. The light was strange too – greenish, and gloomier than usual. When I pushed back the curtain to check on things, angry grey clouds were swirling past in a way you couldn't ignore, but at least the rain had stopped.

Nobody would be coming, not because it was Sunday, which was Mrs Gayle's day off, but because of the floods. I had an awful thought that Mark wouldn't come either, if the puddles were bad in the lane. Dad wouldn't open the mill or the shop, and I would be left a whole day with no visitors and nothing to do. My alarm clock read six fifteen, barely morning. There was a hush over the house, and I longed for a sound – a grown-up moving about, a sister in a bed next to mine – but all I could hear was the Loraligh sign, creaking in the wind.

I kept myself amused for a while, leafing through my favourite Pookie annuals. I kept these hidden under the bed because really I was too old for them, but I liked the illustrations and, truth be told, I liked the stories too. Pookie was this strange, rabbit-type creature, with enormous ears and cute, beady eyes, surrounded by brilliant paintings of fairy folk and insects with human faces. He had a real character too, the sort I could identify with, being the type that didn't always get everything right.

Mrs Gayle sometimes found a spare half hour to read one of these stories to me, once she'd finished all her chores, although she would moan about the amount of words on a page. She didn't seem to mind that I should've grown out of them, even though I'd had my tenth birthday by then. I'd be moving to the top junior class soon, and you always had to have paperbacks and no pictures. She didn't make me feel bad about my Pookie books, but I hid them anyway. Dad sometimes had an opinion about the books I read or the games I played, but he wasn't tuned in to what children like, and Mrs Gayle said I wasn't to mind, because men often didn't understand children the way women did.

That made me even more aware that I should've had a mother around, to fill in all the gaps. When I was little older than a toddler, Mrs Gayle said I went through a phase. She said I would put my hands on my hips and say, all cocky like, 'Men, honestly!' whenever Dad made a mistake. Like with my eggs, forgetting to cut the bread into long, thin soldiers, the way you're supposed to. Cedric and Mrs Gayle had been in the kitchen at the time and they both laughed out loud. Mrs Gayle said I was a precocious child and wherever did I get that expression from, when we didn't have a television? Cedric blamed Mrs Gayle for putting the words into my head, and she denied all knowledge as usual. Dad didn't bother trying to do my eggs after that, so I suppose it was my fault for criticising. I wondered if he'd always stood back where I was concerned, because I couldn't remember a time when he'd had much to do with looking after me, full stop.

Distracted, Cedric called him. Mrs Gayle responded that he had a lot to be distracted about, and Cedric wasn't to be casting his judgements so easily on others, especially those less fortunate. Then I realised she was talking about my dad.

"Why is Dad less fortunate, Mrs Gayle?"

She was taken aback at first when I said that, and I could tell she didn't exactly know how to answer me.

"Well, at least he's got you, Imogen, and any man with such a sharp lass for a daughter has got a lot to be glad about."

I took that to mean Dad didn't have a wife any longer and had a chance of being lonely, if it wasn't for me.

"What does sharp mean?"

"It means you ask too many questions."

"Cedric, what does distracted mean?"

They both raised their eyes to the ceiling at the same moment, and Cedric made as if he was going to tickle me, and Mrs Gayle told me off for trying out my questions on anybody who would listen. But they never answered, so I had to look it up in our dictionary.

Distracted *Adj: perplexed, harassed, frantic, mad.*

It sounded serious. Mad? Was Dad going mad? The very thought of this definition made *me* perplexed. That *was* a word I knew. I ran back downstairs to ask Mrs Gayle why Dad was going mad, and she grabbed the dictionary.

"Read 'distract' Imogen. What does 'distract' mean?"

She handed me the book, her thumb in the page to keep from losing it, her index finger jabbing at the word.

Distract – verb: turn (the attention) in a different direction, divert; prevent concentration.

I thought about that for a while and then it opened up a whole new can of worms, because I needed to know the different directions his mind might be going and why.

"Is he worrying about Loraligh?"

"He's not so much worrying as looking after it, child. Anyone who has responsibilities has to worry about them to a certain extent, and your dad's no different from anybody else. Now will you stop all your questions and help me fold these towels?"

I gave up asking then, because I knew she'd had enough, but the corner of that page in our dictionary became well and truly grubby after that, with me trying to gain some new understanding about my father, as if reading the words over and over would make a difference.

I gave up waiting for Dad to wake up, put on my gown and crept downstairs in search of something to eat. I moved more hesitantly than usual, worried about what might be waiting for me outside the kitchen door, after the drama of the evening before. But the floor was dry. The flags were always cold underfoot, especially first thing, and I wished I'd remembered my slippers. I looked out into the yard and counted the outhouse bricks carefully, up to the guttering. Thirty two. That was a relief.

Dad must've heard me moving about, because he appeared at the bottom of the stairs and he clearly hadn't had time to wash himself, or comb his hair. He was running his hand through the long part on top, and it wasn't flopping down flat afterwards because it needed a shampoo, and he was pressing his eyeballs in an effort to encourage them into action.

"Morning, Dad."

"You're up then."

He went straight over to the back window to take a look at things.

"It's gone down. I've checked."

Then Dad phoned Mark to put him off – said it was too dangerous; said nobody would want to come out on a day like this anyway. Mrs Gayle rang after breakfast, to check on things back here. I heard Dad ask her about Three Boys, how it had been last night; was there any chance he could get out? Then he passed the receiver to me because Mrs Gayle wanted a word.

"Did you have your breakfast yet, Imogen? Did you remember to turn off the electrics?"

"I didn't do bacon today."

"Oh, all right, pet. You'd better do the dishes. What are you going to do after that?"

Mrs Gayle always worried about how I was going to amuse myself on a Sunday. She had no need because, as she put it herself, I was a resourceful girl.

"I haven't decided yet. Is it really bad out? Are the fields flooded?"

"Pretty bad, Imogen. It said on the radio most of the country lanes are blocked or nearly impassable. Don't let your dad drive out today, will you? Tell him it can wait. There's food in the pantry. You can warm up that stew I left in the casserole dish, and do some carrots and mash. Remember to turn down the heat, once they've come to the boil."

"I will. See you tomorrow then, Mrs Gayle."

She hesitated before putting down the phone, her end. She always did that. I could tell she didn't like the thought of leaving it all to me, but she had no choice.

31

I looked at Dad.

"Why do you always ask about Three Boys, Dad? Why is it so dangerous?"

There was a long gap while he stared at me. He seemed to be looking right through my face. He was either choosing his words, or clearing out his thought path to make way for an answer. It was always the same. Cedric said it was as if my dad couldn't concentrate. Or he was thinking so hard about his own thoughts, he couldn't easily side-track onto yours.

"It's a nasty blind bend, that's all. You meet the oncoming traffic in the middle of the road, if you're not careful."

"Has anyone ever died there?"

"No. I don't know. I don't think so."

"Why is it called Three Boys then?"

Then Dad took his plate over to the sink and dropped it into the bowl. It splashed up his shirt, but I didn't say anything.

"That goes a long way back. You'll have to ask Mrs Gayle."

He collected his waterproof jacket from the peg on the door, shook it out and put it on, pulling up the collar. He always left his plates for me to wash up, or perhaps he didn't even think about who would be doing them. He was used to our housekeeper taking charge of things. Sometimes I wondered whether it occurred to him at all that I did them on a Sunday.

"Where are you going, Dad? You're not driving anywhere are you?"

He was pulling on a pair of socks, and then pushing his feet into his massive wellingtons. He never tipped them upside down first, to check.

"No, don't worry. I'm going to take a walk up the lane. See how bad it is. See if we can get out. You stay here."

"Don't be long, will you?"

I watched him go up the path and open the latch to the side gate. It had started raining again, but it was that soft, fine rain that floats around your face and doesn't exactly respond to gravity. I didn't feel easy about him going out like that, and I watched the space he'd left for a while. The puddle under the gate was smaller than it had been, which should've put my mind to rest, but my teeth would be chewing on my lip right until Dad was back. I went to check on the bricks at the back again, and then I pushed the kitchen step over to the sink and washed up the breakfast things, but I couldn't rest easy and returned to my look-out.

That was when I saw her.

She was standing behind the big, swingy gate, her hands in her coat pockets, her hair scraped back in a ponytail, getting wet and not minding. She was staring at our house. At first, I wondered if she was looking straight at me, but then I thought she couldn't possibly see into the kitchen. I flicked off the light to make sure, and checked again. She was still there, not moving, the feet of her wellies under water.

Every possible explanation was going round and round my brain, but I wasn't making sense of any of it. I'd spent all my life, all the part I could remember, waiting for my mother to come back to Loraligh. I'd spent hours staring at that gate, wishing, waiting, imagining. I'd seen her in that white dress fluttering in the breeze, smiling, waving to me at my bedroom window. I'd imagined the breathless run, the smothering embrace, the kisses and the sorries and the tears. I'd dreamt

33

up her great list of excuses, the way she was going to make up for it all.

But never, in all my day-dreaming, did I imagine this woman standing forlorn and damp, reluctant to undo the latch, her face sad and vacant. And then I realised she couldn't be my mother at all, because her hair was pale and I could tell, even at this distance, her face was wrong and didn't at all resemble the woman in the photograph.

I wished she would go away. I wished Dad would come back. What did she want with us on this awful day? How did she even get here, with the roads so bad?

She was making me nervous, just standing there looking and, for a moment, I thought I'd go outside and shout out that we were closed, in the hopes that she'd clear off. But that took a bit more courage than I felt I had in me at that particular time, so I decided to get on with things in the kitchen. When I looked back again, she was gone. I decided to tell Mrs Gayle about the woman I'd seen, the following day before school.

"Oh, she came again then," Mrs Gayle said in a matter of fact sort of way, while she scraped the spare butter off the knife, as if strangers stand at your gate staring every day. She was packing up my lunchbox, snapping on the lid and saying, there, that'll keep the doctor away, congratulating herself for remembering my apple. She hated me having packed lunches, and wished I could have a proper hot dinner like most other children. They had come to blows over that, my dad and Mrs Gayle, more than once, and she made sure I ate tea with him every day to make up for it. Dad said he couldn't find the extra, and Mrs Gayle said it was a false economy, because a pack-up costs more, when you look at it, and a child's stomach needs a hot meal in the middle of the day. As if there was a rule somewhere.

"Has she been before, then?"

"I've seen her once or twice."

"Who is she? What's she doing here?"

"Fetch your coat, Imogen, and be quick about it. Time's running on."

"But who is she, Mrs Gayle?" I said, as I pushed my arms into the sleeves she was holding out for me.

"Who knows?" and then Mrs Gayle saw the bewilderment on my face and added: "Oh no, Imogen. It's not what you think. She's not your mother."

"No. I didn't think she was."

"Well, that's all right then. Now, you be getting along or you'll miss your bus. You've got five minutes to get to the stop."

I reached up to kiss her cheek, because Mrs Gayle is quite tall and wouldn't stoop down far, on account of her stiff back.

As I walked along to the bus stop, I was thinking about the stranger. Mrs Gayle hadn't exactly answered my question, as usual. But she didn't give the impression of being surprised either. It isn't every day someone gazes at your house for no reason, but to do it on such a miserable day, with the lane flooded and the rain still coming down...

All that day at school, I was thinking up ways to explain who the stranger was and why she would be there. It's alarming how my imagination can run wild, given a bit of ammunition. By home time, I'd convinced myself she was a social worker, come to assess how my father was looking after me, and perhaps she wouldn't be happy about the state of things and would be carting me off to a children's home, miles from anywhere. (I knew all about social workers, because they took Terry Hudson away in the night when he was only seven, because of his mother getting drunk, and our class never saw him again.) So sure was I of the likelihood of this situation, I was sick with panic as the bus swung its usual way around the country lanes.

I walked round the last bend before home and over the humpback bridge, my footsteps slowing in anticipation of the police car that would be parked outside the gate. By now, the woman had changed her clothes into a posh suit, she was carrying a clipboard and her hair was pulled into one of those tight buns ballet dancers wear.

So great was my relief when I turned the corner to see an empty gateway and drive, without a police car in sight, I ran the last bit of the lane, undid the latch of the small gate and pelted down the drive. I'd prepared my question and I was ready.

As I pushed open the front door, kicking off my shoes and already shouting out Hi, I'm home, in that relaxed, end-of-the-day way, Mrs Gayle was already interrupting me.

"We have a visitor."

I looked up.

There she was, right in the middle of our kitchen. My heart flipped. She wasn't wearing the suit or the posh hair-do, but her fair hair was combed out nice and neat to her shoulders. She was wearing jeans, which didn't look right for a social worker, but I knew it was just a ploy to make me feel relaxed. What was more, she had the nerve to be smiling at me.

"Hello, Imogen."

She knew my name.

"I'm not going!" I yelled. "I'm not going anywhere you send me. I'm happy here with Dad, and Mrs Gayle looks after me as well as anyone could, don't you Mrs Gayle?"

I ran across to our housekeeper, hiding behind her and clutching her arm.

"What on earth are you talking about, Imogen?"

She shook me off, embarrassed.

The woman seemed surprised, but I wasn't easily fooled. She looked across at Mrs Gayle and then back to me.

"I know what she wants," I continued, putting my foot in further and further.

"That's enough. I don't know what you're imagining, but you're barking up the wrong tree."

That was one of Mrs Gayle's favourite expressions and I knew what it meant: I had got the wrong end of things. My face was beginning to flush.

"I'm Lorna," the visitor said. She put out her hand. I didn't move a muscle.

"Imogen, I want you to meet Lorna. Lorna…"

"Bennett."

I looked up at Mrs Gayle. I needed more information.

"I used to live here once, Imogen, a long time ago," the woman added, letting her hand drop. "I hope you don't mind. I thought I'd take another look around."

That would explain things, I supposed.

I was looking at my shoes. "Oh. Sorry."

"That's all right, Imogen. No harm done."

I hated her using my name, like she knew me.

Mrs Gayle was fussing around with cups and saucers, preparing afternoon tea for us all and asking Lorna if she took sugar. She was apologising for me all the while, saying she didn't know how I got such ideas into my head sometimes.

Once we were sitting round the table and waiting for the pot to brew, I had to ask a question because things weren't adding up.

"When did you live here, then?"

"Quite a while ago. Before you were born."

She didn't look old enough. I thought the land had belonged to Grandma's family for ever and ever. It wasn't making any sense.

"Did it look the same, back then?" I asked.

Lorna undid the buttons of her cardigan, and looked around the kitchen.

"This room is much the same," she said, "but the grounds are very different. There wasn't a shop, for a start."

"No, that was Cedric's idea," I announced proudly.

"Cedric?"

"He works here, weekdays. He takes charge of the museum and the shop."

"Oh, I see. Good idea," Lorna added. "I expect it makes good money."

"Was it called Loraligh, back when you lived here?" I asked.

"Of course," Mrs Gayle chipped in. "It's always been Loraligh."

It struck me then, how similar the two names were – Lorna, Loraligh. I'd ask about that later, when she was gone.

"Do you know my dad then?"

Mrs Gayle shot her a look and I caught it on the way. Lorna hesitated.

"Your father'll be back in ten minutes or so, Imogen, and he'll be asking if you've done your homework. So drink up now, and then you need to be getting on with it."

Lorna gulped her tea down awfully fast and stood up.

"I really ought to be going, Mrs Stockington. You've been very kind."

For a moment, I wondered who she meant. I'd completely forgotten about Mrs Gayle's real name.

"But you said you wanted to see the grounds. I'll take you for a walkabout if you like. No need to be hurrying off."

I was glad Lorna was going, even though she wasn't a social worker after all. I didn't want strangers in our house, especially ones who had a vested interest in things. And she talked all confident, in her posh voice, and her pale complexion reminded me of the porcelain doll that sits on the three-corner chair on the landing, staring at the clock like a ghost, smelling of old lace. Not like Mrs Gayle's complexion – all rosy and wholesome. Real people didn't have skin like Lorna's.

"No really. It's been lovely, being inside the old kitchen. It's such a cosy room, isn't it? Nothing's changed much in here. It's the outside that looks so different."

Mrs Gayle began placing the cups and saucers back on the tray. Lorna had hardly touched her biscuit.

"Oh, I think you'll find things are quite different these days," Mrs Gayle said. "Andrew will be sorry he missed you."

"Mrs Stockington, would you mind if…well, perhaps it would be better if you didn't mention to him that I was here."

"Imogen. Homework."

I knew from Mrs Gayle's face there was no arguing with her. I also knew she wanted me out of the way, so they could share secrets. I picked up my school bag and began to make my way to the foot of the stairs.

"Goodbye, Imogen. Nice to have met you."

Lorna was smiling at me, while she fiddled in her pocket with her keys. I hoped she wouldn't be coming back. I said goodbye and began to go up, but near the top stair I stopped to listen, being careful not to let the boards creak. I needed to hear what Mrs Gayle had to say.

"Why won't you stay, Lorna? It's all in the past now. He's lonely, you know."

There was a pause.

"I can't, Mrs Stockington. I'm sorry. I can't face him."

"But you came this far. You came through the door. He'll be mortified if he finds out he's missed you."

"I don't deserve that."

"You can't go blaming yourself forever, Lorna."

"No really, I have to go. Goodbye Mrs Stockington, and thank you for everything. I'm sorry."

"Call me Gayle, won't you? And do say you'll come again."

I heard Lorna's footsteps cross the kitchen floor and the door click shut. I hurried across to the landing window, to make sure she left. She must've parked her car up the lane somewhere, because it certainly wasn't in our car park. Only moments after she disappeared, Dad's Land Rover swung in front of the gate and I watched him jump out, undo the latch and push the gate open. Then he carved his usual noisy crescent through the gravel, spinning stones left and right. Dad always drove too fast. Mrs Gayle was always telling him about it, but he didn't listen. He kicked our best cockerel with the side of his boot, and I flinched. They never learned to get out of his way.

I knew not to mention the visitor when Dad was around, but I was dying to ask Mrs Gayle about her. She clearly knew more than she was letting on. I decided to quiz Cedric instead, the next day after school. Cedric never left before five thirty, and I was usually home a good hour before that, so I tended to bother him most afternoons, especially when Mrs Gayle was being less than communicative.

"Did other people live here before Grandma, Cedric?"

"Your Grandma? She lived here all her life, as far as I know."

"Wasn't she an old lady when she died?"

"That depends on your point of view."

"What d'you mean?"

"Well, old to some folk isn't the same as old to others."

"You're talking in riddles, Cedric."

He gave a short laugh when I said that. He knew where I'd got that from.

"For example, I expect you think *I'm* old, although it's five more years before I draw my pension, and your friend Mrs Gayle still calls me young man."

He'd got me there, because I knew it was rude to describe a person as old. But he was – ancient.

"But if Grandma was, say, sixty or something when she died, then Loraligh must've been in our family for at least that many years."

"That's right, but I've a feeling she was older than that."

"So nobody else could possibly have lived here before, who would be younger than sixty now…at least."

41

"True. Why are you asking?"

"Well, because this woman, called Lorna, has been hanging around the place, claiming she used to live here. But she can't have done, because Loraligh has always belonged to our family. So she was lying. I could tell she was lying anyway."

"Now hold on, young lady. We can't go accusing people of telling lies until we have our facts straight."

Cedric was counting up loose change and putting it into neat piles, before he bagged it up. He was only half concentrating on me.

"I do have my facts straight. She said she used to live here. And Mrs Gayle said she definitely wasn't my mother. I'd know anyway, from the photograph."

Cedric stopped what he was doing, and his eyes looked concerned and thoughtful. He pushed the fringe out of my eyes.

"I'll have a chat to the old dragon indoors. See what I can find out for you."

I smiled when he called her that, because she wasn't a dragon at all, and I knew Cedric was, in truth, very fond of her. But I knew what he meant. She had the upper hand where most things were concerned. Wore the trousers, you might say.

When I tried Mrs Gayle before tea that evening, she was decidedly cagey and I didn't know whether or not to believe her. She was spreading the cloth over the kitchen table, and gave two corners to me and said perfect timing, Imogen.

"Perhaps your grandmother took lodgers. It's quite likely, you know. Money got tight for a while."

"Dad would know, wouldn't he? Shall I ask him?"

"He might've been too young to remember. Knives on the right."

"But Lorna looks younger than Dad. Wouldn't you say, Mrs Gayle?"

"I didn't pay much attention. That spoon's dirty."

"Yes she did. She looked much younger. Dad's going bald at the front."

Mrs Gayle laughed.

"It's called a receding hairline, Imogen – not going bald. He's only early forties, you know."

"All the same. Lorna's younger, I'm sure of it."

"If you say so."

Mrs Gayle was doshing out carrots and trying to get the numbers even.

"Hold your plate still."

"So Dad would remember her, wouldn't he? Even if she was a child, and it was her parents who were the lodgers?"

At that moment, Dad appeared in the kitchen and used the step to remove the heel of each boot.

"Remember who?"

"Never mind, Andrew. Your daughter's getting the wrong end of the stick as usual."

With that, she shot me one of her best which meant, and that's enough of that now Imogen. She had a way of opening her eyes wider than usual and piercing them right into mine, or pressing her lips together in that firm, no-nonsense way of hers. I'd have to save my questions for later.

All the way through the meal, even though Dad was telling Mrs Gayle about this man's head that was found in a bag in the stream at Hutton, I switched off because I was trying to imagine Lorna lodging at Loraligh when it was Grandma's.

Where would she have stayed? Which bedroom? Why wouldn't Dad have remembered her? It was useless interrogating Mrs Gayle any longer. I would have to rely on Cedric to do my detective work for me.

Four

Mistake

The next Saturday, Mark heard no end of it.

"She said she couldn't face him. My dad, she meant. What could she have done that was so terrible?"

"God knows. Perhaps she hurt him or something, when they were little. Or got him into trouble. Kids can be horrid to each other."

"I suppose." What did I know, being an only child?

I was stamping the labelling machine onto the bottom of the latest set of Loraligh mugs, and I liked clicking the trigger, the way it made a definite snap.

"Make sure they go on straight, Immie. Cedric'll throw a fit if he sees them all crooked."

I peeled a couple of labels off again and put them on by hand, as straight as I could, licking my lips to help me concentrate. Mark used to tease me about that.

"These are nice," I said. "Better than the last lot."

Cedric had asked the company to redesign the emblem on the side of the mugs, using the silhouette of a deer, picked out in gold, on a dark red background.

"Yeah. They look kind of classy, don't they?"

"Why do you think she didn't want to see Dad? Why wouldn't she want to say sorry?"

"She bottled."

"Then why bother to come all the way into the house? Why stand outside staring, and then pluck up the courage to knock on the door and come right inside, and then just disappear before she had a chance to say anything to him?"

"I really haven't a clue, Immie. Could be something else completely. Something we haven't guessed. Why don't you ask your dad?"

"You have to be kidding."

Mark took each mug from me after I'd priced them up, and he arranged them neatly in rows on the shelf, making sure the deer was at the front.

"What's so bad about that? He is your father, after all."

I gave him the last mug and stood up. My legs had pins and needles from sitting scrunched up for so long.

"Would you ask *your* dad?"

"I haven't got one anymore. But if I did, yes I would. What's the worst he could do?"

I mulled over that one while Mark was ripping off the sticky brown tape from another box. This box was a different shape. Cedric had ordered some new lines in souvenirs, and Mark and I were excited about seeing what was in there.

"He hates me asking questions...and if we're right about Lorna, he'd definitely hate it even more."

He peeled back the side flaps and lifted out a wad of bubble-wrap.

"Wow! Look at these," Mark said.

We peered inside.

Several ceramic ornaments of animals lay in compartments: there were deer, some of single stags with grand antlers, others of a doe with a fawn, each engraved with

46

the Loraligh name. There were woodland creatures too – squirrels, foxes and frogs with wide grins. They were glossy, as if they'd been polished.

"Children will like these. *I'd* like these."

"So will their grandparents. Neat idea," Mark added.

"Sorry about your dad."

"S'okay."

I thought I'd better not mention the father problem again, what with Mark's home situation, so I changed the subject.

"Can I show these to Mrs Gayle? I bet she'll love them."

"Just one then, but carry it carefully."

"You can come too, if you like."

"Better stay and mind the shop. It's a nice day. We might get visitors."

I carefully wrapped my favourite ornament of the baby fawn in some bubble-wrap, and carried it across the car park to the house. A strong breeze was blowing and I had to hold extra tight. The front door was open and I could hear Mrs Gayle talking to Dad in the kitchen. My father sounded agitated and she was trying to calm him down. I waited outside, listening.

"Why didn't you call me? Why didn't you make her?"

"She's a grown woman, Andrew."

"But you knew how important it was to me."

"I couldn't force her, could I?"

I heard a chair screech.

"Don't let it get to you so. She'll come back."

"Wasn't there a car? A number?"

"She must have left it up the lane. You only missed her by a hair's breadth."

47

There was a long pause. I was about to decide that it was safe to go in, when Dad started up again. This time his voice was quieter, sadder.

"What did she look like? Was she the same?"

"You're forgetting. I didn't know her, Andrew."

"Yes but, the papers. You must've seen a photograph?"

"I might have."

"Well, has she changed?"

"Her hair's shorter, maybe. Shoulder length. I can't tell. I didn't know her, back then. Still pretty."

So, she had long hair when she was young. I could imagine that – her face like one of Pookie's elves, with its thin nose and small features, blonde hair down her back or in a neat ponytail. I knew now for sure, they were talking about Lorna.

"If it helps at all, she mentioned she wanted to see you. Or she did at first, before she changed her mind. Why else would she have come? Maybe she lost her nerve."

"Lorna doesn't lose her nerve."

By now, I was scared I would drop the ornament because I'd stood still so long, and that wind was whipping my hair like a loose flag. I elbowed the door open and walked in.

Mrs Gayle looked across at me, brightly.

"Hello, Imogen. What have you got there, lass?"

Dad shifted in his seat. I'll swear he was wiping a tear as he looked away. He couldn't speak to me, not a word.

"I wanted to show you this. It's new in the shop."

I unwrapped it carefully and stood it on the kitchen table. Dad got up from his chair and walked out. He never even took one look at the fawn.

"That's grand, Imogen," Mrs Gayle reassured me. "It looks exactly like the deer in our meadow. That'll sell as well as anything, won't it?"

"Yes," I said, but my mind wasn't on it anymore. My eyes followed my father, until the office door shut behind him.

Mrs Gayle had picked up my treasure and was turning it round, this way and that.

"It's even got Loraligh written in gold."

"That was Cedric's idea."

"What would we do without him, eh?"

I was trying not to cry.

"I'd better put it back in the shop now. Mark said I wasn't to keep it for long."

"Oh well, if *Mark* said…"

Mrs Gayle was smiling and I knew she was teasing me. I wasn't much in the mood to smile back, and felt her gaze following me across the car park to the shop. Sometimes, you could sense when Mrs Gayle wished she could change things, even when there was no chance.

Dad was quiet for a long time after that. He was even more distracted than usual and I noticed he'd stopped joining us for tea. There was always some excuse: he wasn't hungry, he had work to do, he'd eat later. Sometimes, I could tell Mrs Gayle was about to argue with him. She'd open her mouth, about to say something, and then close it again and put his cutlery back in the drawer. She always saved him a plateful though, and kept it warm in the stove.

It must've been well over a year had passed – I know because I wasn't far off starting secondary school – when Mark and I were down at the river's edge, our trousers rolled up to our knees, and he said:

"Hey Immie, you'll never guess what."

"What?"

Mark grinned at me and then he reached down into the water and scooped a whole handful of it up in his palms and hurled it at me, with all my clothes on. I shrieked.

"*Tell* me, Mark Wheeler!"

"I saw your dad in town yesterday."

"Is that all? What was he doing?"

"*And*, he was sitting in the window of Tony's café, you know, the one near the station…with a *woman*." And he said 'woman' like it was dead mysterious.

"So."

"She had fair hair."

I stopped wading and looked across at him.

"So."

"Aren't you bothered?"

"Anyone would think you wanted me to be bothered."

"I was thinking. It might've been that woman who was knocking around here, a while back."

I lost my appetite for playing in the river and went back to The Beach, where I sat down on the dead tree trunk with all its twists and curves. I started banging at the pebbles with my long stick.

"What were they doing?" I asked eventually.

Mark came over to join me.

"I'm sorry, Immie. I didn't mean to upset you."

He put his arm around my shoulder and I liked him doing that, so I carried on being serious for as long as I could.

"Were they talking?"

"Yes, I s'pose so. Your dad had one arm stretched out across the table, as if he was going to touch her."

"Was he smiling?"

"No, most definitely not smiling. But he was looking at her, intently like."

"Did he look cross then?"

"I don't know. Blimey, I only saw them for a split second. I was just walking past."

He took his arm away then, and I wished I hadn't always got the urge to ask so many questions.

"If it was Lorna, they could've met by chance. He could've run into her when he was shopping or something. It doesn't mean anything, does it?" I said.

Mark was squatting on the beach, both hands gripping his stick, gouging a hole out of the ground between his feet and pushing the stones back behind him like a dog.

"Would you mind if it did?"

"Yes." It came out sulky, although I never meant it to.

"Why though? If your dad had…you know, another woman in his life. He's been by himself a long time now, Immie. He must be lonely."

"He's not lonely. He's got Mrs Gayle and me. He doesn't need her. He doesn't need anyone."

"It's not the same thing."

"Besides, Cedric says Dad's a loner. He doesn't need people like some folk do."

"That's because…" and then Mark went quiet and he refused to finish that sentence, even though I begged him to.

I worried for days and days, and had trouble falling asleep at night, after what Mark had seen. I figured out for myself the

51

ending to his sentence. Dad was a loner because Mum had left us. It wasn't exactly hard to work out. I wished Mark hadn't told me he'd seen him with Lorna, because there wasn't a single thing I could do about it, and I couldn't exactly ask Dad, could I?

In the end I didn't need to, because he came right out with it one Friday afternoon, when I arrived home from school. He'd asked Mrs Gayle to stay on and look after me for the evening, and she'd said, well all right then, just this once, but I do have a family of my own you know. Dad had given her a look, the sort that stood still in mid-air, and Mrs Gayle said: It'll do you good, Andrew. Of course I will.

"Where's Dad going then?" I asked her, as he was climbing the stairs to get ready. It was unheard of, Dad going out of an evening.

She looked at me and smiled. "I believe your father is going on a *date*."

I took one look at her, dropped my bag in the corner by my shoes, and ran up to my room. And there it started. I screwed my eyes up tight in an effort to stop the tears coming, but they had a mind of their own and began to flow in full force. And then the noise began too, even though I was burying my face in the pillow.

The problem was my imagination. It often made things out to be worse than they were. In my mind, the woman who was supposed to come back and have a date with Dad was my mother. And I knew for a fact this wasn't her. Then there was the possibility that this was the start of something big, something everlasting, because otherwise why would Dad announce it publicly to Mrs Gayle and me, if it wasn't?

52

The more I let my thoughts carry me away, the worse it got. My mother was turning up at the gate in her lovely white dress and her wavy hair blowing in the wind, and there was Dad telling her we didn't need her anymore. Telling her to go away.

By the time Mrs Gayle walked into my room, I was in a complete lather, gasping for air because of all my sobbing. That's when the idea came to me, forcing its way in between all the other thoughts with a way of its own, which was pretty much beyond my control.

I began to wheeze and cough, my face pressed into the pillow. Mrs Gayle was already on her knees, rubbing my back and giving her usual instructions. I thought I'd add a bit more drama to the whole thing by screwing up the sheets, and mixing in a whole croupy noise, which sounded especially good against the depths of the pillow.

Mrs Gayle became really alarmed then. She flipped me over to face her, hooked her arms under my armpits and pulled me up straight, in an effort to help me breathe properly.

I'll never know whether she understood what was going on before, or after, she slapped my face. Whichever it was, the slap caught my performance completely off-guard and, for a second or two, our eyes made contact and held each other there. I was so shocked, so maddened by the sharp crack of her hand on my cheek, I stopped still. That was when she must've guessed, because if I hadn't been faking it, the wheezing and whooping would've taken their own course, slap or not.

"Dad! *Daddy!*" I shrieked, but he was already in the doorway.

It was that look – the look Mrs Gayle gave me when I yelled for Dad – that was when I knew I'd lost her forever. That she would never forgive me, no matter what I did or what I said thereafter.

"What's the matter, Imogen?" Dad asked. "What's going on?"

He looked from me to Mrs Gayle, and back to me. My hand was pressed to my cheek where it had started to burn. My head went down. I was looking at the lines on my shirt, the way they curved around and got lost in the creases, like the roads on our moor. I couldn't look her in the eye again. I continued wheezing, although the purpose had gone out of it. Mrs Gayle stood up and made to leave the room.

"What do you think, Mrs Gayle?" he asked her. "Is it a bad one? Perhaps I should stay in after all."

"Do what you like. She's your daughter."

She walked straight past him standing there in the doorway and didn't say another word. I felt mortally ashamed. I ran across to my father and wrapped my arms round him, burying my head in his shirt.

"Don't go, Dad. Please don't go."

I felt his hand briefly touch my hair, but it dropped away again. I felt his sigh. When we went downstairs, Mrs Gayle was already putting on her anorak and collecting her things together. She left without saying goodbye to either of us. Dad watched her go. He didn't know what to say.

He told me he had to go to his office. Had to make a telephone call. His eyes were dull and he looked sad, so I hadn't gained a thing. I sat at the kitchen table and began crying all over again – for the need of Mrs Gayle's hug and smile and kind words, which I knew full well I would never feel again.

When I'd done with crying, I sat at the kitchen table, picking at the grooves with my fingernail, the other hand covering the burn so Dad wouldn't see. I had to keep the wheezing going, although I was making it calm down fast, because it felt like the wrong thing to be doing.

I could hear Dad's voice in the office, but his words were muffled and I couldn't work them out. He would be telling Lorna he wasn't coming out. He would say Mrs Gayle had had to hurry home. He would put down the receiver, his heart heavy, and I had made it like that. It was easy to hate myself then – to know that I had spoiled Dad's night out, the only one he'd had that I could remember. Inside, a part of me was glad he was staying in with me, but the other part was telling me how miserable and hateful and totally selfish I'd been. Hateful enough for Mrs Gayle to hit me. Hateful enough for her to leave and never come back.

After what felt like an hour or more, the office door opened and Dad came into the kitchen.

"All right now then?" he asked.

I had nearly dropped off to sleep and his voice sounded strange, as if I was still in the dream. I looked up at him.

"Yes, Dad."

"Better get off to bed then."

"Sorry about your night out."

He stared at me. He thought I wasn't sorry, but I was. It was awfully quiet in the kitchen. It didn't feel right to fetch a glass of milk, with him watching. I went to the doorway and paused by his side, wondering if we should kiss goodnight there and then, but he didn't stoop down for me to reach him.

"Good night, Imogen."

"Night, Dad."

Five

Mad

Mrs Gayle didn't come over that weekend. I knew she wouldn't. When Mark turned up for work, I couldn't wait to see him to explain what I'd done. Dad didn't join me for breakfast and he had that far-away look. He mumbled something about getting a part for the Land Rover and I was to stay and mind Loraligh until Mark arrived. Someone needed to be here to let him in. And so Dad left, and I had to push his bacon into the bin because he wasn't hungry.

When I'd finished washing up, I spent a while staring at the telephone, wondering whether or not I should ring Mrs Gayle to apologise, but I couldn't summon up the nerve. I was willing it to ring of its own accord, to be her, to say she'd forgiven me. The time dragged and Mark was late. When he finally opened the gate, I ran across the car park to meet him and burst into tears. I didn't mean to, but I couldn't help myself.

"Hey, what's up Immie? What is it?"

I buried my face in his parka and wouldn't come out. I didn't want him to see what a mess I was in.

"Where's your dad? Where's Mrs Gayle? Has something happened?"

"I've done something bad. Really bad. She's never coming back."

Mark took me into the shop where he got the whole story out of me and then he sat down on his chair, behind the cash register, because he said he needed to do some thinking. After a long silence and a couple of false starts, when he seemed to have got the answer and then changed his mind, he began to give his verdict on things.

"She shouldn't have hit you, Immie. Whatever you did. She shouldn't've done that."

"No."

"Did it hurt?"

"Yes. Well, not much. Not as much as this hurts."

"I don't follow."

"Not seeing her. Sending her away."

Mark got thoughtful then, and began fiddling with things in the shop that he needed to do. I tried not to watch him. I wasn't sure what he thought of me now, if he would see it from my side. I undid a packet of crayons from the shelf and began arranging them on the carpet, because I always like them to look like a rainbow, not a muddle. I was itching to try them out in one of the new colouring books, but I was in enough trouble.

"The way I figure it," he added eventually, "is that she, Mrs Gayle that is, thought she ought to shock you. You know, bring you round, out of your hysterics."

"It wasn't hysterics."

"Sounds like hysterics to me. And then, she did it so quick, she didn't have time to think about it."

"Maybe."

"And then, once it had happened, she must've felt so bad she couldn't face either of you. That's why she left straight away."

"D'you think she was worried my dad would find out?"

"I think she thought he already knew."

"Mm."

"And now, she feels so bad for what she's done, she can't face you either."

I needed time to think about that. I was scratching the pattern on the carpet with the wrong end of a crayon, running it along the lines of the cord. Needlecord, Cedric said it was. Cheap. Just like Andrew, to buy cheap.

Then I began shaking my head.

"It's me she doesn't want to see, Mark. She hates me now, I know she does. I can feel it."

"Where is your dad, anyway?"

"He's gone into town. To the garage. He needs a spare part."

"He doesn't usually leave you by yourself, does he?"

"No."

Mark had noticed the significance of that fact. Things were going to be different from then on. There was no housekeeper to look after me, and Dad couldn't be expected to do it all the time, now I was eleven. I began imagining the empty days ahead, with me doing all the cooking and ironing, because Dad didn't have a clue did he? It wouldn't only be Sundays I had to wash up – it would be every day of the week – and the thought of it all sent me into another wave of misery.

Mark didn't know what to do with a girl who wouldn't stop crying, but I couldn't. The tears were stinging my eyes and making them bleary. The hopelessness of it all had no answer. Mrs Gayle had become a sort of mother to me, and losing her was as hard.

"Immie, I know what we'll do. When it's my break, we'll go down to The Beach and build a dam. My mum always says activity's the best cure for being down in the dumps. We can find sticks and stuff from the wood, and build a big dam right across the river. Just for the hell of it. What do you think?"

He was rubbing my back through my jumper, and it felt comforting.

"Won't we get into trouble? Won't the water build up?"

"Not with a bit of engineering."

"What does that mean?"

"You'll see."

In the end, Dad didn't arrive back at Loraligh until after twelve, by which time I was frantic. I'd spent half the morning sitting on the gate, watching out for him. He might've had an accident. And besides, if he didn't come back, Mark couldn't have a break because there was no one else to ask. When Dad finally turned up, I pushed the gate open and ran to meet him before he'd even turned off the engine.

"You've been ages," I said.

"They didn't have the part. I had to try somewhere else."

"Oh."

"Did Mark come?"

"He's in the shop. We want to go down to the river for his lunch break. Can we, Dad?"

He didn't look pleased. It meant he'd have to mind things.

"Any visitors today?"

"Not a soul." Mrs Gayle's words.

"I'll lock it up for now. If anyone arrives, I'll see from the house."

So we were free, but only for an hour or so.

Down on The Beach, Mark and I got collecting. We picked up anything and everything that was loose: old branches that'd fallen from the larches and junipers and oaks; twigs, sticks, boulders. You name it, we used it. Mark said that if we created a hole in the middle of the dam, enough water would keep flowing through so as not to block it up. Not to make it dangerous. He explained that that was how dams worked. He said if beavers could do it, so could we, and they'd had no training.

It took us ages, especially at first, because as fast as we added bits to the dam, the water dragged them along downstream. But once we'd piled things higher and higher, I could see we were gaining ground. It was the river against us, water against man, and man was winning. Mark was feeling victorious, you could tell. He was moving fast, laughing and shouting at me to collect more and more. Then he carefully climbed on top, to test it out – holding out his arms like a trapeze artist.

"Wahoo!" he yelled. "Come on up, Immie!"

But I was watching what was happening behind him. A pool of water was growing, gradually covering over the pebbles on that section of beach. We stood and stared as the water level rose.

"What's to stop it?" I asked.

"It'll settle in a minute. Give it time."

Mark climbed down onto the stones and found a particular boulder, one with a stripy pattern on the top that was easy to remember.

61

"We'll use this as a marker."

He placed it a little way away from the water's edge and we both watched, checking the pool wouldn't come up as far as the stone.

"That's clever," I said.

"Nothing to it."

Mark liked it when I paid him a compliment, even though he brushed it off. His face coloured up and he got extra busy. Once the water had settled and a steady flow was trickling through our hole, we sat back on our piece of driftwood, tired out. We'd sat on that particular tree trunk so many times, it had worn a shiny curve the shape of our backsides. I was watching the ripples spreading out in neat, steady lines, and how the water boatmen rode over the humps, gripping on for dear life.

"What do you think I should do, Mark?"

"About Mrs Gayle, you mean?"

"And Dad."

"I'd leave it a day or two. She's bound to get in touch sooner or later. Your Dad's more difficult to work out."

"Why?"

"We don't know if he knows, do we?"

"No. He's not exactly easy to ask, either. I never know what to say to him."

"If he knows, about her slapping you I mean, it could be that he wouldn't have her back anyway. Or...he might think you deserved it, in which case he wouldn't mind what she did, and he's probably wondering right now how to approach her."

"Maybe."

"One thing's for certain, Immie. You can't come right out with it. You have to go about these things carefully. Be diplomatic. People can be very complicated."

I knew he was right about that. Even though there weren't exactly many people in my life, the ones there were had never been straightforward. Except Mrs Gayle. She was as straightforward as a bill for the electrics dropping on your doormat. That was what Cedric always said. You got what you expected, no surprises there. Until I reminded him that Dad said the last bill was much bigger than he'd thought, so Cedric had to think again.

"What ever happened to that woman? Did she come back?"

"Who, Lorna? Not as far as I know."

I wished Mark hadn't brought that up again, because things were bad enough in my head as it was, without her to worry about. But since he had, it started me wondering about her all over again.

"Mark?"

"What?"

"You remember that day the new souvenirs arrived, ages ago, and I overheard Dad talking to Mrs Gayle in the kitchen?"

"What of it?"

"Dad said something about the papers. I wrote it all down in my diary, so I wouldn't forget. I keep going over it. He said *You saw the papers*. What do you think he meant?"

"It usually means the news, newspapers. Or it could have been legal documents, that sort of thing."

"He said *her picture*. You must've seen her picture in the papers. So it wasn't, what you said, legal papers. They don't have pictures do they?"

"Not as far as I know."

"So, Lorna could've been in the news."

"But when? We have no idea how long ago they were talking about."

"And now we never will, because Mrs Gayle won't be here to ask."

Mark was lobbing pebbles at his marker boulder and they were bouncing off at random angles into the water. The splashing sounded loud in the peacefulness of Shallow Falls, and echoed, because of The Slopes rising behind. I could smell the sweat on his shirt, from all his cavorting about, but I didn't mind.

"There's always Cedric."

"I don't think he knows anything. I asked him about it all, the next day in fact. He wasn't keeping any secrets, I could tell."

Mark rested one hand on my thigh then, and the other was round my shoulder. He caught my bare skin, because I'd got my pleated skirt on for a change, and his hand felt warm. We leant our heads in together and I wished and wished he wouldn't have to go home. That he lived at Loraligh with Dad and me. But not like a brother. Never like a brother.

Then Mark looked at his watch.

"Bugger, it's nearly quarter to."

He grabbed my elbow and we began running through the trees to the meadow.

"Come on, Immie. Run faster."

He had an amazingly short memory for a bright lad, because you'd think by now he'd remember about my asthma.

"I can't."

I stopped running and held back.

"You keep going. I'll catch you up."

He stalled a moment, yards ahead of me up the path, looking back and wondering what to do for the best.

"I'll be fine, Mark. You go on ahead."

He left me then, because he had to get back. He couldn't risk being late again. I figured there wasn't any point in hurrying up to the house. There was a month-old fawn standing in the middle of the path, yards from its mother. It stood stock still, staring at me, not sure whether to scarper or stay right there. It wasn't as used to people as the rest of them. Mostly, they'd hardly bat an eyelid when folk came near.

I edged towards him. How much I wanted to stroke his hide, to feel how smooth it was. I reached down carefully and pulled up a handful of grass to entice him towards me, all the time speaking softly, the way Mrs Gayle had shown me. But right at the last second, when I'd got so close I could feel the warmth of his flank, he darted off across the grass to his mother.

A sadness swept over me then. Not because of the fawn, exactly.

It began raining after that. Not that soft, downy rain that drizzles on interminably. These were great big splats of rain, each drop big enough to drink from the palm of your hand. I noticed the sound of it before I actually saw it. The whoosh was several yards behind me at first, sweeping across the meadow, loud enough to make me swing round, loud enough to make me say – what on earth? I hurried back to the house

65

and Dad was relieved, because he said he'd seen me from the window and he was worried. I couldn't understand it. He didn't usually have a problem with me wandering around unsupervised. I wondered what was making him so jumpy.

"Best stay in now, Imogen."

"Okay, Dad."

"You were gone a long time. What on earth do you two get up to down there?"

"Nothing much," I lied. But it wasn't exactly a lie because although we'd been busy, it wasn't anything that counted. It wasn't anything you'd have to admit to.

Dad gave me a strange look then. His gaze lingered longer than I felt comfortable with.

"How old were you last birthday?"

Wasn't that an odd question for a father to ask? And then he didn't wait for an answer, which was just as well because, with my annoyance at him not remembering, my words had frozen up.

"I don't know how we're going to manage without her, you know, Imogen. With you growing up so fast."

He was pacing the room, hands deep in his pockets, looking out of the window. Then Dad sat down at the kitchen table, one elbow on the surface, his head in his hand. It can be dark in our kitchen with its low ceiling, but the light comes in from both sides, because it's a big room which runs from front to back, with no porch. It's sunnier out the front and later in the day, when the sun's low. On this particular afternoon, the light had all but disappeared, because of the intense rain. We didn't have the lights on yet, and I remember this strange, green glow of leftover day was casting its colour on Dad's side, picking out the veins that were sticking out above his wrists, and the lines around his eyes.

He was looking at me as if I had all the answers.

"She's upset, you know."

My head went down.

"Yes, Dad. I know."

"There are times when we all need to say sorry – for anything we might've done or said."

I waited a while before I could think what to say next.

"It won't make any difference," I added eventually. "She won't come back."

I thought it strange that Dad wasn't asking what I'd done. As if he knew. But if that was the case, why wasn't he punishing me like I deserved?

The rain went on and on that day and Dad sent Mark home. On the Sunday, I slept in. Nobody woke me and there was nothing to get up for. Dad's bed was empty when I finally surfaced, and he wasn't in the kitchen. His office door was shut, but when I summoned up the courage to knock and go right in, he wasn't in there either. I looked for evidence of breakfast, but the kettle was cold and the sink empty. I began to panic. I hurried into my jeans and top, and went out to look for him.

The sight that met my eyes when I turned the corner by the outhouses took me by complete surprise. Water, great pools of it, was sloshing across the west side of the meadow, forcing the deer across to the other side. The river must've burst its banks from one side of our garden, right down to Murderers' Wood. Several small trees were poking up out of the water's surface, like a swamp. It was surreal. That's what Mark would've said, surreal. That was a good word for it. I knew it had rained hard, but not *that* hard. Not enough for a flood.

I found my wellies and ran down the path, most of which, fortunately, was on higher ground. It isn't easy running in wellingtons, because they feel too big and your socks slip under your heels, and I was doing my best not to trip. All I could think of was Dad – perhaps he was out there somewhere, perhaps he was in trouble. When I got to The Beach, I caught sight of him. I gasped. He was mid-river, up to his thighs, and I thought all the rain running down from the hills must've raised the water level much higher than usual. He was frantically removing our dam, piece by piece, throwing it across to the bank on the other side.

At that moment, Dad stopped and looked across at me. I thought he'd ask me to help. Or I thought he'd tell me not to come in, it was too dangerous, stay at the side. But Dad didn't do either of those things. No.

With a steely gaze fixed right on me, holding me there as if I'd be in so much trouble if I dared to look away, he stopped what he was doing and began walking towards me, striding through the heavy water. He was getting quicker and quicker as he got nearer, and when he reached me, he raised his arm and struck me so hard on my back, I fell forwards and nearly lost my balance. He hit me again, and then a third time, and I was yelling at him, Dad, Dad don't, Dad stop! But he was like a man possessed and he couldn't stop, and I ran screaming and crying away from him, through the trees. I was the one being murdered in our wood and nobody would be there to know. Nobody was watching and there was nobody at the house to run to.

I realised, half way up the meadow, that he must've given up chasing me, because there was no sound from behind, but there was no way I was going to stop running. My lungs hurt. My heart hurt. My back hurt where it could still feel the shape of his hand. I was wheezing badly, but I knew I had to keep going. I didn't turn round to look until I'd got to the outhouses at the top of the garden. I leaned against the wall and tried to gain my breath back, but it hurt so much. I slid down the brickwork until I was crouching, with my arms wrapped tight around my knees. My brain was desperately trying to work out what to do. It was clear I couldn't stay there. Dad had turned into a madman and there wasn't another soul in the house. I must have done something wicked. My whole body was trembling, my heart thumping so much it hurt, but I wasn't crying. Not then.

The town. I'd have to go to town. Find Mark. Find someone. I'd need money for a bus. I'd need my coat.

I fled through the house, grabbing Dad's loose change he keeps in a dish on the mantelpiece, and my anorak. I stuffed two apples from the bowl into my pockets and then, as an afterthought, in case I was never going back, I grabbed Mum's photograph too and pushed it in with the apples. It ripped the pocket, but it was vital I had it with me. There was no other way I was going to find her, without that picture.

I was running along the lane, over the bridge, all the way to Three Boys and then the crying began. Rivers of it. The noise I was making was alarming, even to me, but it sounded outside of me.

I wanted Mrs Gayle then, so badly. I wanted Mark or Cedric. I wanted my mother. But most of all, I wanted Dad. Not this Dad, with crazy, angry eyes. My Dad.

Six

Runaway

I don't remember the rest of the journey to town. I know I
didn't get the bus because it never came – Sunday timetable.
When I finally reached the High Street it was virtually empty.
The roads were wet, but the traffic was moving well enough.
I'd expected bad flooding all the way, but that only seemed to
be at our mill.

The Wimpy bar was closed and so was Tony's café. I
walked on to St Simon's, even though I was exhausted, it
being the only other place I really knew, apart from my
primary school and the library. Several kids, much older than
me, were knocking around by the school gate. A couple of
them were up on the wall where I didn't think they should be.
They were passing round a packet of fags and having a joke.
In September, I'd be one of them. But right at that moment I
felt young, too young. I'd only just started developing. Mrs
Gayle had noticed. She said I'd need a bra soon and I turned
hot when she said that, and I said, no I don't. I don't need a
bra. But that night she suggested it, I looked at myself in the
long mirror inside Dad's wardrobe when I was changing for
bed, and I could see what she meant.

I had an idea then, but it involved interrupting their conversation. It took one hell of a lot of courage to do that, but what other choice did I have?

"Excuse me."

They stopped and looked at me, all four of them at once. I hoped they wouldn't notice I'd been crying.

"Do you know Mark Wheeler? He goes to your school. He's in the sixth form."

"Why?" The lad who answered me was wearing a cap the wrong way round.

"I need to find him."

"We might," another one answered. I didn't think they were going to be awfully helpful, but I'd started so I might as well carry on. The way I saw it, I was running out of options.

"Is he your brother then?"

"No, but I know him. He's a friend. He works at our shop."

That seemed to satisfy them.

"He lives up the avenue, off the top. The close, off the top."

"Do you know which house?"

"Search me."

I began walking away then, after I'd said thank you, and one of them shouted after me:

"His dad drives a Skoda! It'll be parked up front."

They all laughed. I knew there wouldn't be a car, Skoda or otherwise. Mark's dad left ages ago.

The avenue was a climb and a half, and I'd already walked miles. I sat on the road sign at the top, to get my breath back, and ate one of the apples because my mouth was dry as dog biscuits. The hems of my jeans were soaked, and water was seeping half way to my knees, but at least it wasn't raining. I looked up the close. Hazel Close it was called, although there wasn't a tree in sight. Chestnut Avenue, Larch Way, Hazel Close, and the only trees I could see were the ones round the back of a few gardens, and they weren't up to much. Not very good at naming things, our council. Not like Mark and me.

I counted four houses up the left side, three up the right and two face-on at the end. I could see them all, from where I was perched. All semis, brick at the bottom, rough granite at the top. Black and green paint, and doors with the glass high up that you can't see through. Nothing special. Council, Cedric would say. I knew about council houses, because he and I had watched the news programme together once or twice, since Dad had relented and bought us a television. I'd been on at him for ages, because everyone in my class had a telly and it didn't suit me to be the odd one out. Cedric always had something to say about the public they interviewed on the news. Where *do* they get them from? – he'd say, when someone was giving their point of view on the latest situation. Can't they ever find someone articulate? And Mrs Gayle would reply that he was a snob and a fine one to talk.

I looked at the cars parked out front – not that it would help much, because of Mark's dad. I walked round Hazel Close on the pavement, up one side, across the top and down the other, back to my road sign. I looked in the windows of the houses and I looked for Mark, but I couldn't spot him. What were the chances, after all? He'd be up in his room, looking through his football stickers, or out with his mates.

After what felt like at least half an hour, with me wondering what to do, getting cold and knowing I couldn't go back home, a lady came out of one of the houses. She was young, lots of lipstick and a shiny plastic coat. She stooped down to look at her reflection in the window of a parked car, and she fluffed up her hair, tugging at the fringe and making a face.

It was my only chance.

"Excuse me, Miss. Do you know Mark Wheeler?"

I took her by surprise and I thought she was going to be cross, but then a smile spread across her face. She had orange lipstick on her teeth.

"Aye, pet. I ought to know Mark Wheeler. He's only my brother, isn't he?"

Connie or Denise, it had to be.

"Do you want to see him?"

"Yes please. If he's in."

"I'll go'n get him for you."

I don't know what she must've thought, me only eleven and Mark about to leave school. Like her brother's own fan club. She went back into her house and called up the stairs.

"Mark! You've got a visitor." She turned to look at me then and grinned, like it was all very amusing. You'd have thought she could tell I was upset.

I could see the bottom of the staircase inside his house. It had one of those carpets that don't fit the width of the stairs, and the sides were painted white gloss, but they'd gone yellow with age, and the stair rods had lost their shine.

She gave me a little wave and left me to it, tottering past on her high heels. Mrs Gayle would've said something about those shoes, because she didn't look at all safe in them.

Mark came to the door. He wasn't dressed yet and it was a bit embarrassing, him standing there in shorts, with his bare chest and his hair needing a comb.

"Immie?"

He looked genuinely surprised. Not happy exactly. I couldn't tell. It didn't feel the same, on his patch instead of mine.

"Sorry…I had to come."

"I didn't think you knew where I live."

"I don't. I didn't. I went to your school. Some boys told me."

He must've realised the way I was feeling, because he told me to wait a minute, he'd be right back. He always had an instinct about other people, did Mark. When he came out again, he was wearing his Arsenal shirt and jeans, with a denim jacket on top and his trainers.

"Come on. We'll go for a walk."

"You weren't coming to work, were you, today?"

"No. Your dad phoned. He said it was too wet."

I wondered if that was before Dad saw the damage, or after. We walked for a while and the relief of having him there, having *someone* there, should've lifted my spirits, but I felt so bad inside.

"Was that Connie or Denise?"

"Denise. Connie doesn't live with us anymore. She's moved in with her boyfriend."

So that was the headache halved then.

"Something terrible's happened, Mark."

I stopped walking. I was looking up at him and he towered over me. He had grown so much taller lately. Mrs Gayle said her David grew like that when he was a teenager, and she said girls didn't put on a spurt, the way boys did. She'd know after all, because she had three girls to one boy.

"What is it? What's happened?"

I told him then. I told him about the flood in the meadow and the trees shooting up out of the water. I told him about our dam clogging up, and Dad being livid about that and hitting me three times. I told him I could never go back. There was no one left there for me now anyway.

Mark's face looked dead serious then – a hard, solemn look – and his eyes were far away and then suddenly they weren't. They were fixed right on mine and he was deadly earnest.

"Immie, your Dad won't want me working at Loraligh anymore. It was my idea, the dam. He'll know it was my idea. I won't be allowed back after this."

He took my shoulders and was squeezing them a bit too tight. He was frightening me.

"You'll have to go home, Immie. Your dad'll calm down. He won't be mad for ever. He's all you've got."

I was trying not to cry, but my bottom lip was trembling.

"Bloody hell. I never thought it would do that. How the hell did it do that?"

He was walking again now, purposefully, faster than I wanted to but I had to keep up.

"It rained really hard in the night."

"Yes, but we left a big hole didn't we? We checked it."

I didn't have an answer.

"He's a bit neurotic, my dad. That's what Cedric says."

"It's for the best, with me going away in September. I couldn't stay on much longer, as it is."

A black cloud came over me when he said that, because I knew it was the truth of things, but I was trying not to think about it. There was I, about to start at St Simon's, and Mark was leaving. One in, one out. It was bad luck we couldn't have overlapped by one year at least. Sod's law.

We walked for ages all round the town. We passed the shops in the High Street, which were shut, and under the railway bridge through all the pigeon muck. You always have to walk through there as quick as you can, to be sure to get through alive. There must be a hundred pigeons living under those arches. The pavements smell of wet tarmac after the rain, and you have to keep to the inside to avoid the spray as the cars pass. Especially if it's one of the sixth formers, just passed their test and showing off. They do it on purpose.

Then Mark diverted off the roads into the graveyard and round the outside of the church, him going too fast and me trying to keep up. Once or twice, I begged him to wait for me, but he didn't hear. He had no idea how far I'd walked already. My legs were aching and my feet were sore underneath. Finally he slowed down and we spent a while reading the inscriptions on gravestones. There was one of a two-day-old baby, which made me sad to read: Winifred Gable, taken too soon. Given to God, 1911.

"Why would a two-day-old baby die, Mark?"

"Lots of reasons. Cot death, illness, maybe it was born premature. Lots of babies didn't make it in those days. They didn't have the technology. Or the medicine."

"Her poor mother."

I got to thinking of the sadness of all the mothers who had ever lost a baby. Imagine, all that grief put together in one, enormous pool of tears. Enough for a whole lake. Enough for an ocean. And my mother's tears were all mixed up in there somewhere for me. And I didn't even die.

We could hear the organ playing and people singing inside, *For those in peril on the sea.* I like that hymn because it conjures up images in my head – small fishing boats, red and blue, tossed about on the waves in the inky night, the moon picking out the white spray of the sea foam. It makes you feel safe, to be in the school hall with the doors and windows shut and the lights full on. I'd never be a fisherman.

As we passed the front door of the church, it creaked open, which made us both jump, and who should walk out but Mrs Gayle, clutching her handbag and looking much smarter than I was used to. First Mark and then her; what were the chances of that, with the way my luck went? Mark and I were standing not five yards away, so I couldn't pretend otherwise. She looked shocked to see us but sort of pleased at the same time. Or perhaps she was embarrassed, I couldn't tell.

"Good Lord! What ever are you doing here, Imogen?"

I thought that was funny, her saying Good Lord like that when she'd just been singing about him, and you weren't to take his name in vain, especially in a church. And she was still in the porch.

"Boy, are we glad to see you," Mark said. And I was so relieved, I ran up to her and buried my face in her coat and clung on for dear life. I expected her to brush me off, but she rubbed my head and said there, there, pet lamb, it's not as bad as all that.

She suggested we went to her house after that (which surprised me, since she'd always found a dozen excuses not to let me in the past) because she said the roast was on and it would spoil if she didn't get back, with only her son watching over it, and he wasn't to be relied on. Not at his age. Mark explained a few things on the way, because I couldn't speak.

77

He told her about the dam clogging up, and the flood, and Dad losing his grip. Mrs Gayle was nodding her head and saying I see, goes to show, now it all makes sense. I was glad it was making sense to someone.

It was weird, going into her house. I'd heard about it so many times, I had a picture in my head of what it might look like inside. But it wasn't anything like I'd imagined. There were four children raised in that house, and there was hardly room to swing a cat. I'd envisaged a big, grey, stone house on the edge of town, a bedroom for each child and a dresser full of china and family heirlooms in the kitchen. Mrs Gayle was a family-minded person, I knew that, even though she'd spent more hours a day at ours than hers. But the only evidence I could see of her children was a photograph of each one on the sideboard, as teenagers. Not one of them when they were little. They weren't exactly a handsome group either, except the youngest daughter, who had deep, dark eyes that grabbed at you. The rest were pasty and uninteresting, with freckled skin and eyes that disappeared into their faces. Which was surprising, because Mrs Gayle was handsome enough in her way – that's how Cedric had described her, and I thought for a while that perhaps he was sweet on her, but nothing ever came of that.

They'd all grown up and gone but David. Mr Stockington, whose christian name wasn't revealed to me at that time, had gone missing when the children were in their teens, and you weren't to mention it. Dad told me. Never ask, he said, because it was too hurtful. It wasn't the *lost* kind of missing, Dad said, when you had to keep looking and worrying. I hadn't understood at all, because I was only five when the whole subject of Mr Stockington had been raised, but Dad said it was the kind of missing that only adults understood, and it meant he didn't want to be found. I worried about Mrs Gayle, because I thought she might be sad about that, raising four youngsters all alone, but I had to admit there was nothing about our housekeeper that seemed sad or incapable, so I gave Dad the benefit.

Mark said he wouldn't come in, but Mrs Gayle insisted. Come on, have a cup of tea at least, won't you?

"Sit down now, you two. Take the weight off."

She checked the roast and basted it and popped it back in the oven, without its lid, to brown off. The smell was amazing: onion and gravy and crispy chicken skin. It reminded me how hungry I was. When she had five minutes to herself, she rubbed her hands on her apron and sat down beside me.

Then Mrs Gayle did the strangest thing. Or rather, she said it.

"Come and sit on my lap, Imogen Wise. I have something to tell you."

It was odd, because I hadn't sat on anybody's lap, not for a long while, but it felt so warm and nice, being wanted like that. She cuddled me up in her rough, no-nonsense way, and Mark turned to look out the window because he didn't know where else to look.

"Imogen, I know you were a naughty girl, and you did a very naughty thing to me last…well, you know when. I'm not excusing what you did and I'm not saying it wasn't a very dangerous thing to do, pretending like that…and to *me* of all people. But I'm not past apologising for my actions either. I did you wrong and I want you to know that I'm sorry. There are other ways to discipline a child. I know that. And I chose the wrong one."

I was so surprised, with Mrs Gayle apologising to me, instead of the other way round.

"No you didn't," I said. "Mark says you have to smack people in the face when they're having hysterics. He says that's the only way to stop them."

She looked at him then and grinned.

"There's not much you don't know, is there Mark Wheeler? Well, that is sometimes so. Now, Imogen, what are we going to do about you?"

"You won't make me go back, will you? Dad was angrier than I've ever seen him. He'll kill me. I'm not pretending about that, I'm really not this time."

She looked down at my face, which must've been appealing with every ounce of appeal I had in me, and she laughed.

"I've no doubt he was mad, child. I know Andrew has it in him to get mad sometimes. But if I know him, he'll be regretting his actions as much as I did mine, by now. And he'll be frantic with worry about where you are and what's happened to you."

"He will, Immie. She's right."

So now there were two of them onto me and I didn't stand a chance.

"He was bound to be startled, what with the land disappearing under water, and all completely avoidable if it hadn't been for you two."

"We didn't know it would do that."

"Plainly. Never mind that now. Your father turned up in time, just. And there's no point crying over spilt milk. We'll have to get you back home, so as you can have the opportunity to apologise and put things to rights."

"Mrs Gayle's right, Immie. He won't be mad for long. My dad never was."

And all I thought was, your dad was so mad he left you all, Mark Wheeler.

"But first you can both stay to dinner, because there's more chicken than the two of us can eat, and then I'll take you home. I'll explain everything to your father, and I'll make sure he has a good understanding of things before I leave. How will that do you?"

At that moment I loved Mrs Gayle more than I had ever loved anybody, ever. Even my father. Even Mark. She had that way of making me feel safe, the way no one else could.

After dinner, Mrs Gayle washed up and Mark and I wiped. David had scarpered, even before the treacle pudding, because he had friends to meet in town. I wondered what on earth they'd find to do there, with the Wimpy bar shut and the weather so cold.

It didn't take long, with three of us on the job. While I was waiting for the others to get ready to go, I scanned the family photographs and I discovered the strangest thing. There was a photo of me, right there in the row of her girls, with David on the end. I must've been about two. It was definitely me, although I'd never seen that particular one before. I couldn't believe I was so important, that I deserved a place in her living room.

When Mrs Gayle came downstairs and caught me looking at it, she got all flustered and went pink in the cheeks.

"You've always been like another daughter to me, Imogen. I've been looking after you since you were knee-high. You

81

know that, don't you?" she said, taking the frame from me and putting it back next to the big girls.

"Who's who? Tell me their names."

"Well, this one's Mattie. She's thirty four now. She's got two of her own. And then this one's Hayley – she's thirty one, she's got two daughters, and then my Karen's the youngest of the girls."

"How old is she?"

"Twenty six, last week. So you see, they're all grown up now. They don't need me for anything."

"Has Karen got any children?"

"She's not the maternal sort."

She took my chin in her finger and thumb, and turned my face to hers. Her eyes were serious, sort of concerned.

"I *am* sorry, pet. Sorry I hurt you and sorry your dad hurt you. It's not easy for an adult sometimes, to admit they were wrong to a child. Adults are very proud people. They like saving face. You'll understand that one day. But I shouldn't have laid a finger on you like that. You, of all people. You do believe me, don't you?"

I nodded, unable to take in all this apologising in one go, when I thought I was the worst child in the world. I'd deserved it, pretending to her like that. Me, of all people, she said. And then Mrs Gayle reached down and kissed me on the cheek, the side she'd slapped, and gave me a long hug, and at one point I thought she might be sniffing.

"You see, Imogen, I know why you did it. I understand why you tried to stop your father going out. I've had time to think it through since the other day, to try to see things from your point of view. You were only protecting things from changing. It isn't hard to see. But there are things you don't

82

know, child. Things I can't tell you. You have to trust me to know best."

Mrs Gayle had a way of saying things, putting a final stamp on it, which stopped me asking more questions, even though I desperately wanted to know what she meant. Of one thing I was sure – I could trust her. Of all the people I knew, I would always trust her the most.

So now everything was better, because she was back in my life and back at Loraligh where she belonged, and whatever Dad said or did after that, it would never be so bad as losing my wonderful Mrs Gayle.

Seven

The Goodbye

Dad never knew how to hug a child. He wasn't good at saying sorry either, not the way Mrs Gayle had. But the look in his eyes when the three of us turned up, was as near to sorry as he could get.

Mark came along too, because he wanted to assess the damage to the grounds, and to see what he could do to make up for things. He didn't expect his job back, but he said he had to face things like a man. There was an awkward moment when neither of them knew what words came next, but in the end it was clear that Dad had forgiven him and wouldn't hold a grudge, so both of them went out the back to see what more needed to be done.

I watched them go, two skinny men, rubbing their chins and scratching their heads. It didn't look that bad to me, from where I was looking. The flooded riverbanks had left huge muddy patches all over the flattened grass and round the tree roots, but most of the water had sunk back into its proper channel, and the herd of deer were now edging their way back across the west side of the meadow.

Mrs Gayle stood beside me, an arm around my waist, and I reached for her hand.

"He's going soon, you know. Mark, I mean."

"I know, lass. You'll miss him badly, won't you?"

"That I will."

"Well, you've got one summer left now, haven't you? So there's no point in moping around. Life has to move on, Imogen. We all have to make changes, and we never know what new opportunities life will bring. And you're off to the comprehensive, and that'll be something new and exciting for you too."

"I know, but it's still hard. Do you think Dad'll let him stay on in the shop until September?"

"I should think so. As long as you're both good and don't get up to any more antics."

And I was good, extra good after that, to make sure we had the whole of that last summer. Mrs Gayle took me shopping in town the next week. She met me at the school gate and took me to Bainbridges, where they measure you for a bra. Dad had obviously suggested it, which was dead embarrassing that he'd noticed.

The shop assistant took me into a cubicle, and I had to take my vest off and hold my arms out. The tape measure was cold and so were her hands, so it wasn't a pleasant experience all in all, but she was quick about it. 32A, she said I was, and I'd been a helpful girl and wasn't I sweet? Hardly worth spending one pound forty nine on, Mrs Gayle said, but she was unclipping her purse, and it was Dad's money so I know she wasn't that bothered. She bought two of them, one in white so it wouldn't show under my school shirt, and the other the same style in pink. They had a small, satin bow the size of a penny-piece, right in the middle. I liked the pink one best, but she said it wasn't to be worn at school. It would be too obvious. The pink one was for special occasions, and I wondered what the point of that would be, with no one to appreciate it. And besides, I didn't have the need to wear best clothes that often. Not at Loraligh. But Mrs Gayle said real ladies care about what they wear underneath, because it makes them feel they've made the effort. That made me wonder what Mrs Gayle wore under her skirt. She didn't look like a woman who would want anyone to know.

I stood for ages in front of the mirror inside Dad's wardrobe, practising with my pink bra on, and wishing Mark could see it. It gave me that tingling feeling you get between your legs, and I climbed under Dad's covers, trying to make it go away. I imagined Mark looking at me in my bra and kissing me as we lay on the bank. This was one of my favourite dreams I saved for bedtime, and I would turn it over and over in my head, trying to add to it and improve it, without changing things too much and spoiling it all.

I could see what Mrs Gayle meant about it hardly being worth it, because I only had small bumps at that stage, and if I stood face-on to the mirror, they disappeared completely. Not like Mrs Gayle's; hers were huge. I could tell her youngest daughter took after her mother, because in the photo she was showing her cleavage and there was plenty of it. I was surprised Mrs Gayle chose that picture of Karen to be on her sideboard. You'd think she'd have a better one than that. Something more respectable.

Mark and I had to make Dad some promises, after all the trouble with the dam. We promised not to build any more dams, for a start. And we promised not to interfere in any way with the structure of Shallow Falls, or any other part of the land, come to that. Dad explained, using all his technical terms, about water supply and the water table and natural drainage, why the working of the waterwheel rested on a highly balanced system, and that interfering even slightly with that balance, was dangerous and foolish. Mark looked shame-faced while he was listening, and I was just relieved that he was allowed to stay until he went to Sheffield in the autumn. I didn't know what Polly was, but I knew it was something to do with more studying, and it wasn't the same as university because he wouldn't have the grades for that, which I was surprised about because of his maths. Polly was an odd name for a place, I thought, because it always made me think of the nursery rhyme about putting the kettle on.

Cedric was the only person at Loraligh who didn't mind about it being Mark's last summer, and about him leaving soon. If he ever caught me looking glum, or making comments about how quiet it was going to be in October, Cedric would brush it aside, as if Mark was as easily dispensed with as an old sweet wrapper.

"Plenty more youngsters looking for a job where he came from," Cedric would say. "You wait and see. Half the sixth form will be looking for work out here. It's a plum job."

"They have to have transport, Dad says. School children can't get here easily, especially on Sundays," I reminded him, knowing full well that Mark nearly always got the bus. When he first came to work for us, he used to get a lift half the way and then walk the rest. That was before his dad left.

I could see I wasn't getting any sympathy as far as Cedric was concerned. Mrs Gayle said he did it on purpose, that he was being deliberately *obtuse*, which wasn't a word I understood, so I had to look that one up in our dictionary. She said obtuse was a useful word for old men and I wondered why they had to be old, before it applied.

"Men turn grumpy and difficult as they age," she said. "They've decided how the world works and how they like it, and they can't stand anything getting in the way of their interpretation of things. And then if it does," she added, "they dig their heels in and are about as difficult as they know how to be."

It made me think about Mr Stockington, when she said that. I wondered if that was why he'd gone missing – because of being obtuse. I thought Mrs Gayle was possibly glad he'd gone missing after all, because it might've been less trouble that way.

"And," she added, "they realise they're not getting any younger and they feel, well, usurped – by younger, stronger men, who've got more pulling power than they have."

I thought she meant like farm horses, pulling a plough like in the old days – until I was older, that is, when I realised there was another interpretation for it. I was surprised Mrs Gayle knew expressions like that, because I always had her down as an old-fashioned type. She could surprise you sometimes.

She told me it was all to do with the alpha male, and she used the deer in our meadow to explain what it meant, and how a stag couldn't bear to lose its position as leader of the herd, the king of its kingdom. That got me to thinking about Dad: King of Loraligh. It was an amusing thought, him sitting at the top of The Slopes, a crown on his head, ruler of all our land. It didn't feel right though, because Dad had never been the bossy type. Added to which, I always felt Mark was the

King of Loraligh, and I was the Queen. Dad didn't really figure at all.

"Your father's never had any competition, has he?" Mrs Gayle said. "You wait 'til you're old enough to bring home your first boyfriend. You wait and see what he makes of that."

I told her I'd never have a boyfriend. I meant, never unless it was Mark, but I wasn't going to admit to that, was I? She teased me often enough as it was.

The summer passed too quickly. Mark never kissed me at the foot of The Slopes, even though we lay next to each other countless times, me with my head propped up, chewing a blade of grass, pestering him with questions, and him flat on his back, watching the clouds. His body grew longer and longer, and by September, I barely reached his shoulder. I used to purposely slide higher up so our heads were level, and I'd wear my pink bra in case, and leave my legs bare, but he never even came close. The longing was terrible, all mixed in with the sadness that our time together was fast coming to an end. Sometimes, the conversation got round to wondering what it was going to be like in Sheffield, and how exciting it would be in a big city, with more than Tony's café and a Wimpy bar and only two screens at the Empire to entertain you.

It was being left behind that was so hard. He had loads of new things and places and people to look forward to. I had nothing and nobody.

"One of my brothers needs a job, Immie. He's always skint. Do you think your dad would let him take over from me?"

I hardly cared. I didn't want his brother.

"How old is he then?"

"Fifteen. And a half."

"I don't know. Dad was asking Cedric if he thought I could do it, you know, on my own, at weekends. He said he'd pay me."

"What did Cedric say?"

"He didn't. He just frowned and said whatever you think, Mr Wise. It's up to you. But I could tell he didn't approve. He doesn't think I'm up to it."

"Do you want the job? Do you think you could do it?"

I hunched my shoulders and didn't know what to think. I couldn't even imagine standing around in that shop all weekend, with no company and nobody to talk to except the odd visitor. Nothing was ever going to feel the same again.

In the end, it was Mrs Gayle who decided for us, because she said eleven was far too young to join the world of the employed, and I should have my freedom to run around and play, after working hard at school all week. Besides, she said, I'd have to be concentrating hard on my studies at secondary school, to make sure I didn't miss anything and fall behind. I'd need to be making an impression.

So Mark brought his brother Philip along to meet us all, the Saturday before he left, and Philip wasn't a patch on Mark in any way that I could see. He wasn't much taller than me, and he had a mole under his eye, the shape of Ireland. Standing next to each other, Philip only served to highlight everything Mark was to me. I realised how handsome Mark had become, even more than my imagination of him – how tall. Mrs Gayle said he was going to be a winner. Bees round a honey-pot, she said. Until she caught me scowling, and then she quickly changed the subject.

The next day was our last. Mrs Gayle offered to man the shop for a while, and said we could have longer than usual and she'd turn a blind eye. She even packed sarnies for us, wrapped in tin foil, with corned beef, because Mark was a man now and not a schoolboy any longer. I noticed he didn't run down Deer Meadow anymore, or grab loose branches from the trees and whack away the undergrowth as we went. His movements had become more deliberate. Heavier. His sleeves didn't reach his wrists, and his forearms now had veins that stuck out, and silvery hairs which caught the sunlight.

Something as wide as our river was opening up between Mark and me. Was it his age, or his height, or the quiet that was growing between us? I remember, for the first time ever on that last day, I felt I didn't know him so well. We'd become more like strangers and it didn't feel natural, being there at the water's edge where we'd built that dam in our frenzy only months before, and he'd been firing instructions at me and getting so excited. I thought of the emeralds and gold we used to gather from the riverbed, and wondered if Mark would think that was a silly game to play. Or the way we hid from each other behind the hawthorn bushes that dotted the foot of The Slopes.

"Will you be all right then, Imogen Wise?" he asked, "without me to keep an eye on you?"

I remember that he was smiling kindly when he said that, and he drew my forehead in and bounced it gently onto his chest. I was looking at our feet, one pair of trainers twice the length of the other.

"Guess I'll have to be."

"You need to have a few friends round, Immie – your own age. You need to work on your dad. It isn't right, you being by yourself so much."

"He won't let me."

"That was before. You need to try again. I don't like to think of you being lonely when I'm gone."

"You won't have time to think about me, Mark."

I was fishing for sympathy and I knew it, even at eleven, but it was hard not to look out for myself. There was nothing in the whole of this situation that was going to benefit me.

"I can come and see you in the holidays if you like."

"It won't be the same, you not working here at weekends."

And I was thinking, although I was trying my hardest not to let the thought worm its way in, that he might have a girlfriend by then, and if he did, I sure as hell didn't want to know about it.

"I'll always remember this place, Immie. It's very special."

I wanted him to add, and you're a very special person, and in my day-dreams of our last day together, I added that line on again and again until I could hardly separate the reality from the part I'd made up.

The actual goodbye took place up in the car park. It was all a bit awkward, with Dad shaking Mark's hand, and then Mark reaching forward to hug me, but because it was in front of Dad, he felt wooden and strange. And then he just went – through the side gate – with a click and a wave and an apologetic smile, sorry he couldn't make things better for me.

There were yards of space and air and emptiness between Dad and me then, which he didn't try to fill up, even though he must've known how miserable I was. We watched Mark's jacket and jeans and trainers disappear round the bend in the lane, and in my head I could see him continue on, over the bridge to the bus stop, or past the stop if he couldn't be bothered to wait, walking all the long miles into town. He didn't mind. He hadn't wanted a lift. Bit like going to the airport, he said, but I didn't know what he meant.

That night, as I lay in bed not sleeping, I carried on my idea of him, of his actual body and hair and flesh and bones, his arms and legs, his face; of the distance that would gradually increase between all of that and me, all the way to Sheffield. I made myself a promise that I wouldn't forget his face, not ever. But I couldn't help it. In the end, I only had an idea of the expression he wore, but it was blurry and wouldn't fix in one place. I thought his eyes were deep blue, and maybe they were, but I couldn't be sure. Mrs Gayle said what a pity we hadn't taken a photograph, and she'd ask Philip if we could have one for the album.

Eight

Revelation

Lorna disappeared off the planet for a long while, and I thought she'd gone for good, which didn't bother me one jot back then, because I was a child and only interested in myself. But when she resurfaced, I'd turned thirteen and Mrs Gayle described me as a 'self-possessed young woman', which I took as a compliment because she recognised I wasn't a child anymore. She said I wouldn't be needing her much longer – that there wasn't much I couldn't do for myself now. But I argued the point, considering she'd been around for as long as I could remember, and she was family as far as Dad and I were concerned. We'd be a pretty poor excuse for a family without her – that was for sure, seeing as Dad had fewer words for me than I did for him, and that wasn't saying much.

I remember the day as clear as anything, when Lorna turned up. Dad was upstairs, Cedric was finishing up in the shop, and Mrs Gayle and I were peeling potatoes and setting the table for tea. Mrs Gayle saw her first. She dropped her potato into the bowl of water, splashing it up her frock because she'd forgotten to use an apron. And I said, what is it, Mrs Gayle? What's the matter? – because she was peering out of the front window and looking bothered.

She turned to face me then, that serious look of hers pressing down on me.

"Now don't you go overreacting, Imogen," she said. "It's Lorna. And whatever it is she wants, we'll wait to find out and we won't go off the deep end."

By which she meant *you*, but she had a way of sharing the blame sometimes, for my sake.

Mrs Gayle went to let her in, and I carried on laying out the knives and forks, as if nothing out of the ordinary was occurring, and desperately hoping I wouldn't be laying for another, once Mrs Gayle's generosity got going.

"Come on in then, Lorna. It's nice to see you again. You remember Imogen?"

"Yes, of course. Hello, Imogen."

I nodded, which wasn't too friendly and I could tell Mrs Gayle wasn't pleased with me, but it was hard to make an effort when you wanted someone to go away.

"I was wondering, is Andrew in? I'd like to see him if possible."

"He's in his bedroom, I think, pet. I'll go and get him for you."

She disappeared upstairs, leaving Lorna, me, and a gaping silence that neither of us knew how to fill. I'd wrecked things before and wasn't about to repeat my behaviour, but it was hard to know what to say. I didn't understand how things stood between my dad and her, or whether I'd ruined things permanently. It annoyed me, Mrs Gayle calling her pet, because Lorna was a grown woman and *I* had always been her pet anyway. I could be childish when things weren't going my way, although I didn't like to admit it.

95

"You've grown," Lorna said. So *she* wasn't much good at breaking silences, either.

"I'm thirteen."

"My goodness. Has it been that long?"

"I'm at secondary now."

"Yes, you must be. Do you like it there?"

Well, what was I supposed to say to that? It was school, wasn't it?

Fortunately, Dad came downstairs at that moment. I examined his face, to see what he would do when he saw her. I had so many questions going on, about what these two were to each other, or what Lorna had been doing at Loraligh, and I wanted answers. I wasn't going to be fobbed off, not at that age. It was time for everyone to stop hiding.

If I could describe exactly what happened to Dad's eyes when he was in Lorna's company, I would, but it's hard to explain how they changed. Their usual murkiness, the drift, the glazy distance, cleared like our river on a still morning after a storm. You could see right into the back of them, as if everything made sense, and was filled with light and worth being alive for. Yet nothing was making any more sense to me than it had before. I remember that he leant forward, that his shoulders sat up and became brighter, that he reached for her hand with both of his and held onto it for longer than he should. I remember that he smiled, and the smile made me jealous, that I'd never seen it before with exactly that radiance.

Lorna stayed to tea of course, there was no getting around it, and when Cedric came into the kitchen to drop off the keys, he was pulled into proceedings too, so we were a complete *party.*

"I want you to meet Lorna," my Dad said. "She's…a special friend," he added, and we all knew what that meant.

It wasn't during the first course, or pudding, or even when we were sipping our mugs of tea afterwards, that the bombshell was dropped. I'd been wheedling away all that time for the truth of things, so I suppose you could say it was my fault. It might as well have come crashing through the roof like one of those V-2s we'd learned about in History. No warning. Just a pause, a silence, and then Blam! Blasting the house to kingdom come. Wrecking my life and everything I'd imagined to be my world before that moment.

Cedric had gone home, straight after the rice pudding with its nutmeg on the top, the way he likes it. Mrs Gayle was looking nervous, clearing away dishes and glancing across at Dad and then me. You could tell something was up. I realised, after the bomb, that they'd been planning to tell me all along, one day. But Mrs Gayle had looked genuinely surprised when Lorna appeared at the window. I don't think she knew the exact timing of things. That's what I mean about knowing looks and adults and secrets. I was *meant* to be left out of things. They decided what I was allowed to know and what I wasn't, so I was powerless and at their mercy, even though I was almost a woman now. Unless I managed to sneak around, picking things up, listening in. And I'd got quite good at that.

I remember the moment exactly. Mrs Gayle had picked up the last knife from the table, and turned her back to us. Her head was bobbing up and down furiously, while she scrubbed the dishes. She didn't want to be involved – I know that now – but she was tied to me and my feelings with that invisible thread that had held us since I was small, and she could no more abandon me at that moment than leave her own children.

Dad reached one arm across the table and was resting his hand on top of Lorna's, and she was letting him. There was a hole in the conversation, a huge, black hole, and it felt like we were all suspended in the air, looking at each other and waiting.

"Imogen, we…that is I…have got something rather difficult to tell you."

I'd made up the next line for him, but I was wrong.

"I suppose I haven't been entirely honest with you, all these years. It wasn't because I wanted to keep the truth from you."

Mrs Gayle glanced over her shoulder and looked away again. She stopped crashing around in the sink, and her movements became slow and suspicious. I was staring at Dad, feeling sick. If they asked me to be a bridesmaid, I'd run away.

"The thing is, I was trying to protect you from having to know…things that might hurt you, that might make life more difficult for you. I suppose I didn't think you'd ever need to know."

The course of this conversation was veering off track and the riddle of it all was irritating me almost beyond my endurance, but some little voice inside me was, unusually, telling me to keep quiet this once or he might never get to the end of it.

"You see, Lorna isn't quite the person you might think she is."

Lorna looked across at my dad when he said that, and then down at her hands. Dad was rubbing his thumb over and over her knuckles, in that kind of reassuring way he'd never once done to me.

"You remember Lorna told you she used to live here, at Loraligh?"

I waited for the rest. Words were beyond me.

Lorna spoke up then, taking over, because Dad was finding it hard. She spoke quietly and carefully, felting each word like a cat.

"I lived here, Imogen, because I was married to your father. I was his wife and Loraligh was our home."

I stood up, and my chair screeched on the flags as it shunted back. I was shaking my head, unable to make sense of anything. I fired my statement at Mrs Gayle next, then Dad and Lorna, my eyes flashing from one to the other.

"But you said she wasn't my mother. She can't be. She doesn't even look like her."

Tears were already springing out of my hot, angry eyes and I was beginning to boil inside. Mrs Gayle turned to face us, and she wiped her hands on the towel.

"Lorna's not your mother, Imogen. I told you that and it was true."

"Then…then you had another wife before my mother? You married twice?"

Dad was already standing, coming round to my side of the table, holding up his hands in the space around my shoulders, but afraid to make contact.

"I'm sorry I didn't tell you before, Imogen. There was never the right moment. I wasn't purposely trying to…deceive you."

It was all too much. I fled from the kitchen, ran upstairs and flung myself down on my bed. My Dad, married before

99

my mother. Two wives, two lives. And now the wrong wife had come back, and all my dreams were dashed and destroyed, because it was quite plain who he loved and who he wanted back.

I cried hard into my pillow, wishing I hadn't heard a word of it. Wanting a different truth – the one I'd dreamed up, played with, carried around all my life. The ground had been pulled away from under me, leaving me somewhere strange, somewhere else. Somewhere I didn't recognise.

After a while, I heard Mrs Gayle's footsteps at my bedroom door. There's a board that creaks as you come in. I heard her cross the room. She began playing with my hair, trying to soothe me and stroke all my bad thoughts away, but it was no good. Every part of me had gone numb. What was the difference between one lie and a hundred lies? I didn't understand anything anymore.

I detected the shuffle of her anorak, so it was obvious she was intending to leave. Back to her house and her chores and her son, back to her life – while mine was in shreds.

"Your father's right, you know, Imogen. He was acting in your best interests. He wasn't to know Lorna would come back. Try not to be too hard on him."

But I was only thirteen, wasn't I? I wasn't about to put anyone else's needs and wishes before my own. He'd lied, and pretended, and hidden a secret from me. A monumentally huge, important secret. Nothing would surprise me now. For all I knew, I wasn't even his child. He didn't have my brown eyes, for a start. He was skinny, while I was getting curvier by the week. No, I probably wasn't even his. At least that would explain why he and I had never been close – why he found it so hard to show me any affection. He'd adopted me, found me on a doorstep, taken me on as a favour for somebody else – a promise he wished he'd never made.

"I'm sorry, pet. Truly I am. It's a lot to take in, I know."

She paused.

"This'll take some getting used to, Imogen. It's not what you would've expected, I can see that. But it's really not as bad as all that."

"Yes it is!" I hollered at her through my pillow.

I felt her hand on my back.

"It feels like it at the moment. I understand. But in time, you'll see. She meant a lot to your dad, did Lorna."

I turned to face Mrs Gayle then, furiously wiping the wet off my cheeks, although there was plenty more where that came from.

"If he liked her so much, why did they split up? Why did he marry someone else? He must've loved my mother more."

She stood up then, smoothing down her crumpled skirt and rubbing her chin, in that what-shall-we-do-with-Imogen? – way.

"Life is never that simple, child. Not black and white. I'm always telling you that. Other things get in the way of happiness sometimes – things that are outside our control."

As if I needed telling.

"Can't I go home with you, Mrs Gayle? Please. I can't stay here with him. I can't bear it."

"I don't think that would be a good idea, Imogen," she replied, saying it gently. She never liked to reject me outright. "That would be running away, wouldn't it? You need to stay and sort things out with your father. You need to come to terms."

She had no idea how huge this was. I was never going to come to terms, was I? – because that meant giving up hope.

Mrs Gayle left shortly after that, because David needed his tea soon, and I couldn't help wondering why a grown lad couldn't get his own, with me doing carrots and mash at nine years old. I was left on my bed, staring at the cracks in the ceiling where the damp got in, listening for Lorna's car, so I would know when it was safe to go downstairs again. I wondered then, about what might have happened to Dad and Lorna in the past that got in the way of their relationship. What could Mrs Gayle have meant? I wished I hadn't got the habit of butting in or waltzing off, when there was a chance I'd have been told the answer if I'd stayed long enough to listen.

If Mark had still been around, I'd have sounded him out the minute I got the opportunity. His brother wasn't remotely like him, and had a way of avoiding conversation of any importance. It was a two-way thing though, because I wasn't exactly forthcoming with him either. It wasn't Philip's fault. He was never going to match up to his brother and that was that.

If Mark had disappointed Cedric, because of the bins and the lack of sufficient soap, Philip was even worse. Philip made mistakes. He misread labels and gave the wrong change. He forgot to re-order the bags when they were running low, and had to do absolutely everything on a calculator, because his brain didn't work the way Mark's did. Added to that, he had a splatter of spots in a runway down the middle of his face, which made you avoid looking right at him when you were talking. Philip's voice was breaking too. He would be using his deep, I'm-a-man-now voice at the beginning of a sentence, and suddenly it would jump up high and throw you completely, and then you couldn't concentrate on the meaning of what he was saying because you were trying not to show you'd noticed. And so was he.

However, the one useful thing about having Philip around was that he provided a useful telegraph wire to his brother – a conduit, Cedric would say. He'd explained about conduits when he was putting the electrics into the store cupboard in the shop. Philip told me everything Mark was doing, and sent messages back for me. And from time to time he'd bring in a photograph – Mark outside their house with his trunk labelled up, ready for Sheffield; Mark with a group of friends, all shiny-faced and arms round each others' shoulders, holding beer glasses; Mark in his jeans, thumbs up to the camera. On one of them, he'd written a message to me on the back, but it just said 'Hi Immie!'

Which didn't impress me much.

Once, during a particularly boring and pointless Biology lesson – which was about genetics, and by the time Miss Mercer had tried to explain the third generation of blue-eyed offspring and their chance of being able to roll their tongue, she'd utterly lost me and I couldn't care less anyway – I drafted out a letter to Mark. Carrie was sitting next to me, and I didn't want her to see what I was writing, but I needn't have worried because she was dipping splints into the Bunsen burner and fiddling with the gas tap.

The letter was about Lorna and Dad being married before, and I was asking him for suggestions about why they might have split up, and what I could do about things. I knew Mark wouldn't have all the answers, but I needed him to know. I needed confirmation that I was right about Lorna. If Dad had given up on her once, he'd do it again. There must have been a reason. She'd let him down. We knew that already.

I gave Philip the letter when I'd checked it over carefully, and asked him to write Mark's address on the envelope. He took it with him after work and I thought he'd post it straight away, but weeks later there was no reply, and when I asked him, the stupid idiot said oh yes, that letter, that's still in my room. I forgot all about it. Sorry. I'll do it tomorrow. I was fast losing patience with Philip.

I decided not to show him the places at Loraligh I'd shared with Mark. They were ours and they were special. I knew: I knew he'd not come back. He'd be twenty one when all was said and done, and he wouldn't return to Loraligh, or a job for two fifty an hour, or a teenage girl with puppy fat and brown hair and freckles. So The Beach, and Deer Meadow and Murderer's Wood became names in my head and nowhere else. Only The Slopes were mentioned again, and only because Dad was insistent I wasn't to go up there. It was daft. What harm could I come to?

Dad finally appeared at my bedroom door. It was at least an hour later, because by then I'd dried my eyes and put on my pyjamas and was staring at the ceiling again. I realised I'd crossed my hands over my chest and must've looked like the Lady of Shalott, but really I was hanging onto myself, trying to work out who the hell I was.

"She's gone," was all he said, but I knew he meant just for now, not gone for good.

There wasn't an answer from me.

He came over to my bed and sat half on the edge of the mattress, even though there was plenty of room.

"Imogen, I should have told you that I was married before. It was wrong of me."

That was a surprise. I slowly turned to look at him. I needed to see if he meant it. He caught my eye for a second, but then he looked over to the window. The light made his eyes turn to glass and took him far away. I swivelled onto my side, and looked right at him. It wasn't that I was ready to forgive him, not by a long shot. But a question had come to mind while I'd been mulling things through, and he was a captive audience for once.

"I've been wondering, Dad. Why weren't there any photographs of Lorna around anywhere, not even in our albums? I swear I've never seen a single one."

He couldn't answer at first, but I wasn't surprised at that.

"I couldn't cope with it – her not being here. I must have taken them all away."

"Don't you remember?"

"No. I...I mainly tried to forget."

He didn't offer more, even though I bit my cheek to stop butting in, and waited an age. Eventually I had to ask.

"Why did you split up with Lorna then?"

That did it. He got up from the bed and walked over to the window. He was running his finger down one edge of the window frame and rocking on his heels.

"It's complicated."

I thought, I'm thirteen now. I can deal with complicated. But those were the kind of words you thought, with my Dad. You didn't say them.

He wasn't about to answer, so I changed tack.

"How long after Lorna did you marry Mum?"

He sucked in a great breath. It was all too much thinking.

"It was several years later I met your mother, Imogen. I can't exactly remember. Maybe five or six."

I didn't know it then, but Dad lied to me again during that particular conversation. Or *was* it a lie? Did he simply leave out part of the truth, after I'd jumped to conclusions and made a mistake? Is an omission as wrong as a lie? Perhaps, by then, Dad had got so used to lying to me, it had become a bad habit.

I know he left my room pretty soon after that, with all the questions still floating around in the air, and me feeling entirely dissatisfied with how we'd left things. When he'd gone, I dug around in the roof cupboard, looking for our old albums. I needed to be sure, even though I'd seen them countless times when I'd been searching for a glimpse of my mother. She wasn't there either, not one picture, not even caught by chance in the background. Both wives from Dad's life, obliterated.

There was a picture of Grandma standing behind the front gate, holding a baby in her arms and smiling directly at the camera. That baby must've been Dad, because the photograph was tiny and crinkled at the edges, and Grandma looked quite young. Besides, she died before I was born, so it couldn't have been me. There was even one of her with a man, walking arm in arm on the promenade, and some beautiful writing in ink under the picture said *'Mary and Binks – Scarborough.'* Binks was my Grandad's nickname and that was the only name I ever knew him by. Then there were two or three pages of Dad growing up. He got skinnier in every picture, rather than filling out like you'd expect.

Then there were a handful of photos of him as an adult, even one of him with me when I was little. I was sucking the end of my plait, and Dad was holding my tricycle. But not one picture of him with a woman. I decided to rummage deeper into the cupboard thinking, there had to've been a wedding album. People would surely have a separate one for a wedding. But I knew there wouldn't be one, as hard as I looked. Would he have thrown it away? Burnt it? I wouldn't have had Dad down as a man who would do something so drastic. At least, not before the episode at Shallow Falls when he'd gone mad. Now I wasn't so sure. An image came to mind then, of Dad dancing round a bonfire, his eyes alight with fury, the fire filled with every possession of the women who had abandoned him. But then I realised they didn't both leave him at the same time. And if I'd been one of them, I'd have left him too.

Nine

Difficult

One Saturday out of the blue, when Mark had been gone two years already, a postcard came. He wasn't up to letters, so I shouldn't have been surprised about that, but a postcard was something. The words read:

Hi Immie, Having a great time. Brilliant city. Tons to do here. Got your letter. Sorry didn't reply yet. Been busy - they set you loads more work in the third year. See you in a fortnight, Mark x

I didn't know whether to be happy about that message or not. So, he was too busy to find time to write to me, even though anyone could tell how upset I was. *And,* he was finding stacks of things to do. Sheffield was obviously so much more exciting than the countryside. But he'd put a kiss at the end, and I held onto that kiss, loading it with far more significance than he probably ever attached to it.

I was fourteen when I became a woman, and the oldest girl in my class to start. Mrs Gayle said she couldn't understand it, because needing a bra and starting your periods often went hand-in-hand, and her concern was beginning to rub off onto me. I didn't want to be one of those women I'd heard about who couldn't have a baby, oh no. I'd got that part of my life all planned out, and I was going to do it so much better than my mother had. No baby of mine was going to be abandoned, not in a million years. I wasn't about to be infertile. I was going to have at least four, and it didn't matter if they were boys or girls or some of each, because preferring one or the other would've meant feeling disappointed, and there was nothing worse for a child than that.

My children were going to be loved like no others. I'd often imagined myself grown up and surrounded by a car-load of kids, all bouncing and happy on the back seat, driving off to Scarborough or Whitby, with the boot full of buckets and spades. In my mind, I'd grown slim, with well-behaved hair like Mum's, cut shoulder-length, and my lipstick as red as a pillar-box. I'd wear a pretty frock, nipped in at the waist with a shiny white belt, and my children would all be beautiful and do as they were told.

Dreams and the reality of things, as you'd expect, were a hundred miles apart, which was brought home to me time and again. I only had to look into the long mirror Dad had fixed in my room. Mrs Gayle said I needed one of my own, now I was older, and I couldn't be expected to keep going into Dad's room, so he bolted it straight onto the wall because I don't have a wardrobe. I have to stuff everything into drawers, except my uniform, which hangs on the back of my door, reminding me daily of school.

The Imogen Wise that looked back at me from my new mirror was fatter than the last one had been. I was shocked at first, and kept trying to hold the image for five seconds from my own mirror, and then running over to Dad's one, to compare. There was definitely a difference, and I got Cedric

109

up there once, after work, because he'd used the lavvy upstairs, and I told him to look at himself in Dad's mirror and then in mine and tell me what the difference was. He wasn't comfortable about going into Dad's room, but I was insistent.

"Still bloody beautiful," he said, tugging at the hair above his ears.

"*No*, Cedric. I mean, do you look *fatter* in mine? Wider?"

"Don't know what you're talking about, lass," he said, and then he added, "Don't know why you're asking me, any road. It's not as if I can see 'owt, these days."

I tucked my arm into his elbow then, because I loved Cedric nearly as much as I loved Mrs Gayle, and I hated either of them getting older. But they were, and I knew he wasn't joking about his eyesight. The lenses in his glasses were getting thicker every time he got a new pair, and that made his eyes look bigger and bigger. Which meant you could see how the hoods over them were hanging heavy now, and the whites of his eyes had changed colour.

When the Easter holiday finally came, I badgered Philip for news about when Mark was coming over. He had said he would come, in his postcard, but I didn't see how that was going to come about, with him not working in the shop and having no reason to visit. I'd seen Mark during the holidays a couple of times since he went away, but the purpose had gone out of it. That first summer he came back, we even took a walk down to The Beach together. The long grass at the foot of the bank was filled with meadowsweet that day, which looked like white froth and had a lovely scent. I'd taken my socks and trainers off and rolled my skirt up to stop it getting wet, but Mark was watching me from the edge, and I remember suddenly feeling awkward about him seeing the mottled patches on my thighs, so I quickly dropped my skirt and came out of the water.

"I'll ask him," was all I got, and I wasn't likely to trust that response, was I, with Philip's track record? So I wrote down his home phone number and decided I'd leave it a week and see.

But a week of the holiday went by and three more days after that, and Mrs Gayle caught me more than once, hovering over the telephone, trying to pluck up the courage.

"Why don't you invite Mark over next Saturday? I could do you up a picnic. The weather's set fair, considering it's April," she said. How on earth did she know what I was thinking? She was a wily old bird. Cedric was right.

I felt myself going red in the face; that happened more and more. Blood was a funny thing when you were fourteen. It had a way of affecting your life, and could be more of a hindrance than a help.

All the same, I followed her advice and dialled Mark's number. I told Mrs Gayle to go out of the sitting room because I couldn't find the right words if someone was listening in, and I wasn't allowed to use the phone in Dad's office. My heart was banging like a tin drum, and my hand was so sticky the receiver might slip right through it, but the need to see Mark was burning.

There'd been other boys I liked. There was Brian Stokes, who'd taken to wearing a leather bomber jacket round the town and had a way of making you feel he was interested. But the trouble with Brian was that he used that trick with all the girls, until you realised you were nothing out of the ordinary. I also liked this boy called Darren, but he was a high-flyer in the top stream, so I didn't see him that often, and that meant engineering ways to bump into him accidentally on purpose down the corridors, which didn't always come off well. But apart from Brian and Darren, there had never been any boy that interested me, not nearly as much as Mark.

A woman's voice answered.

"Mrs Wheeler?"

"Speaking."

"It's Imogen, from Loraligh. I was wondering, is Mark there? Could I speak to him please?"

"Oh, hello Imogen. I'm sorry, duck, he's gone off fishing with his dad and his brother. They've taken a tent. They won't be back 'til Sunday night."

My heart sank like a stone in a river.

"Oh. Okay."

"Shall I give him a message?"

"No. It's all right."

"Shall I tell him you called?"

"Um, yes okay."

"I'll do that, then."

"Thank you. Goodbye Mrs Wheeler," and I placed that receiver back so quietly, in case my heart cracked. The disappointment was unbearable. Mrs Gayle came back into the room and squeezed my shoulder. I knew she would listen in.

"He's busy then."

"He's gone fishing. With his dad. She said with his dad, but he left them years ago."

"That's good then. A chance for them to get together again, wouldn't you say, Imogen? Might be just what they need."

I didn't believe it, about the fishing.

112

"He didn't even call me. He's been back for nearly two weeks, and he didn't even call."

I could tell Mrs Gayle was upset for me, but as usual she tried to make light of things. She was always having to pick me up, and I was fed up with being the hurt bird all the time.

I mooched around for days after that, and spent a lot of time in my room. Dad had often been out in the evenings, and I knew he was with Lorna but we didn't discuss it. He was well aware he was on dodgy ground, and the words were better left unsaid. As long as they didn't do it right in front of me. As long as they didn't involve me.

I couldn't understand how Mark could have ignored my letter. It was obvious I needed help, and the holiday was nearly over. I thought ahead to the summer and realised it was Mark's last year at the polytechnic. A smile slipped across my face, in spite of my mood, when I remembered learning that word. We'd been having careers advice at school, and our tutor group had been taken for a guided tour of the Careers Room. That was a joke, because it basically consisted of several index boxes full of cards showing you all the jobs there were to do in the world, in alphabetical order. Except they weren't all the jobs you could do – they were only the ones the school would tell you about: doctor, fireman, lawyer, nurse, politician, shop assistant, teacher. As if anyone wanted to be a teacher. There were a few posters stuck around the walls with drawing pins, covered in pictures of young people with insane grins and whitened teeth, advertising the Police or the Forces. Have you thought about? Why don't you try a career in? Don't throw away that education! Anyway, the point is, that's when I learned about polytechnics and universities and colleges of education and suchlike. So Mark had never gone to Polly after all.

Sometimes I think that's a pity about growing up – that children's words are better.

I got under the bedcovers and was trying to squeeze back the tears. They had a way of welling up when I felt sorry for myself. Mrs Gayle said it was my own fault, because moping around and chewing things over was bound to lead to misery, and it didn't cure a thing. The answer, she said, was to keep busy and not to *dwell* on things. I liked that word – dwell. I decided that's what you had to do at my age. It was a way of making sense of the world which, after all, was a crazy place full of crazy people, who did nonsensical things and made stupid decisions half the time – which screwed up everyone around them, but they were usually too preoccupied with themselves to notice.

On the Monday, school started again. I'd had a useless Easter holiday. Not one thing had gone well. Dad hadn't had time to take me anywhere, and Cedric had been off ill, some problem with his waterworks. That was how he put it, and it didn't sound like something I wanted to visualise. I'd been helping Philip in the shop half the time, because I was old enough to be trusted now. Actually, I was a damn sight better at it than he was, but I was glad Dad hadn't given him the sack, because that would've been my weekends tied up for evermore.

When I hopped off the bus at the end of the day, I had the shock of my life. Mark was standing there, leaning against the bus stop in a relaxed, I-could-wait-here-all-day sort of way. He was wearing a jacket that matched his jeans, had his hands in his pockets, and his smile went up one corner and down the other.

"Good afternoon, Imogen Wise," he said, all posh, and he bowed low, pretending to have a big hat in his hand. As if he ever called me that.

I couldn't help smiling back, but I wished I'd known he would be there. My hair was a mess, and I'd have given my mascara another coat.

"What the heck are you doing here?"

He leant forward and kissed me on the cheek.

"I said I would."

"You were supposed to come in the holidays."

My inclination to sulk was getting the better of me, but I was trying to keep it in. I didn't want him to turn right round and leave me to it.

"I know, I'm sorry," he said. "I forgot you only get two weeks off. I'm home for another week."

"Oh."

We crossed the bridge together, and I noticed how much longer his shadow was than mine.

"How's it been then, Immie?"

"Okay, I suppose."

"You didn't sound so good in your letter."

We went quiet for a while then, walking in the sunshine, with me trying to smooth my hair down because I could see in my shadow that the sides had gone frizzy. It started playing up when I turned a teenager – something to do with my hormones, Mrs Gayle said, and there was nothing I could do about it if the air was damp. Eat your greens to make your hair curl, she always said when I was a child, as if curls were something to aspire to. The hours we women used to spend, she'd say, putting our rollers in and wishing for waves like yours, Imogen.

I pushed open the small gate.

"Let's not go into the house yet, Immie. Why don't we go down to Shallow Falls? I fancy a paddle."

It was the first time anyone had used our name for it for so long. I slung my bag outside the front door and pulled off my jumper too, because the afternoon was warm and steamy. I'd be in trouble for not changing out of my school uniform, but there wasn't time and I'd always done what Mark said, regardless.

We cut through Deer Meadow, and he chatted to me about his course, and his finals coming up, and some of his mates who he shared digs with. Then we made our way through Murderer's Wood, and Mark asked if anyone had been killed there lately, and I said not since Dad nearly killed me that time. And that got us reminiscing about the dam we'd built, and then I started giggling.

"It wasn't the best idea you ever came up with, Mark Wheeler."

"I'm not just a pretty face, you know."

"You're not even that," I laughed.

"I'm prettier than Philip."

"Anyone's prettier than Philip."

We arrived at The Beach, and Mark got into a playful mood and began scooping up water and hurling it my way. It was like the old days, even though he was twenty by then and stood a good clear foot taller than me. I ran shrieking across the river and kicked the water back at him, telling him to pick on someone his own size, which was funny, because you'd be hard-pushed to find anyone as tall as Mark.

116

We crossed the river and slunk down on the grass at the foot of The Slopes, to dry off our legs. Mark lay on his back with his hands behind his head, and shut his eyes. He looked contented. I remember clearly what he said then:

"D'you know, Immie, whenever things get bad and my head needs somewhere to go, this is where I come? To Loraligh and our river."

I loved it when he said that. To think that my home meant so much to him. But I was confused too. What could be so difficult in his happy-go-lucky life that would trouble him? I'd never imagined Mark letting anything get to him much.

"That's brilliant," I said. And I thought, what a stupid word when you needed a better one, and I wished I'd been more poetic.

Then Mark spoke very gently, as if each word was loaded with meaning.

"Immie, I want to know everything that's happened to you. Tell me what's making you so sad."

It was amazing, wasn't it, that a grown man of nearly twenty one, whose life had taken such a different turn, would have even five minutes to care about me? The feeling choked me, that I was worth bothering with.

"I don't know where to start."

Mark waited then. He wasn't about to put words into my mouth.

"I can't remember how much I told you."

"It didn't make much sense. Start again from the beginning."

So I related the story then, about Dad being married before. About all his lies and the shock of finding out that a grown-up could be so deceitful. And about everyone else knowing, except me. Even Mrs Gayle. How could she have kept that up so long, with me no longer a child?

Mark didn't answer for quite a while. He was gazing at the clouds, and I was sitting beside him with my arms wrapped round my knees. It made the fat round my waist bunch up and I realised how much bigger I must look, so I stretched my legs out in front and leant back, to pull me out thinner.

"Are they going out together now then? Your dad and Lorna. Are they an item?"

"Search me. Nobody tells me anything."

"You must know if your dad goes out once in a while, even if he doesn't tell you where."

"Yes, I suppose he does. More often in the day time than the evening, Cedric says. And on Saturdays sometimes."

"Hmm."

I lay down, even though the grass smelled strong, and I watched the clouds too, to see if I could guess what he was making them into, and Mark did his best to persuade me it was a good thing, because Dad wouldn't be lonely and that would mean, eventually, that I wouldn't be lonely either. It was also a good thing for me, he said, having another person around. Especially a woman. He didn't understand one bit what I'd been going through, and it was making me begin to feel angry inside, that someone my own age didn't get it. But then, Mark wasn't my age was he?

"You don't know what it's like. Your father never told you a bunch of lies, all your life. You can't imagine what it feels like, to find your whole childhood turned into...I don't know...one big joke."

"My father left us."

I went quiet then, because there wasn't an answer to that. I didn't know what was worse – what Mark had suffered, or what I had.

"You know what your trouble is, Immie, don't you?"

I turned to look at him through the grass and buttercups.

"You made up a story for yourself, years ago, when you were a kid. You decided what the future would hold and you wrote the script...and then life didn't turn out the way you intended. But it doesn't, Immie. That's what you learn when you grow up. It just doesn't."

He was patronising me, pulling the I'm-much-older-and-wiser-than-you card. But he was right. I *had* written the script and it most definitely wasn't going to plan. My own mother hadn't materialised, and all the evidence would suggest she was never going to.

I changed the subject after that, because Mark wasn't going to be my ally over that one, and because he was irritating me, not being on my side. And I didn't want to wreck my idea of Mark, which I'd kept going for all the years he'd been gone.

We chatted about our memories of the mill – the kid who'd lost his shoe when he'd been horsing around in the car park, and flicked it off right over Dad's fence, and how it made a perfect arc into the water. The way all the kids gasped. We laughed about his teacher's face when she realised there was no retrieving it, not with the waterwheel turning that day and the depth of the water. She'd grabbed the boy by the collar of his blazer, and marched him back to wait in the coach. That wiped the smile off his face.

The mood was lighter, remembering the old days, and I was relieved that I hadn't wrecked things between us, because

119

at one stage I felt myself sinking into a hump, and I desperately didn't want Mark to remember our time together that way. But when he'd gone and I was back on my own again, I felt sad because I'd put all my hopes into Mark being the one who'd help. And he hadn't.

On the Friday after school that same week, my friend Carrie spotted Mark again, as we were walking for the bus.

"Hey Imo, isn't that your lover boy?"

I looked across the street, thumping Carrie's arm for winding me up. Mark was loitering outside Boots, and his arm was round a girl's shoulder. She wasn't anyone I recognised, not even from his sixth form. She was tall, like him, and her arm was round his waist. It hurt like hell, seeing them there like that, and my cheeks turned hot. Thinking back, it was probably the first time I'd ever truly felt jealous over a boy, and it twisted my stomach.

"Is that his girlfriend?" Carrie asked. She was some friend, wasn't she? Sometimes, Carrie could be so bloody thick.

"I only asked," she added, when she realised how much she'd upset me, because the words were stuck in my throat and I couldn't answer. I walked on fast, concentrating on the toes of my shoes.

"He isn't my friend anymore. Thinks he's so special. Thinks he's better than me."

Carrie was galloping beside me, in a sort of sideways step, because she was trying to keep up and trying to appease me at the same time. I knew she hadn't intended to be mean. It wasn't her way.

"They always get like that when they've left home. My brother's the same. Treats me like a kid. Drives me mad."

120

We had to cross over to Mark's side, for the bus stop, and I caught sight of his face as he turned round. He didn't see me because he was looking at her, and she was terribly pretty, which I was hoping she wasn't. That made it so much worse.

Mrs Gayle took half an hour or more to get it out of me, when I got home in a stomp. I would always refuse to tell her anything at first, but she had a way of winning me round and wheedling things out of me.

"It's for the best, Imogen. You know that, really. The way of the world."

I had absolutely no idea how she'd come to that conclusion, but my mouth hadn't loosened up enough yet to argue back.

"He'll be off to pastures new, soon enough. You need friends your own age."

"I've got friends my own age."

"I know you have. I'm only saying. Aren't there any nice boys in your class?"

I laughed when she said that, but it wasn't a happy laugh.

"You have to be kidding."

Mrs Gayle was rolling out pastry, which I thought was odd for that time in the afternoon, with her going home soon. I usually liked watching her make a pie. She was so hard on that rolling pin, and so quick and careless, but the pastry circle always came out exactly the right size and thickness for the tin, and when she cut around the edge to slice off the extras, there was hardly a scrap to spare. When I was small, she let me have the leftovers. I used to roll them into sausage shapes to cook and eat later, dipped in the jam pot. But I'd outgrown all that.

"What's the pie for?"

"Your dad's got a visitor."

I knew what that meant.

"Are you staying, then?"

"No, lass. I have to be getting back. My David's been for an interview and I want to know how he got on."

I was mildly interested in that, despite my sulking over Mark.

"What's it for?"

"A clerical job at the Civic Centre, but it's a start."

I knew she was putting on a brave face. David had never been going anywhere and we all knew it. He'd be living at home for ever, the rate he was going. Cedric told me David was a waste of space, but then Cedric said that about most people. Nobody in our generation was ever going to match up to his – that was clear.

I wondered about that expression, a waste of space. It made me think about the actual amount of space in the air that each human being takes up, and it isn't really that much. The cubic capacity of air isn't exactly the point; it's the fact that we all keep moving, so the space we take up changes shape all day long. And then there's the much bigger space we need – the bed, the bedroom, the bathroom to wash in and the kitchen to cook in, and then all the space in schools to educate us, and that needs teachers, so then there's all the space to train the teachers and the homes they have to live in. And on top of all that, there's the space in the police stations to control us, and the supermarkets to feed us, and the space to grow all the crops for our food, not to mention all the space we need outside, just to get from A to B. Thinking about it like that, I began to see that each one of us actually takes up acres of space, so we'd better put it to good use. Not like David.

Mrs Gayle had already left when Lorna arrived. She drove right into our car park, even though it was after closing time. Dad made me go and open the gate for her, and Lorna gave me a little wave and a smile, despite the scowl on my face. Cedric hates me doing that. He says it's most unbecoming of a young lady, and Mrs Gayle reminds him that I'm a teenager and that's what teenagers do. They wouldn't be normal if they didn't. Mrs Gayle is a world expert on teenagers.

I turned my back on Lorna and went indoors before she'd even got out of her car. I couldn't help it. I knew I was being rude, but I didn't want her there – it was that simple. I did manage to leave the front door ajar, and Dad pushed past me to let her in, a pathetic grin on his face. He didn't even acknowledge my existence.

"Lorna. Hi." That wasn't a word my dad *ever* said.

"Hello, Andrew."

He probably kissed her at that point, but I'd already made it over to the kitchen table and was repositioning the cutlery, so that she wouldn't be sitting opposite him. I couldn't stand them gazing into each other's eyes all the way through the meal. I figured that, if I put her next to me, with Dad at the other end, they'd have to talk across me instead. That would put me in control to some extent. They'd have to include me then.

"Nice to see you, Imogen."

I managed a fraction of a smile.

"Thanks for letting me invade your tea time."

I guessed she was trying to be funny.

"You haven't."

123

Dad started to shuffle, and I caught his steely glance in my direction. I didn't want to repeat history, because I knew by then how mad I could make him. It wouldn't be in my interest to push him too far, so I thought I'd better at least be civilised, if not exactly sociable.

That was the funny thing about me, back then. I could actually observe myself putting up brick walls and being deliberately difficult, and I didn't like the person I was looking at, but there was something exciting about controlling things, about being in charge of the atmosphere. I knew Dad didn't like me and I didn't care. I didn't like him much either, and I definitely didn't like Lorna, so what did it matter if she didn't exactly take to me? If I did a good enough job of putting her off, she might even take a walk. For good.

After the soup, Dad told me to get the pie out of the oven, while he dished up the runner beans. Once we'd all been served, and Dad had exhausted every possible conversation about how the mill was doing, and the shop and the weather, Lorna changed tack.

"Imogen, I think we ought to talk a little more about what happened the last time I was here, don't you? It doesn't do any good, burying things. We've been thinking: it must have been an awful shock for you – finding out that Andrew, I mean your father, was married before and you hadn't ever known."

I glanced at her, and then at Dad, who was looking decidedly twitchy.

"The thing is, Imogen, your father had his reasons for not sharing that with you. He's not a lying man. You know that, deep down, don't you?"

I couldn't stand her trying to tell me she knew my dad better than I did. I hated the posh way she said 'father', and I couldn't stand her calling me I-mo-gen either, the way she drew it out. She sounded like a teacher when you're in trouble. She was trying to worm her way in and get round me. As if she could.

Dad spoke up then, because I clearly wasn't going to.

"We've talked about this, Lorna and I. We do understand how you must feel. We know it can't have been easy for you."

I couldn't believe it, my dad talking like that. He hadn't once given me the slightest evidence that he understood how I was feeling. Not about anything. I doubt if he'd ever taken the trouble to work it out. He was always so wrapped up in his own problems. This had the mark of a woman stamped all over it.

I still didn't reply. It was interesting, watching them both squirm. Besides, what exactly could I have said? That I didn't mind? That it was okay, finding out that your whole family history was a pile of lies? That it was wonderful, knowing your dad had loved another woman enough to marry her, before your own mother?

Lorna tried again.

"What would you like to happen now? If you had the power to change things, what would you choose, Imogen?"

She was good, I'll grant you that. The ball was in my court, as Mrs Gayle might say, and I hadn't had time to think this one through.

"I don't know," I answered. Which was pathetic. "I can't have what I want, can I? I never can."

"No, possibly not this time," Lorna replied, checking with Dad and then back to me. "Life doesn't always give us exactly what we want, does it? But sometimes we have to veer off in another direction and have a rethink. And sometimes, good can come of that. New things. Better things. Sometimes, life can surprise us."

She was certainly right about that. I watched her expression while she was speaking, in spite of myself, because her eyes had this way of dancing and smiling, even when her mouth wasn't. I could see why Dad found her so appealing. She was almost taking me in, and I had to look away quickly in case I gave her the impression I was paying her much attention.

"How old are you now?" Dad said, which was at least the second time he'd asked. I shouldn't have been surprised, but it always narked me that he couldn't remember. I rolled my eyes. My bad mood had taken over. It was Lorna's fault.

"You must be fourteen or fifteen," Lorna chipped in. *She'd* worked it out. I liked the idea that I might look fifteen.

"You're probably old enough to understand how things can be between men and women," Dad said. God forbid, he wasn't about to give me some rendition of the birds and the bees was he?

"Adults need the companionship of people their own age, in the same way as children do," he went on.

And then Lorna added: "It doesn't mean your father doesn't love you. You know that, don't you? It's not the same sort of love."

This conversation was fast becoming the most embarrassing thing that had ever happened to me in my life. Dad and I didn't talk like this. Our family wasn't a discussing-our-feelings sort of family. But Lorna didn't know, did she? She hadn't sussed us out at all.

126

I ate my dinner in silence and didn't have much appetite to finish it, so I got down from the table and left them to their pudding. I felt the weight of Dad's sigh, and the hope in Lorna's smile. She could wash up, this time. On the way out, I grabbed the photo of Mum and me, and took it upstairs. They must've noticed but I didn't care.

I lay on my bed, staring at that photograph. I held it over my face, so that Mum was looking down on me, the way she would have if she'd seen me lying there so sad. If she'd been around. Her eyes were dreamy and caught the light, like the opals in my bracelet – the one Grandma left behind. *Oh Mum*, I said out loud. *Why have you forgotten me?* Why won't you come and get me? Don't leave me here with them. I can't bear it. Why can't I come and live with you?

I realised how pointless those words were. If she'd cared at all, she'd never have left in the first place. But the thought of staying at Loraligh, with Lorna moving in on my life and Dad so besotted, was becoming unbearable. It hadn't been so bad, just Dad and Mrs Gayle and me, with a dose of Cedric thrown in now and again. But adding Lorna into the mix was going to muck up everything. I'd have to think of a way out of there. No way was I going to stick around while they dripped and mooned all over each other. No way.

It was while I was mooching over this dead-end line of thought, that I heard the two of them talking downstairs in raised voices. It was so unusual – like a quarrel – that I moved to the top of the stairs to listen.

"You'll have to tell her, Andrew. She's not a child."

"How could I do that, after the way she reacted, finding out about you? I can't make things worse."

127

Lorna paused then, and I imagined him pawing her arm, and her searching for the right words.

"But it's ridiculous, letting her believe all that rubbish about her mother. You know it is. She's bound to find out eventually. She's going to be an adult one day, with a child of her own. She has a right to know."

"But I can't do it to her, Lorna. I'd make such a pig's ear of it. You know what I'm like. I wish I'd told her when she was small."

"Hasn't she wondered why her mother never came back?"

"She never lets the subject drop – at least she used to. The girl's infatuated with that damned photograph. What was I supposed to do?"

"She's already asked what went wrong between the two of us. What if she asks again? What are we going to tell her?"

"I'll come up with something."

"You can't keep fobbing her off. It isn't fair."

By this point, I'd crept to the top stair and sat down as quietly as my creaky knees would allow, straining to hear. My heart was thudding so hard, I could've told it to shut up. Then I heard a click, after which their voices became instantly muffled. Someone had shut the kitchen door. I couldn't believe it. They'd closed the door on the secret of my life, which I evidently wasn't supposed to be privy to.

It was a waste of time, sitting there any longer. If I barged in on them, they'd stop talking. But I had gained one thing at least; I'd found the one person who didn't believe in keeping secrets.

Ten

Chance Encounter

Our Geography teacher arranged a field trip that summer. His name was Mr D. Larkfield, and Nicola found out that the D stood for Dudley. She'd overheard the Deputy Head speaking to him in the corridor. Would you just do that for me, Dudley? – she'd asked, and she tossed her mane of dyed-red hair and squeezed the leather pad on his elbow. Nicola passed that juicy bit of information on to me, because she thought the two of them were having an affair and this was undeniable evidence. We were always working out who was getting off with who, at our school, because two of our teachers were discovered in the stationery cupboard.

Personally, I doubted if anyone would have an affair with Mr Larkfield, in spite of his poetic surname, because when he talked, little pools of spit clogged up in the corners of his mouth, and you had to look away because it was revolting. Added to which, he sweated like a wrestler and always wore blue shirts, which didn't hide a thing, even on a cool day.

The field trip was to Scarborough, which was really an excuse for a day out at the beach. Nicola wanted to bagsy a seat next to me on the coach, which created a problem because who would Carrie sit with? Mrs Gayle said nice to be popular, Imogen, when I asked her what I should do about it, so that was hardly a solution was it? She made me up a special packed lunch though, with cheese triangles, iced-diamond biscuits and a drink in a carton with a straw. Nicola said I was daft, getting excited about a pack-up at our age, but I didn't go for days out, hardly ever, and I couldn't get to sleep the night before.

In the end, Carrie couldn't go, because her Nana had died two days before our trip, which was a shame but it solved the coach problem. We had a great day, Nicola and I, despite the long coach drive. Mr Larkfield let us all go off in groups for a couple of hours, as long as we did some proper research, which basically meant collecting things in plastic bags and prodding around in a few rock pools. We each had a clipboard, for jotting notes and sketching interesting patterns on stones, but it was a flaming nuisance if you ask me, because it wouldn't fit easily into your bag and the paper got wet, so it was as good as useless for recording anything.

Cedric was always moaning about clipboards on school trips. He said kids knocked everything off the shelves because of those damned clipboards, and couldn't their teachers just let them explore the world properly, using their eyes and ears, instead of having to write it all on a bloody piece of paper? He said David Livingstone never discovered the Zambezi with a bloody clipboard.

Nicola and I joined the queue for an ice-cream, even though it was yards long and the others didn't want to bother. Mrs Gayle had given me two pounds spending money, because she said I was a good girl and didn't ask for much, and it was her pleasure to spoil me now and again. Dad would never remember to give me spending money on a school trip, because he wasn't that kind of dad. She'd get it out of him later, she said.

So there we were, standing in the queue, and I was watching people up the front, how much time they wasted faffing around, trying to choose which ice-cream to go for, and then discovering that that particular variety had sold out. So they'd spend ages making a different selection, and when they'd finally chosen one which *was* in stock, they had to find some money to pay for it. As if they hadn't realised.

I was getting impatient, turning the coins over and over in my hand until they were hot to touch, when I suddenly saw her because she turned round. And I thought, I know that face. Why do I know that face? She was reaching down, passing a lolly to a small child by her side, and he was looking up at her, all expectant, taking the lolly stick carefully. She was saying, don't drop it will you, and he was concentrating so hard on not dropping it, he couldn't speak. Then she turned her back and paid the ice-cream lady.

My brain was flick-flacking through my memory bank of all the faces I'd ever known, because I knew that face. Then the young woman and the child turned towards us and, as they walked past, I caught the flash of her eyes, and she held my gaze for a split second longer than was usual. Probably because I was staring so hard. I knew Nicola was trying to get my attention, but my brain was somewhere else entirely.

"Imo?"

I nudged her elbow and tried to point, without making it too obvious.

"You see that woman? I know her from somewhere."

Nicola was used to me garbling on about my mother, and she sighed.

"Not again, Imogen. She can't be your mother. She's far too young."

"Yes, I *know*," I said. "I didn't mean *her*."

"Who then?"

We bought our lollies and found a wall to sit on, so we could dangle our legs and look at the waves, and that's when it came to me.

"Karen! Mrs Gayle's daughter. That's who it was. Her youngest daughter. They're all grown up now, her kids."

"How many does she have, then?"

"Three girls and a boy. David, Mattie, Hayley and Karen. I'd remember her eyes anywhere. Brown as conkers."

"Did she recognise you?"

"No, we've never met, but I remember her from the photograph on Mrs Gayle's sideboard."

In that photograph, Karen was wearing a top with too much cleavage showing, and her long brown hair was parted at the side, so a slick of it was hanging over one eye, and it was shining like in the shampoo adverts. But this time it was divided straight down the middle like a Roman road, and she was wearing massive hoop earrings which nearly reached her shoulders. She was a bit overweight too, but that was understandable because she'd had her child not long ago.

I bit all the crunchy chocolate off the outside of my lolly, until I got to the gooey bit in the middle, and all the time I was deep in contemplation.

"The funny thing is, though, Mrs Gayle said Karen didn't have any children, and that was definitely her child. I heard her telling him to say Ta Mummy."

The two of them, Karen and the boy, were sitting on a blanket next to a windbreak, half way down the beach, more or less in front of us. Karen, if it was her, was looking after the toddler really well, helping him with the last bit of his lolly, so it wouldn't drop off the stick. After that, she found him a woolly, because the wind was cold, and then she plonked him down on the rug next to her, and was helping him spoon pebbles into his bucket.

Not the maternal sort, Mrs Gayle had said, yet this woman was definitely doing a good job of mothering her little boy. I felt kind of jealous then – watching the two of them. I wished I had a mother to care about me like that.

I went on about it, and Nicola was getting fed up because I didn't want to leave our look-out spot, but then Karen started packing her stuff into a holdall. She was clearly about to leave, and I had this sudden urge to follow her, or to introduce myself. What harm would it do? But I couldn't pluck up the courage to speak to her, in case I was wrong and it wasn't her at all. So instead, I got off the wall and decided to go after the two of them, to see where they went.

Nicola was moaning, because there wasn't anything in it for her and she couldn't see the point. But there was something about Karen's eyes, the way they enchanted you, as if they were hiding a chest of secrets. There'd be things she could tell me about Mrs Gayle. Things I'd always wanted to know. Like, how come she got to spend so much time with us, when she had a whole brood of her own to look after? And why her husband went missing all those years ago. And what was he like anyway?

"Just for a bit," I said. "Go and join the others if you like. I won't be long."

Nicola tutted and sighed, but she didn't want to leave me. She tagged along a few steps behind, dawdling on purpose

133

and making me feel guilty for wasting time. We hadn't put a thing in our plastic bags yet.

We followed Karen and her toddler along the pavement, and I made sure to keep well back because I didn't want her thinking I was weird or anything. But then she stopped at the bus stop. No car, then. I should have realised there wouldn't have been a car. I was stumped, because it would've looked strange, us waiting at the bus stop and then not getting on, so I gave up at that point and we veered off, back to the beach. But I thought about Karen and her son all the way home on the coach, and I quizzed Mrs Gayle about it the next day.

"Does Karen live in Scarborough?" I asked her, while she was scraping the skin off an onion.

"No, she lives in a village a few miles out of town. Whatever made you ask that?"

"Because I think I saw her yesterday, on our school trip. I'm sure it was her."

I could tell from Mrs Gayle's expression that she was interested, so I carried on.

"She had a little boy with her."

I watched her closely, to see if she was surprised, but that knife kept scraping away without a moment's hesitation.

"I see." That was all she said.

I decided to lay the table mats, but really I was stalling for time, trying to work out my next line.

"I thought you said Karen didn't have any children."

"I never said that."

I went to find us a glass each and a jug of water. You did, I was thinking. Yes you did. But that would've made Mrs Gayle out to be a liar, and I knew she wasn't that.

She started frying the onion in hot fat, and it was fizzing and spitting. Then she told me to dice the potatoes and carrots, ready to put in the pan with the onion, and she stood over me to make sure I didn't lose a finger.

"Don't put them in yet. Let the onion sweat first," she said. "Let it brown up nicely."

Then she sat down on a kitchen chair, with her forearms resting on the table and her fingers laced together, and she looked across at me.

"His name is Sonny. Odd name for a child isn't it? He'll be three next birthday."

I carried on stirring, trying to work things out. "So...I would've been about...twelve, when he was born?"

"That's right," she said.

Strange, I was thinking. Why didn't you say at the time? You never even mentioned another grandchild. Why wouldn't you tell Dad and me? Wouldn't you be as proud as anything, having another little grandson?

"I know what you're thinking," she said. "You're thinking I never told you about Sonny being born. Aren't you, Imogen?"

I came to sit at the table with her, but at that moment Dad came through the front door, slamming it behind him and hanging his jacket on the hook, which was completely bad timing as far as I was concerned, because I was sure Mrs Gayle was about to explain things to me. He had this habit of turning up at exactly the wrong moment.

"Evening, Mrs Gayle...Imogen." He gave me a nod. "What's for tea? I'm starving."

Funny how he never kissed me hello. Even Nicola's dad did that when he came home of an evening. I knew that, because she wrote it in her diary for homework – An Ordinary Day in my Life – and she read it out in class, and I thought her dad sounded nicer than she'd let on.

"Evening, Andrew. Fried mince and vegetables; apple crumble and custard for afters if you're lucky. Had a good day?" (She always added on the bit about being lucky when it was custard, because she was none too confident. Mrs Gayle could cook anything and everything, she said, but custard has a mind of its own.)

"Not bad, but there's a strong wind brewing."

That would explain his chirpier spirit. The weather had a way of affecting my father's moods, more than the average person. The wind always whipped him up, and the rain, especially heavy rain, would stir him into a frenzy of activity. But when it was sunny and calm, Dad would change to the exact opposite and become quiet and depressed – which wasn't at all in tune with the effect of the sunshine on me. We didn't have much in common, me and my dad.

"I was about to tell your daughter about Sonny, my latest grandson."

I looked across at her in surprise. I'd banked on that conversation coming to a definite halt for the time being.

"Oh yes?" Dad said, pulling up a chair and pouring himself a can of beer. It was amazing how he never thought to help with serving up. Unless Lorna was there. He always left it to us.

"Unusual name, isn't it?" he said, more of a statement than a question.

"Karen was never one to follow the crowd," Mrs Gayle answered. "I never liked the name, though. What will people

136

think when he's older? It's all right for a tot, but you can't imagine a grown man with a name like that."

I had to agree. Sonny was the sort of name Cedric called small lads when they were in trouble for handling merchandise in the shop, that they'd no intention of paying for. Not a real name. It certainly wasn't a name for a man. Not like Mark.

"Was he actually christened that, or is it short for something else?" I asked.

"I don't think he's been christened at all," Mrs Gayle said, and I looked at Dad and he looked at me, and I thought – better not say anything about that – but I know what he was thinking. Because a baby should always be christened, in case it dies.

For all the mistakes my mother made, I know she and Dad did do that for me, at least, because I had my own silver christening cup, engraved with my initials: I.M.W. The M stood for Mary, which was Grandma's name, and it made me feel safe when I was little, because I was closer to Grandma in her grave and closer to Jesus. I also had a tiny bracelet, which squashed in smaller or stretched out longer according to the size of my wrist, but it wouldn't fit anymore, so I kept it in the glass cabinet in the sitting room, together with the silver cup and a porcelain Beatrix Potter bowl, with pictures of Peter Rabbit and the soporific Flopsy Bunnies dotted around the edge.

"Doesn't Karen believe in God, then?"

"Oh, if I know my daughter, she's got her own special brand of religion. She likes to do things her own way. We don't discuss it."

With that, Mrs Gayle dolloped the last of the mince onto her own plate. It was sloppier than usual, and nearly ran right onto the tablecloth. She caught it with her finger which she licked clean, even though the gravy must've been piping hot. Old people don't feel hot things the way young people do; I've noticed that before. And Cedric says he's losing his sense of smell, which can be a bad thing or a good thing, depending.

"Have you got a photo of Sonny, then?" I asked her. "When he was a baby."

"I'll have a look," she said, and she reached for her bag on the spare chair, and shuffled around in her purse. Dad hadn't waited to start. He was piling into his spuds, digging the fork in deep and putting them in whole. I was always embarrassed when he did that. You were supposed to cut them up. The older I grew, the worse my dad's table manners were becoming.

When she pulled out the photograph, a whole pile of others – small enough to fit in a purse – came spilling out at the same time. There were pictures of all Mrs Gayle's children and a few of her grandchildren, and I saw one of Karen holding Sonny when he was first born, in the hospital, and one of him as an older baby, sitting on her lap with a rattle in his hand, showing two teeth in his bottom gum. There was also a photo of me in there, and I felt pleased when I caught sight of it, although it didn't surprise me as much this time. Mrs Gayle was embarrassed to be getting out all these photos when we were supposed to be eating our tea, so she quickly tapped them two-ways into a neat pile and put them back in her purse, but she let me keep out the one of Sonny on Karen's lap, to study it.

"He's got her eyes, hasn't he?"

"Aye, he's a lucky lad. He's inherited her complexion too. She never goes red in the sun, not like the others."

Mrs Gayle was right. Karen did have a nice complexion – smooth as an olive, and not a freckle to be seen. She didn't look exactly English. Her shoulders had been tanned, that day at the beach. I noticed, because she was wearing one of those tops that are supposed to slip down over your shoulder, even though your bra strap shows. Mrs Gayle would say she'd never get the hang of modern fashion, and Karen was making a spectacle of herself. And her opinions were rubbing off on me, because I didn't approve either, showing your bra strap in public. I was glad my mother wasn't that sort of woman. I could tell, even from a photograph. My mother would wear a petticoat from the lingerie section in Marks and Sparks, and it would have pretty broderie-anglaise round the hem. And on top, she'd wear a cotton frock and a belt and a hat, with a blue satin ribbon to match the daisies.

Dad was getting annoyed, so Mrs Gayle took the photo back, snapped her purse shut and started to eat. She ate tea more often with us in those days, and I figured David was out more than in. Dad never wanted to be bothered with photographs and I could tell he'd wanted Mrs Gayle to stop talking about them. He did his best to change the subject, and asked all sorts of boring questions like have you done your homework, Imogen, or do the animals need feeding?

We'd expanded our range of livestock recently, from chickens and deer to two fat pigs (who'd had a litter of seven piglets, much to my excitement, although Cedric complained because he reckoned he'd be the one cleaning them out), and Dad made an open pen for rabbits and a couple of guinea pigs, because the toddlers, who visited in the daytime with

139

their mothers, loved petting them and holding out cabbage leaves. Sometimes they hugged them too hard though, and you had to hover around and keep reminding them, because their mothers were too busy nattering and turned a blind eye.

Having to answer Dad's questions was annoying, because in my head I wanted to concentrate on the curious situation of Sonny. There wasn't a grandmother in all the world who'd want to keep quiet about a new baby in the family. Yet now she seemed all too happy to talk about him.

I waited until Dad had gone to his office, and then I asked her outright.

"I've been thinking," I began, "you're right – when I asked about your girls, you didn't say Karen hadn't had any children. I think what you actually said was, she's not the maternal sort. Which isn't quite the same thing, is it?"

"You're a canny lass at times, Miss Wise. What a memory."

"It was a bad day. You always remember things on a bad day. But I was only eleven then. I was about to start at St Simon's, wasn't I? And if Sonny is two, coming up three, he hadn't been born then anyway. You remember. That time Mark and I visited your house?"

"I remember."

"So, he must've been born quite soon after that."

"Right again."

Mrs Gayle was washing and I was wiping, and I had to remember to let things drain for at least thirty seconds first, or the tea towel would get soaked. And it was the one covered in pictures of places in Yorkshire which Mrs Gayle had got for her birthday, from her Mattie. She thought I ought to know more about the county I lived in, and I could learn as I wiped.

"Why didn't you tell Dad and me about Sonny back then?"

She put the jug on the drainer. It was the pale green one we'd had ever since I could remember, with a crack up one side, but Mrs Gayle didn't believe in throwing things away.

"I had my reasons. They were good reasons then, but things have changed."

It wasn't only Cedric who talked in riddles.

"Karen's…well, she's a complicated girl. But then she's not a girl anymore. She must be, what, thirty now? How time flies."

I kept quiet because I didn't want to interrupt her flow, now she'd got going.

"She didn't easily take to motherhood, my youngest daughter. She wasn't the responsible type. But who knows, she seems to be doing a pretty good job with Sonny."

"Yes," I said. I detected that Mrs Gayle had been disappointed with Karen at one stage, although she didn't want to admit it.

"Do you get to see him often? Sonny, I mean."

"She brings him over most Sundays. She works at the King's Arms, waitressing. I have him a couple of nights a week too, so she can bring in a little extra."

"*Do* you? You never said." This was getting stranger and stranger. All this was going on, and she never let on. Not a word.

"We all have another life, Imogen. I'm not only a housekeeper, you know."

And I thought – I don't. I don't have another life. I only have this one. The one you know about. And nobody tells me anything, even though I'm virtually an adult now. I don't even

141

know where my mother is, I thought. Or why she left me, or what she's doing now.

Mrs Gayle could probably tell that I was cooking up inside, because she took the soggy tea towel from me and told me to go on and leave her to finish off. I could put my feet up or watch the television. But I wasn't in the mood, and took myself off to my room without saying thank you.

Before she left that evening, Mrs Gayle put her head round my bedroom door. I didn't look up from the book I was pretending to read, but I could see her out of the corner of my eye, and I heard her say, I know it's hard for you to understand, Imogen, but one day it will all become clear – when you're old enough – and you'll see I was right to…to keep things back.

She went quiet after that. I suppose she was waiting for me to respond, but I was fed up with all the secrets and I didn't feel like letting her off that lightly. I was already old enough. I could even have a baby if I wanted one. I made my mind up, there and then, to interrogate Lorna the next time she was over. She was definitely my conduit to the truth of things. Mrs Gayle was a dead loss.

Eleven

The Phone Call

Mark rang early one Saturday morning, out of the blue. It was near the end of the summer holidays and he'd already sat his finals. I guessed he'd got his results in the post and wanted to tell me how he'd done, but it wasn't that.

Philip hadn't even arrived in the shop yet, and I was still in my bedroom, fiddling around with my make-up bag, when Dad called up the stairs:

"Imogen? It's the phone, for you."

This was more than a little unusual. Nicola and Carrie had long since given up ringing me, because Dad didn't like me tying up the phone. Mrs Gayle was already scattering chicken-feed across the car park, so it couldn't be her. I'd seen her from the landing window.

"Who is it?"

"It sounds like Philip's brother. The one who used to work here."

I clicked my tongue, because Dad had already forgotten Mark's name, even though he'd worked for us for a couple of years at least. I tried not to hurry to the phone, because I didn't want Dad to think I cared, but all the way down the stairs I was thinking, I wonder what Mark wants. I wonder if he's going to come over.

"Mark? Hi, it's Imogen," and I could've swallowed that back, because *he'd* called *me*.

"Immie, how you doin'?"

He was being casual. Like a student.

"M'okay thanks. You finished at Sheffield now then?"

"Yup. But that's not why I called."

His voice had become serious.

"Oh?"

"The fact is, I've got something to talk to you about. It's kind of very important, Immie. I don't want to discuss it over the phone."

"Okay," and my mind was already flooding with possibilities, about his job, or his dad, or his girlfriend, or maybe his mother had cancer, or he was moving away, or he'd seen Dad and Lorna in Tony's café again and they were having a row.

"Do you want to come over here? We could go down to Shallow Falls or something."

"No, I don't think that's a good idea. It'll be too crowded, won't it, in the summer holidays? We need somewhere quiet. Can you get into town later, about ten o'clock?"

"I could get the bus…um…the nine twenty gets in just before ten."

"Fine. Where shall we meet?"

"There's always Tony's café," and I wished I was more sophisticated and knew of somewhere better.

"Yup, guess that'll do."

"Will your girlfriend be there?" I added, thinking – I don't want to go if she's there.

"What girlfriend?"

I realised I had jumped to conclusions, but it was pretty obvious.

"I thought...I saw you with someone in town. Ages ago, last holidays, even. I thought..."

"Oh, that was Ange. Yeah, we were going out for a while. No, she's not here."

"See you about five past, then."

I put the receiver down. I couldn't tell, from what he'd said, if *Ange* and he were still together or not. I knew I was being silly. After all, he was twenty one now. The way he spoke made him sound like a hippy or something. He didn't talk like the Mark who left Loraligh on the bus, all that time ago. It was all a bit affected, if you ask me. I expected he would be smoking fags and asking for a beer instead of a Coke, just to impress me, but when I arrived at the café, Mark was already inside with a mug of coffee on the table.

He was stirring his spoon round and round, and seemed lost in his thoughts, but he got up as soon as I walked in, and offered to buy me a drink. I couldn't think of anything else to ask for, so I said a Diet Coke please, and then I wished I hadn't said the diet part, because it only drew attention to my shape, which wasn't all I'd wished for, although I knew I wasn't fat. I suddenly felt self-conscious. Mark towered above me, more than he had even as a sixth former, and he was growing a beard which you could still see his chin through. It made him look much older. Like a man. He'd ditched the Arsenal shirt and was wearing a black one instead, with a button-down collar, a pair of black jeans and a loose jacket with loads of pockets. I must've looked ridiculous next to him, because I hadn't even had my fifteenth birthday yet.

145

Luckily, the café was nearly empty, except for an old man sitting by the window with his back to us, reading the paper. The girl serving behind the counter looked as bored with us as she was with her job. By the time we'd sat down, she'd taken out a nail file, and sat herself cross-legged on a tall stool in front of the portable telly. It's a grim place, Tony's café: the ceiling tiles aren't fixed properly, so you can see the electrics, and the lino's ripped, and people have been picking at the table tops for years on end, doodling into the surface with blue biro. Probably school kids. Susie loves Kev, and an arrow through a heart – that kind of thing.

Mark started to explain that he hadn't known whether to contact me or not. He wasn't sure if it was the right thing to do. The thing was, he said, he'd come across some information – mind-blowing information, about my past – and he'd battled with the decision about whether or not to share it with me. It was all beginning to sound like the same treatment I got at home, with everyone deciding for me what I should and shouldn't know, but then Mark said he'd come to a decision and he hoped it was the right one.

He'd broached the subject with his mother, and she'd said ah yes, she remembered something about all that, back in, what was it now, '66 or 67? And Mark said no – it was 1965, November. And his mother had said oh yes, course it was, 'cause that was the winter of the terrible flooding. The whole town had been talking about it. Well Mark, she said, if it was me, I'd want to know, wouldn't you? After all, Imogen might find out for herself one day. So he decided to go ahead, and desperately hoped I wouldn't be traumatised afterwards, or wished I'd never found out.

You can imagine that by the time he got to actually spitting it out, I was going berserk.

"It would never've happened...I mean, I wouldn't be here saying any of this if we hadn't pulled up the carpet in the sitting room," Mark began. "Mum decided the old one had to go out, it was so threadbare, and she couldn't have people round with it so bad in the doorway – she wouldn't be seen dead. She asked me to see if we could get it up before the new one arrived. If she hadn't decided on having that new carpet, I'd never have known any of this. Then you wouldn't have known either. That's the problem, you see, Immie. That's what I have to consider here – whether or not you were ever supposed to know."

He stared at me, as if he was asking for permission to carry on. But honestly, what would anyone do after that amazing lead-in? There was no way I was going to tell him to keep this great secret to himself, not when I knew it concerned *me*.

"You see," he said, and he was looking into my eyes intently, and I have to admit I was finding it all a bit scary: "when I pulled up the carpet, Mum, or someone anyway, had put down sheets of newspaper all over the floor – they used to do that under carpets, I think it was for insulation – and I thought nothing of it and started collecting them up because, you know, they'd gone all yellow. But on one of the newspapers, I spotted a large photograph of some little kiddies, side by side – a toddler and a baby. They looked so cute and smiley, you couldn't help noticing. And on the same page, tucked in the corner, was a photograph of two people clutching each other and looking upset. I mean, the man's face was obviously in torment. You couldn't see hers."

Mark stopped there, for a breather, like resting on a landing when you've another flight of steps to climb. He waited for me to speak, but I was failing to grasp the significance of this story to me.

"Immie, the next part is really difficult to say," and he took both my hands in his and held them there. God knows what the waitress thought.

"The people clutching each other in the photograph, they were...your dad and Lorna."

I was adding two and two and getting ninety six. Dad and Lorna? Was I one of the children? Did I have a brother or sister somewhere? Was Lorna my mother after all?

"How do you know? You said you couldn't see her face," I said, not believing and not making sense of what Mark was telling me, both at once.

"Because the article stated their names; it's obvious, they always do. Mr Andrew Wise and his wife Lorna, of Loraligh Mill, Eastlye Lane. I recognised his face immediately. But there's more."

Mark took a great gulp of his coffee, and took a packet of Rizla and a small tin of tobacco out of one of his jacket pockets. He licked the edge of the paper and rolled it so thin, I didn't see how it would last five minutes, but he obviously needed it to steady his nerves. His hand was shaking.

"So which one was I? The toddler or the baby?"

He stopped making his roll-up and looked me straight in the eye.

"Neither."

"Neither?" I was almost shouting when I said that, and I didn't want to attract attention, but my nerves were in shreds. The waitress looked across briefly and turned the telly up. It didn't matter. I didn't want her listening in. A small face suddenly peered in at the window, nose pressed to the glass, but his mother grabbed him by the collar and hoiked him off.

"Sorry," I said, "I didn't mean…"

"It's all right. I knew you'd find it hard. I'll tell you everything I know, okay? Give me time."

He inhaled long and slow, and blew the smoke out to one side of his mouth. Smokers always do that. They think it doesn't go in your face – that you can't smell it.

"There was a boy and a girl. The girl was gorgeous, two and a half, a little angel. Curly, blonde hair pinned up kind of to one side, you know, like they used to. You couldn't help looking at her, Immie, she was that bonny. Little dimples, and eyes that lit up. Kinda like…you ever heard of Shirley Temple?"

"Didn't she used to be in those black and white films?"

"That's right. This little girl looked the spit of her, only fairer."

"And the boy?"

"He was only a baby, but he had the same smile. You could easily tell they were brother and sister."

"Who were they? Were they Dad's children?"

Mark rested his fag on the ash tray and took my hands in his again, so I could tell the next part was going to be really bad. To be truthful, I could sense what was coming, because if the ending had been any different, it wouldn't have been so hard to say.

"Yes. They were his and Lorna's. They all lived at Loraligh. The little girl was called Rebecca. The baby was only three months old. His name was Jonathan. They called him Jonno, for short."

149

Tears were welling up, even though we were out in public.

I guessed the next part, because who wouldn't?

"They must've died then," I whispered. It was the only logical conclusion, because they sure as hell weren't around anymore.

"Yes."

That was all he said. Yes. They'd died. And the two adults in the photograph were my Dad and Lorna, bound together in their grief, for their two little children who had *died*. It was unbelievable, but here was Mark telling me he'd read it in the papers, so it had to be true.

"Have you got it with you, the newspaper?"

He stared at me then, his eyes holding mine, and I could feel him gauging my reaction every step of the way. I knew if I went to pieces, if I made a fuss, I wouldn't get to hear the rest and I desperately needed to. The whole story. I'd come this far.

"I've left it at home," he said, "on purpose. I thought it better to…to let you in as gently as I could. To start with."

"Can I see it? Can't we go and get it? You didn't throw it away, did you?"

Mark drew on his cigarette again, sucking in until you couldn't help wonder how his lungs could hold so much smoke without complaining.

"It's incredibly…it's a hard story to read, Immie. I will let you see it eventually, I will. If you really want to. But it's tough, you know? Mum agreed. I should give you an outline first."

I was just about managing to keep myself together. A single tear had spilled onto each cheek, which I brushed away quickly because I needed to be strong. If I wasn't, Mark might have drawn a halt to things – might've decided I couldn't cope.

"Shall we go for a walk?" he said.

I stood up, because walking was a good idea, and Mark paid for our drinks, which he didn't need to, because I'd brought two weeks pocket money with me. There wasn't much to spend it on in our town.

We walked up the High Street side by side, saying nothing, then we turned the bend at the top and branched off into Grove Road, towards the park. It isn't up to much, our park. A triangular patch of grass (big enough for a quick game of footie, if you don't mind the shape of the pitch and make your own goalposts with your jumpers), a handful of benches, a set of rusty swings – one permanently broken – and one of those dragons that seat a few kids at once and rock backwards and forwards, but you have to push it yourselves and it's hardly worth the effort.

We went over to the swings and I sat on one, while Mark leant against the frame. He dropped his stub onto the ground and twisted his heel into it.

"I can't believe Dad had other children and never told me. Why wouldn't he tell me? Why did he go on making me think I was the only one?"

After a long pause, Mark said, "It's because of the way they died, Immie. It's because of that."

My imagination was simmering, and I was even – in some wild nightmarish flash – wondering if Dad had murdered them, or Lorna had, because he'd never liked children much. But I dismissed that idiotic idea almost as soon as it entered my head because, if that had been true, he'd be in prison now, not living at Loraligh with me. And I would never have been born.

"Lorna said – d'you remember, Mark? – Lorna said something about not deserving him. Not deserving a second chance."

I don't know why I was trying to guess the story. Mark already knew didn't he? He'd read it all in the paper.

He came to sit on the other swing and gently rocked his foot back and forth, so I did the same, and the synchronised movement was kind of soothing.

"It wasn't Lorna. It was your Dad."

I knew it. That day at the Falls when he totally lost his mind. He had madness in him.

"What did he do? What the hell did he do?"

"It was more what he *didn't* do," Mark said.

"What? What didn't he do?"

There was another silence and I was feeling horribly impatient, because I wanted all the facts now, and because I was angry that it was Dad's fault. I didn't want it to be his fault, but it obviously was, and there was no changing history was there? I wished Mark would just spit it out.

A couple of girls were cutting through our corner of the park, and one of them recognised Mark and yelled out his name. He looked their way and then, infuriatingly, they began walking towards us. They were teenagers, older than me, with denim skirts and brightly coloured ankle socks spilling over their bumper boots. They had plenty of bare leg showing. When they got closer, I could see they had matching tops too, but in different colours, and Cedric would've said they were wearing too much mascara, because he didn't know the difference between that and a kohl pencil. I couldn't believe the timing of things, with my head spinning from Mark's revelations. Part of me wanted to scream and shout and cry out loud, or run home and have it all out with my dad. But the other part knew that I had, absolutely *had*, to hold it in for a little while longer, because I needed to find out how those children had died.

"Hi Mark. You're back then," the taller one said.

Talk about stating the bloody obvious.

"Yup. Done my time."

"Did yer like it, then, at uni?"

"Great thanks. It wasn't a university though."

"Oh, you know what I mean. Same thing." The girl giggled, as if something was funny.

"Yeah."

It was one of those conversations that was going nowhere, passing on no useful information whatsoever and achieving nothing at all, and I was longing for them both to clear off. But one of the girls sat herself down on the grass by the swings, with her legs crossed, which was a bad idea because you could see her knickers and they were red, and she looked like she was settling in good and proper.

"This is my friend Immie," Mark said to them, and then he introduced them to me too, but I can't remember their names because I wasn't remotely interested.

They said hi, and I knew they were wondering how I could be one of Mark's friends at my age, and I frowned at them and mumbled something which might have been a greeting, but it wasn't a warm one.

"We have to go Mark, don't we?"

Fortunately, he could see my state of agitation and, after all, he'd been the one to arrange our meeting in the first place.

153

"'Fraid so. Things to do. See you around then girls."

We began making tracks, and the girls took over the swings we'd left behind. I'm sure they were talking about me, and you could hear them sniggering for ages, until we were out of earshot.

"Let's go and get the article, Mark. I want to read it. I need to see it for myself."

"Hang on a bit. There's more you have to know first. Let's go somewhere else. This isn't a good place."

We turned out of the far corner of the park, where it meets Alders Road, and then we cut through an alley into Post Office Lane, because the road tapers out into a chalk path if you walk far enough, and then into countryside and the riverbank. The hedges on either side of that path can be draped in old man's beard like net curtains, or smothered with May blossom or wild roses, depending on the time of year, and sometimes they hum with a thousand bees, but I wasn't in the mood to notice.

There's a long granite wall at one edge of the river there, and a couple of wooden benches, but I wanted to sit on the wall, dangling my legs over the water, because it reminded me of the old days with Mark. He was standing beside me, and you could see his shadow, tall and thin, in the water. The river was lazy and slow that day – a deep golden brown.

I wasn't looking up at him. I was sitting on my hands, watching the odd leaf or stick float down with the river's pull. I remember every detail of that day because, well you do, don't you, when something shocks or scares you? You remember it all.

"It wasn't exactly his fault, Immie. Not deliberate, if you think about it," Mark began. "He probably couldn't have helped it. I wouldn't want you thinking badly of him. Then it would be my fault."

Probably. The word stuck, and I tried to let it go so I could concentrate on the rest.

"Was it an accident then? A car accident or something?"

"As I said, it was back in 1965, years ago. Long before you were born."

Mark had come to sit next to me on the wall and I noticed how much lower his legs reached than mine. His voice had turned soft as a cat's purr, and at some point in the telling, he put his arm round me and kept it there. It wasn't a romance thing. It was because he was trying to soften the impact of the story he was unfolding. It wasn't *his* story. I wasn't blaming him, but perhaps he thought I would, because he was the one revealing it.

"It happened in a storm. It had been one of those days when the rain sounded more like thunder, Mum said, coming down in sheets and drumming on the ground with such intensity, you'd stop what you were doing to look out of the window. You'd look up to the ceiling to sense the strength of it, wondering how the roof was going to hold up."

"My God. That's why he's got a thing about rain. That's why."

I looked at Mark and then back at the river, because it was soothing me, and helping the story to flow along.

"It wasn't thundering and lightning, she said. Not that sort of storm. More a rain storm. It had been pouring for days. That was the trouble, Immie, you see. Everywhere was saturated. The drains were full. They couldn't cope with all the water. The fields were flooded."

"Where were they then, Dad and Lorna and the children? Were they out in all that? Were they in a car?"

I couldn't understand why he was going on about drains and fields. My mind was racing on all the time, trying to piece together the story he was unthreading, because I couldn't help myself. By now, I'd started to cry, and I kept wiping the tears away and trying to stifle any full-blown noise, for fear of missing something.

"Lorna was out, but not the others. They were all at home, at Loraligh."

A man walked round the back of us then, a golden labrador lumbering several paces behind him, and we waited for them to pass by and I remember thinking, I don't know why he needs a lead, that fat old dog. He's not exactly going to run off, is he? And I've no idea how I could've been thinking about some old dog at a time like that.

"Like I said, your dad was at home with the children. Lorna had gone away for a few days. Something to do with her grandmother. Anyway, she wasn't there, so your father must've been babysitting."

That was an odd word to choose. Can you babysit, when it's your own children? Isn't it just what you're supposed to do? All these thoughts kept jumping in uninvited, while I was trying hard to concentrate on Mark's story. It wasn't that I wanted to be distracted.

"It seems that the little girl, Rebecca, was downstairs playing in the kitchen with your dad. The article said the baby was in a carrycot on the kitchen floor, I think. Yes, that's right, because your father was beating himself up about not picking it up and putting it on the table."

"But you wouldn't put a carrycot on a table, would you?" I chipped in, although the words came out in a blubber, because I was past defining the shape of anything that came out of my mouth.

"No," Mark said. "Maybe, I don't know. Ours always went on the floor by the dog basket. I don't know if it was to entertain the baby or the dog."

He went quiet for a second or two, allowing me time to absorb each horror, one at a time. Or, looking back on how hard it must have been for him to tell me, he was rallying the strength to go on.

"It seems your dad was hopping up and down, getting anxious about the level of the water outside. He mentioned the back door particularly."

"That would be true. It floods out the back first."

And suddenly I'd got it. Or at least, I'd got the essence of things, because flooding was Dad's big thing. I started to cry properly then, because I knew the children must've drowned. I was already seeing them in my mind's eye, floating around in the dark water, the little girl desperately crying out for help and not being able to swim. It was all too horrible.

Mark held on tight and he was tidying my hair away from my face, and kissing my forehead. He even began to cry himself. Deep sobs passing through the top of my head, mixing with mine. I realised later, how much he might have needed to do that. After all, he'd been living with this terrible story for a while, hadn't he? Wondering what to do with the weight of it.

I've thought about it a lot since then – why Mark was so affected, when they weren't even related to him, those children. I think it's got something to do with Loraligh being a part of his life. You can imagine the accident so vividly, when you actually walk over the place it all happened.

When he'd collected himself, and we'd both hushed for a time, I needed to ask another question.

"But weren't they all safe inside? Why didn't they go upstairs?"

"They were at first. It appears your dad decided to go outside for some reason. To see what he could do, I think. To stop the water rising even higher and coming in. And Rebecca didn't want to be left alone in the house without him. She made a big fuss, he said, so he let her go with him. She'd put on her wellingtons and a rain mac, got all dressed up, like. Your dad mentioned that in the article – about looking after her and doing all her buttons up, and seeing she was well prepared for the weather, with her plastic hat pulled down tight."

I crossed my arms over my stomach while Mark related the next part, because it was the hardest bit and I was feeling sick.

"Nothing happened at first. Your dad was fiddling around with the drain, using a long stick or a rod or something. He'd checked the water level by the wheel, and each of the storm drains, but one of them was clogged up badly and he wasn't able to clear it. The water level in the backyard was already up to the second step. Almost to the top of the little girl's boots, he said. He'd lifted her to higher ground. She was fine, he said. He kept looking over at her and she was fine. Even enjoying sploshing about in it all."

"So what went wrong then?" I croaked, because the full strength of my voice was lost in grief.

"The next part is awful, really horrendous. Are you sure you want me to go on?"

I nodded, pressing my lips hard together to keep from crying. If I couldn't cope, he'd never tell me the rest.

"He turned his back for a moment, a split second, and heard Rebecca scream. He turned round and saw her little body caught in that storm drain. He thought he'd put the lid back on, but he couldn't remember. She was still holding the stick he'd been using. At first only one of her legs was caught, and the wellington was jammed somehow inside the drain. But then she must've, sort of, got sucked down. He ran over to her and held on. You have to understand, Immie, that all this time it was still raining really hard. You know how noisy it is when it rains that hard? You can't hear a thing. You can't think straight."

"He should never have let her go out with him."

"Goes without saying."

"Go on, then. Couldn't he pull her out?"

It was beyond my understanding. Any man could pull a little girl out of a drain, especially when it was your own child. When her life depended on it.

"She was stuck right up to her neck in water. He was holding her under her armpit. Your dad was getting in a state, he said, crying and calling out her name. He was even lying down in the water, reaching into the drain and trying to free her boot. And then the worst thing of all..."

"What?"

"He looked back at the house, to see if there was anything he could use to help him, and he saw the flood water had risen over the top step and water was swirling into the house."

"Oh...God."

159

"He was stuck, you see. If he let go of Rebecca, she was gone for sure. But he could see through the kitchen door, and the carrycot was moving in the water."

"But it would take ages for a flood to rise in a house, wouldn't it? The carrycot would've floated. The baby would've been all right." Little Moses didn't fall out, did he? He went all the way down that river, tucked up in his basket, and he didn't even wake up.

I was thinking, no Mark, please, *please* don't tell me he let go of Rebecca.

"The article doesn't make it clear exactly what happened. It only says he was helpless, that both his children were in mortal danger and that he couldn't save them. It seems the water did rush in very quickly and that the carrycot tipped somehow. It wasn't stable. The baby fell out into the water and started crying, and it's a parent's instinct, isn't it, to go to a crying baby? Mum was the same when we were young'uns. It makes you panic. He must've been torn between letting Rebecca go and saving the baby, hoping she wouldn't slip down any further, and he could get back to her in time."

I cried for a long time that day. I was wracked with crying until my ribs ached, and all the time, Mark stayed with me. I tormented him with questions, most of which he could only guess at. We didn't leave the riverside for ages, until I'd gone quiet and numb and there were no tears left, because Rebecca and Jonathan were my sister and brother, weren't they? Half, anyway. And I'd lost them before I even knew they existed.

We were nearly ready to go, and Mark was swivelling his body round the other way to jump off the wall, when he added:

"You have to feel sorry for your dad, though, Immie. You have to understand. It was the most terrible dilemma for him. Not knowing what to do, who to save."

"Yes," I said quietly. But I wasn't sure I meant it.

Twelve

No Going Back

We didn't go back to Mark's that day, to get the article. I didn't actually clap eyes on it for several days, and when I did, I wished I hadn't. It wasn't that the story expanded much on Mark's version, and the other details I needed weren't included anyway. I'd have to ask Dad or Lorna.

What the article did leave me with were the faces of the children, imprinted forever on my mind. He was right, Mark – they were beautiful children. Much more beautiful than me. Rebecca could've been in one of those bonny baby competitions, with her perfect row of milk teeth and her sparkling eyes. You could tell they were a light colour, even in the newsprint. Eyes you could see through – eyes that gave away feelings. I'd always wanted eyes like that. Her hair was swept off her face by a ribbon, and the crinkles shone where they caught the light. She reminded me of a child in my reading books at primary school. The baby's eyes were darker, but I knew you couldn't always tell with babies, because Mrs Gayle said they change fast in the early weeks. He had a wonderful smile and anybody would love him. Would have loved him.

"What are you going to do now, Immie? Are you going home?"

"Guess so."

Mark's arm dropped away and we began to make our way back to the lane.

"What are you going to say when you get home?"

He looked worried. The responsibility for telling me was all his. I looked away from him then, across the field to the distant beech trees, decades old, centuries even, and their leaves already turning. They had survived everything, those trees. I searched the sky for inspiration and watched a hawk, high in the thermals, without a trouble in the world. I wanted to rise like him, higher and higher, up and away. Far away and never come back.

"I hate him."

Mark stopped dead in his tracks. He turned to me and gripped my shoulders.

"No, Immie, no. Don't say that."

"He has lied to me, all my life. He had two children and a wife I never knew about. *Two children who died.* He could have told me, like a man."

"But you can see it, can't you? He felt that angry with himself, that responsible. You know what a quiet man he is. Not much of a talker, your dad. He's been keeping it in, all these years. That's what men can be like, Immie. I should know."

I looked at Mark for a moment, right deep into his eyes, and I felt brave. I could see my own reflection on the shiny surface, and my troubled face looking back at his.

"I am not who I thought I was," I said.

With that, I turned round and began walking. Mark didn't move for a while, and I couldn't hear his footsteps following mine, but for once I didn't care. Within minutes he'd caught

163

up, and with his big strides, he was beginning to overtake me and I had to quicken my pace. His head was down and his trainers were moving in a determined way, crunch, crunch, on the rough road, and I thought he might be angry with me.

"You'd never do it, Mark. You'd never forgive your own father for something like this."

"I wouldn't bloody know, would I?" he said, and his voice had grown louder. "I never had the chance to yell at my dad, did I?"

"Your dad never killed anybody."

"Oh grow up, Imogen."

Grow up, he said – Imogen. He never called me that, not seriously, and now he was as bad as the rest of the adults in the world. Looking down on me, like he was so much older and better.

He took off then, and there was no way I could keep up with him, so I fell back, and the yards between us grew into tens and then hundreds, because Post Office Lane is the longest in town and it runs as straight as a railway line.

I was raging inside. Raging because of the secrets, because of the not telling. I knew Dad hadn't done wrong, not really. I knew if there had been one single thing he could've done differently that would have saved Rebecca or little Jonathan, he'd have found it. I knew.

But it didn't suit me to acknowledge it, not yet. Forgiveness can creep up on you, Mrs Gayle always says, when you least expect it. Even when you're digging your heels in, it finds a way, and it's time that helps it to come. Well, I hadn't had any time yet, had I? Forgiveness felt a thousand moons away.

I didn't get the bus home. I decided to walk, because walking can be a way of working out the anger and pain, one step at a time, passing it through your feet to the road beneath, leaving each load behind. Added to which, it gave me longer before I had to face anyone.

As I walked, I came to realise that Mrs Gayle knew about Rebecca and Jonathan too. She must've done. That would explain all those strange looks and unfinished stories. She was always telling me: there's things you don't understand, Imogen. Things you don't know about yet. So she'd lied to me as well. Or at least, she'd left things out, which amounts to the same thing when you're supposed to be friends. Maybe even Cedric as well, as far as I knew. Perhaps I was the only wretched person in the world who hadn't known. Me – insignificant, fourteen-year-old me. Neither child nor adult.

My thoughts trailed back through my life, seeking all the evidence of my father's neglect of me. His non-love. Nothing left, was there, after losing two such precious, beloved angels?

I was walking into the wind virtually the whole way back, which was hard work, and I'd forgotten how far it was and how the wind can make your ears ache. My feet were sore and I was desperate for a drink. Every now and then, I'd lean against a gate to get my breath back, and look out at the fields, like a bumpy eiderdown of green patches, with the wavy lines of dry-stone walls like stitching around each one, until far away, they met the moor.

The moor, where it was wild and free and angry. Where you could run and shout and no one would hear you. My place.

I slowed at Three Boys Corner and crossed the bridge thinking, three boys – how I'd always wondered about those three boys – and all the time they'd had no relevance to me whatsoever. It had been one little girl and a baby.

I glanced across the car park into our shop window, and saw Philip's top half moving across the room. He'd be leaving soon. Almost his last weekend wasn't it? Eighteen now, and off somewhere to do his apprenticeship. He'd never be able to follow in his brother's footsteps.

The kitchen was empty and the Land Rover was missing. Good. The back door was open, and beyond the outhouse, I saw glimpses of Mrs Gayle between the washing that was billowing on the line, a peg in her mouth and her flabby arms reaching up. She always strung that line so high she could barely reach it herself. I watched her for a while. Truth be told, I hadn't composed my recitation for her yet. Only the one for Dad. What on earth was I going to say to *her*? I watched her exchanging each peg from the bag hanging round her waist, to her mouth, to the line. A juggling act, with promise of a fine day. Nobody hangs their washing out anymore, Mrs Gayle. Don't you know that? Nothing round here belongs to the times we are in.

She emptied the basket and put the prop in place, raising that line 'til the sheets nearly took off. And then she spotted me in the doorway, staring, and called out:

"Oh, hello pet. Didn't see you standing there. Had a nice time with Mark?"

And I thought, if only you knew. Well, you are about to know, because I'm going to tell you. And your face will turn ashen white, and the guilt will creep up from your neck to your forehead in rashes of red, the way it does, Mrs Gayle. Any minute now.

But before I'd had a moment to think what to say, a voice perked up from behind me and made me jump.

"Hello, Imogen. I hear you went into town."

There was Lorna, right inside our kitchen. She was taking things out of the cupboard, as if she owned the place.

She smiled at me.

"Hungry? I thought I'd make up a salad. I bought some honey-roast ham especially, and prawns. Do you like prawns?"

"Never had them," I replied, because I hadn't. I didn't have the faintest idea what honey-roast ham was either. In our house it was plain ham, like it or lump it.

She'd taken me completely off guard. I wasn't even expecting her to be in the house, let alone moving in on our meal times.

"There's always a first time," she said brightly, passing me a colander full of lettuce that was covered in clods of earth.

"Would you, love?"

I took that lettuce and held it under the tap, which I'd turned on about as hard as it would go, and I glared at it. The bottom had fallen out of my great speech. Nothing was going the way I'd planned. But as my hands worked away, ripping off the leaves and smoothing away the dirt with my fingers, I steadied myself because I was thinking – Lorna could be the one to tell me the rest. Lorna knew everything. It would suit me to keep her on my side, at least on the surface of things.

Mrs Gayle appeared in the kitchen, the empty basket banging at her leg, not at all surprised to see Lorna in there – so that was another conspiracy.

167

"Well? Did you?" she asked again, pausing beside me and jutting her face out. She clearly had no intention of getting on with things until I'd obliged.

"It were okay."

I shook the water out of the lettuce – hard – so that it splattered wildly around me onto the floor and caught our housekeeper on her front, and Lorna's shirt, and I plonked the colander on the table.

"What did you do? Go anywhere nice?"

I threw Mrs Gayle a contemptuous look because, after all, there isn't a single nice place in our town. Not until you get well outside. It was amazing the power I felt, knowing that I held the great secret like a parcel in my hands, the seal broken now, the wrapper wide open, but that no one else in the room knew I'd found out. It gave me the control, for once – the upper hand – so I held on to that little piece of the pie for a while longer. After all, if I let on, Mrs Gayle would probably persuade Lorna to hold back and save the really interesting stuff until I was older. I might even find out about my mother because, when all was said and done, what would be the point in concealing anything else now, with me so boiling angry? But if I kept quiet, if I got Lorna on her own…

"Where's Dad?" I said, more accusing than asking.

"He's gone in search of weed-killer." Lorna was still being bright and breezy, and pretending she couldn't read my face.

"Don't approve of that stuff. Never have," Mrs Gayle responded. "Still, Andrew will do what Andrew will do. Never mind me."

"Don't worry," Lorna said. "I'll make sure he restricts it to the gravel area. We can't have the car park covered in weeds, can we? – or people will think nobody lives here."

168

I couldn't stand that, Lorna talking like she had some stake in the place. But then, in a way, she did. Or at least she had once, because she'd lived here as the woman of the house. Even before Mrs Gayle had. She must've known our mill like the back of her hand, but there she was, pretending it was all new to her, saying where's the cheese grater kept, and do we have anywhere for tea towels?

Dad turned up in time to eat, and he gave Lorna a hug and a kiss, and then Mrs Gayle reminded him that I'd gone to town all by myself, on the bus, and he said well he should hope so, because he'd been getting the bus into town from the age of twelve. I moved the salad round my plate and picked at the prawns, but they didn't taste of much, and I waited for Mrs Gayle to go home. I didn't look at Dad once through that meal. How could I? If I'd said something pleasant, it would've ruined my great oration. It would've taken the edge off.

I tried to imagine him here at Loraligh, with two young children, being the perfect father. I bet he was wonderful with them. I bet he talked to them and told them stories and sat them on his knee – because they were Lorna's too, and he clearly thought the whole world of her.

As I put down my pudding spoon, hiding the plum skins underneath, a brilliant opportunity sprang to mind. A way to get Lorna on her own, because Mrs Gayle happened to mention that I'd need new school shoes, come September.

"Lorna could take me," I said. There was spite in my voice; I couldn't hide it. It had always been Mrs Gayle who took me for new shoes and I knew she'd be offended. Ever since I could remember, it had been Mrs Gayle saying wiggle your toes, Imogen. Walk up and down and make sure they're

169

comfy, because I don't want to be bringing them back in a week, with blisters on your feet. She'd even relented once and let me have the black patent-leather ones, with glossy tops which gleamed in the light. Even for school.

"What fun!" Lorna said. "We could go into town after work one day, couldn't we? I love shoe shopping."

"Which day can we go?"

"The day after tomorrow's free, I think. I'll have to check my diary."

And I thought, oh lah-di-dah with the diary. I bet it's jam-packed with stuff: meetings and appointments and dates with my father. Nice to be so popular – I bet that's what Mrs Gayle was thinking. Nice to be so very important.

"I'll check mine an' all," I said, in the most indifferent manner I could summon, and I saw Mrs Gayle throw me a dubious look, but she clearly detected something was up with me. She didn't push it.

"Mind the heels are no more than an inch and a half," she said. "Nothing too fancy. School rules, not mine."

Lorna picked me up in her Fiesta and drove me to town, making small talk all the way and saying creepy things about how much fun it would be without any men, and she hadn't been shoe shopping in ages. And all the way I was thinking, there's only two shoe shops in our town and neither of them are up to much, so I don't know why you're getting so excited, Lorna Bennett.

"Why *is* your surname Bennett?" I asked, "because you'd have been called Wise, wouldn't you, married to Dad? Did you marry again?"

"No. I did meet someone else after your father, and we nearly married, but in the end…it didn't work out. No, Bennett was my maiden name."

"You didn't stay with him then, this other man."

"We had what you might call a long-term relationship. But it was difficult. It was always your father I loved, you see."

"Why did you split up with him then?"

We'd arrived at the edge of town by now, and she had to concentrate on turning right at the lights, so she stopped talking for a moment, and I hoped she wasn't going to avoid the subject after that.

"Good question," she said. "Adults are the weirdest people, aren't they? Ridiculous, really. Life doesn't run smoothly all the time, Imogen. Things happen, terrible things sometimes. Relationships can't always recover."

I knew exactly what she was referring to, so I zipped my lips at that point because it wasn't quite time to give myself away. Thinking about this afterwards, it must've seemed odd to Lorna that I didn't ask.

"What was he called, your other bloke?"

This was a pointless question and wouldn't lead to a single thing I needed to know, but I wanted to keep her story flowing.

"Arnold."

A little laugh slipped out of me when she said that, I couldn't help myself, and she grinned too because after all, nobody's called Arnold anymore are they?

"Arnold Makepeace."

We both laughed out loud then, and we nearly hit a pigeon and Lorna swerved, which broke the ice because we got the giggles all the way down the High Street.

171

"And then in the end, it was your dad and I who made the peace, wasn't it? Not Arnold at all."

That did it. She was laughing so much, she couldn't drive properly. Her mascara was running and she needed a Kleenex, and she said she didn't have a clue where the box was, but it might be under your seat, Imogen, on the floor. I was surprised, because I thought she'd have kept her tissues in the glove box, or on the back seat, at least. Not squashed and muddy under the passenger seat. I made a remark about that, and she said there were lots of things about her I didn't know yet, and wasn't it great that we were doing things together and getting to know each other?

We found a good place to park, round the back of the High Street, which Mark had shown me because it was usually free, and his mum used it all the time since she'd started driving. Lorna was pleased that I'd saved her putting money in the meter, and she gave my arm a little squeeze as we walked down the alleyway to the shops, and I wanted to hate it, her doing that, but I didn't.

"What sort of shoes are we going for then?" she asked, a few yards before the shop doorway, as if she was going to wear them too.

"Anything I like. As long as they're black or brown," I lied.

"Do they have to have a strap? Can they be court shoes?"

"What are they, court shoes?"

They sounded medieval.

"You know, open shoes without any laces or straps. Like I've got on, more or less," and I looked down at Lorna's shoes, looking so elegant with her camel-cord skirt, and I thought my legs would never look like those, not in court shoes or any other type of shoes, come to that.

I tried on more than ten pairs, and all the time Lorna was telling me how nice I looked and how they flattered my legs, and it was funny how I could get away with so many different styles and still look good. And I thought, I know you're sucking up to me, Lorna Bennett, but I quite liked it anyway.

We landed on a black pair, no straps and a low heel, not because I was trying to please anybody, but because I'd never been able to walk in heels for long, and we had three tall staircases and miles of corridors at St Simon's. They had a cute little diamond motif to one side of each shoe, which glinted in the light and made them more eye-catching. Mrs Gayle would have something to say about that, but I didn't care.

"Do you like them?" Lorna asked, as the girl was wrapping them up in tissue and closing the lid. "Are you happy?"

"Mmm," I nodded. "They're really nice."

"Good. Now where shall we go next? What else do you need? Got enough shirts?"

I needed to play for more time, but it was difficult quizzing her for information, walking round shops.

"Can we go to a café?" I asked. "I'm thirsty."

"What a splendid idea," she said, as if anyone said splendid round here. "The cafés in town are pretty dull, aren't they? I know a much better place."

We got back in the car and Lorna drove us out of town, a couple of miles or so, to a large, white building set against the hill. It was framed by trees that were already speckled in gold. There was a pretty beck cutting across the front garden, which

173

ran right under the driveway. White flowers that I couldn't identify were sprinkled across the lawn, mingled in with tiny blue ones that, close-up, might have been speedwell, and golden water irises stood up tall, near the water's edge. There was a rockery, too, filled with heathers every shade of purple. It looked like a birthday card. The entire front of the building was made of glass, with the name 'Grasslands' over the door, in green joined-up writing.

"Is it a restaurant?"

"Kind of, but they do afternoon teas as well."

It was fabulous, inside and out. Better than anywhere I'd ever been with Mark, and I was already concocting a way we could go there together one day. It was so much more romantic than Tony's café.

Lorna asked for a seat right by the window. The Conservatory, she called it. Lemon trees with realistic lemons, sat at intervals along the window side, with each set of furniture nestled in between. There was a monster vine, draping leafy branches across the ceiling and down around the windows.

"Lovely view isn't it?"

I had to agree. We were both looking out at the countryside, where the winding road curved down and away beneath us, into town, or up into the hills where the moor began. Every now and then, the road would disappear, and you'd spot it again like a grey ribbon, twisting around the fells, getting smaller and smaller. There were fewer walls and fewer trees, the higher the road went, until the grass took over like a green cloak. Moor grass is different from the grass on Loraligh – mossier and spongy underfoot. It's nice to run about on. And sometimes there's cotton grass, and dozens of wild flowers, like harebells and vetch and yellow toadflax. Mrs Gayle taught me the names. In the summer you can find rock roses and milkwort, and later, the brightest blue gentians and masses of heather, which takes over the moor. If you're lucky, you might even spot a blue butterfly.

I loved it there. I could imagine being up there with Mark, and lying under the ferns, trying not to think of adders, and listening to all his stories.

"Is it on a bus route?" I asked.

"I think so. I'll find out for you, if you like. You could come here with your dad sometime, couldn't you?"

Not with him.

Lorna ordered tea, with interesting sarnies she called sandwiches, with the crusts cut off, and a double-decker cake stand of fancy cakes and fruit scones.

"Funny your father hasn't brought you here before," she said, and I thought, no it isn't – it doesn't surprise me at all.

"So tell me about you and Dad," I began.

"What do you want to know?"

"Everything. Well, not *every*thing."

Lorna smiled. She took a slice of lemon from the tiny dish and dropped it ever so gently into her tea, which was served in a glass cup, and I watched the colour from the bag slowly spreading into the water. I'd never seen tea do that before. Our tea always came milky brown in big, fat mugs.

"Tell me when you first got married, that sort of thing."

"We married way back in 1962," Lorna began. "You know, the age of the Beatles and all that. It was a great time to be young and in love. I'd met your dad at a party my mother held for all her friends and neighbours. Andrew didn't want to come, but his mother – your grandmother, Mary – insisted he came along. She said it would do him good to get out once in a while. She couldn't stand him festering at home."

She began to butter her scone, and I watched her carefully, to see if she did butter, cream, jam, or butter, jam, cream.

"Was Dad a hippy?" I couldn't imagine it.

Lorna laughed.

"Andrew? No, not him, but he did wear his hair to his collar. All the boys did. Mary never approved of that. Long haired yobbos, she called them. My parents too. No, your dad was never the type to let go. Not a rebel, him. But he refused to let his ears show."

It was odd, my father ever being young.

"Did he take drugs?"

"Your dad? He wasn't the type. Never much one for parties. Of course, I was there at this party, with my sister Susan. We were bored witless, because the house was full of grown-ups being terribly dull, and my mother was trying to show me off to all and sundry, like they do…"

And then she realised she shouldn't have said that, so she quickly changed the subject.

"Your father…ha! He was like a fish out of water, I can tell you. If ever there was a boy at a party who didn't want to be there, *he* was it."

"Was he only a boy then? How old was he?"

"Um…no, let's think, he was twenty two by then. But he wasn't very, shall we say, experienced when it came to girls, relationships, that sort of thing. I don't think he'd ever had a proper girlfriend before me."

He sounded like a right drip.

"Where did you live then?"

176

"Just over the way, on our farm. You know the one, on the other side of your hill. You have to turn a sharp right, back on yourself. A pond in front, and a huge oak tree over to one side?"

"I know it."

"You have to go the long way round, from Loraligh. It's quite a trek unless you cut across the footpath. Our parents knew each other better than we did. Anyway, your dad and I got talking at this party, sharing horror stories about how parents embarrass you and so on, and one thing led to another."

"Why do you speak posh, then, if you lived up north?"

"Do I? When your father and I separated, I moved away to London. I think I needed to be as far away as I could. That's where I met Arnold. I did a shorthand and typing course, and got a job as a secretary for the company where he worked. I guess the southern accent must have rubbed off on me pretty quickly."

"When did you get married to Dad?"

"Only a few months later, after the party. We didn't waste any time, did we? I was glad to get away, to be honest. My mother was hard work. That's when I came to live at Loraligh with your father and Mary. Your grandfather had already died."

"Dad said he died young."

"It was a great sadness to your grandmother. She loved him very much."

While she was talking, I got to wondering whether Grandma had been alive when Rebecca and Jonathan were born. Mark hadn't mentioned her in the newspaper article.

After all, if Grandma had been there, she could've saved the baby, at least. She'd have been in the kitchen.

"Mary didn't live long after Binks died. It's funny how people can die of a broken heart, isn't it? Well, not funny. You know what I mean."

Mrs Gayle would say funny peculiar, not funny ha ha.

"How long did she survive after Grandad, then?"

"Not long. I can't remember exactly. Your father and I had Loraligh to ourselves for most of our marriage, though. She left the mill to Andrew when he was still a young man. That was quite a responsibility."

A little question was beginning to form in my mind while she was speaking – a very important, poisonous little question – which went along the lines of: why didn't you have any children, then, Lorna? But that might have really upset the apple cart, so I decided to save that one for later.

"Were you happy together at first?"

"Oh yes, terribly happy. We had so much in common you see, born and bred in similar situations. Your father, he wasn't one of those moody men with nothing to say. We always had plenty to chat about, and he was a very affectionate man."

I didn't see how we could both be talking about the same person. She was full of surprises, this woman.

"So what went wrong? Why didn't it last?"

"It was a good thing for you it didn't, or you wouldn't be here right now, talking to me."

That was quite a thought. The way her story was unfolding, half of me was wishing the ending had been different, but she was right – I would never have been born.

"No, but why? Why didn't it last?" I wouldn't let it go.

Lorna put down the rest of her scone and looked at me.

178

"It's a very sad story, Imogen. Something happened at the mill, a tragedy. We never got over it. We tried hard for a long time, but we couldn't."

At last, an adult who wouldn't lie to me. I didn't speak then, partly because I knew exactly what she was talking about, but also because I could see she needed more space to find the words.

"I know your father hasn't talked to you about this, Imogen, because I've asked him. He probably doesn't want me to tell you now. But the way I see it, you're virtually fifteen, aren't you?"

I nodded.

"You have a right to know these things. So if I tell you, do you promise to bear with me? Try to understand that your father might be...rather cross."

I realised she didn't want to provoke a major row with him, and a day or two earlier I might have seized on this as the perfect opportunity to rake things up between them, but as we sat there in that lovely place, with Lorna treating me like a real grown-up, levelling with me the way she was, some of the anger melted away inside me. I wanted to hear the story the way it was for her, and this time I didn't want to be responsible for any rift that might develop between them.

"Are you ready?" she began, "because this is going to be a considerable shock, hearing this."

I nodded, thinking keep quiet, Imogen Wise, and don't put your size sevens in yet.

"A short time after we married, less than a year, we had a baby. A little girl..."

She told me the story, more or less as I imagined it, and I pretended to be surprised now and again. And now and again also, the waitress came to top up our tea and ask if everything was all right, and we nodded and smiled politely. Lorna clearly found some of it painful to relate, because she was having to remember her children, and I expect, over the years, she'd managed to put those memories away in their own compartment from time to time.

When she got to the day it all happened, I sat up straighter and concentrated as hard as I could.

"Why weren't you at Loraligh?"

"My own grandmother was ill and she had to go into a nursing home. Mum couldn't take her, because she'd just had a hip replacement and couldn't drive. So I went to Ripon where my grandmother was living, and looked after her. Mum and I visited the home together, to get her used to it. And once she was in, it was my job to clear her house. Susan joined me there, because it was more than one person could manage."

"You were staying away then? It wasn't a day trip?"

"No. I'd already been gone two or three days when it happened."

"How did you find out? It must have been terrible."

She went quiet and gazed out of the window. She was trying hard not to cry, for my sake.

"It's as if it happened yesterday. I remember every painful, minute-by-minute detail. The way it was for me. Andrew phoning in the middle of the night – not being able to get the words out. He told me later he wished he'd waited until I'd come home…that it must've been a dreadful way to find out…but of course he couldn't have done that. I wasn't due back for another week. I had to know."

She looked straight at me then and even managed a little smile. And I thought, you are one brave lady, Lorna Bennett. That's when I knew I'd shifted. Perhaps I grew up a little at that very moment, because I realised that relieving her of the pain of having to go over all this, rather than satisfying my quest for more information, might matter more.

"You don't have to go on, if you don't want to."

She reached forward and placed her hand over mine, and it was surreal, because it reminded me of how my dad had done exactly that to her, in Tony's café, that time. I knew then, the power you feel when someone likes you.

"You deserve to know, Imogen. It's years behind me now. I need to deal with it."

"Tell me what happened when you got back to Loraligh."

"It was early the next morning. As you'd expect, the police were all over the place, and two fire engines. There was no ambulance. It had taken…our children away, hours before."

I was wondering how they'd managed to get Rebecca out, but this wasn't the time to ask.

"Were you allowed to see them?"

"I went to the hospital later. I needed to say goodbye."

I couldn't bear to ask what they looked like, even though a strange part of me wanted to know. I'd never seen a dead person. Still haven't.

"What was Dad doing when you turned up?"

"I remember clearly. He was in the back garden. There were a couple of chairs we used to keep there. We'd take our coffees outside and look out across the meadow, watching the grass blow wild. Don't you love that? The patterns it makes in the wind? Or the hills, the way they turn golden in the late sun. It's always been such a lovely place to sit and talk."

181

"Your father was sitting bent over, his arms wrapped round himself, rocking back and forth, moaning. It was a terrible sound, Imogen. Like a cow wanting its calf. Sometimes I wake in the middle of the night, and I can hear him making that noise in his sleep, even now. There's no end to it."

I looked down at my plate, because I couldn't bear the pain in Lorna's face. Or perhaps it was my own vision of how my father must have looked, and what he must've been feeling inside, the hours after it happened.

"The worst of it for him, I suppose, was being completely helpless. Knowing he was the one person there who could have rescued them, and he hadn't. Knowing he'd put them in danger in the first place. It never mattered what I said to him over the years after that. Or anyone else, for that matter. Nothing took the responsibility away. He had to learn to live with it and he couldn't. He just couldn't do it."

"Did you hate him for what he did? Did you blame him?"

"I've thought about that a lot, over the years. At the time? I loved him. I couldn't hate him. But later? I'm not sure. I felt unendingly sorry for him. I suppose I wanted to hate somebody. I blamed God for letting it happen to our perfect little children. I didn't understand why any god would allow it. At first, when Andrew told me over the telephone what had happened, I was in terrible shock. I thought I'd misheard him – that he was talking about somebody else's children. That he must have made a mistake. I was screaming and screaming down the phone, madly trying to invent a different truth because the one I was being told was too impossible. I couldn't take it in, you see. I couldn't believe that they had gone. I barely heard any of the details, not until much later.

Susan had to take the phone from me, and she was crying too."

"It must have been awful."

I felt choked then. I didn't have an appetite for the rest of the cakes, which was a shame because they looked so good.

"Oh, listen to me," Lorna said, "upsetting you with all my stories. I'm sorry, Imogen. I'd meant this to be a nice girls' outing, just the two of us. I never intended to say all this, not today."

"It's all right. I did ask. You're the only person who ever tells me anything."

"Are you sure? As long as you want to know."

"What happened then, when you saw Dad in the garden, sitting on the chair?"

"I think...I remember walking over to him. We couldn't speak. I stroked his hair...and then...he buried his head in me and held on. He was gasping for air. He couldn't breathe."

I could see it all, and yet I'd not once seen my father cry.

"It was strange. I wanted to protect him, to make it all go away for him. I was looking around, expecting Rebecca to turn the corner any second, jabbering to her teddy, and then spotting me and being cross, asking where I'd been to for so long."

"He told me everything, eventually. There was a policewoman standing well back, at the end of the path, waiting. Andrew couldn't speak clearly. He was tripping over his words, and the policewoman stood like a sentry with a completely blank face. She was getting on my nerves. I wished we'd had some time alone together first."

"What was she waiting for?"

183

"To take Andrew to the police station. They questioned him for hours, into the night. They had to."

"But he hadn't done anything wrong had he?"

"Nothing criminal. But when children die in tragic circumstances like that, they have to rule out parental neglect."

And murder, I thought.

"And did they? Did they rule it out?"

"They described it as a tragic accident, but your father never saw it that way. He wished they would lock him up."

I was quiet for a long time. We both were. The waitress came to give us the bill and Lorna signed a cheque, and then I said:

"I'm glad they didn't. Lock him up I mean. I'm glad they didn't."

That was the first time a slice of forgiveness found its way in, like Mrs Gayle had said it would. It was out of my control.

Thirteen

Secret Out

When I arrived back home, the kitchen was unusually quiet, even though I knew Mrs Gayle hadn't left yet, because her car was out front. I walked in and saw her sleeping in the rocker, chin to her chest, her mouth slightly open and a faint snore rising and falling. I watched her awhile, because I'd never once seen her asleep and I thought – you're getting old, Mrs Gayle. It was the first time I'd noticed. Her fingers had swollen, so her rings looked tight. Her hair was mostly grey now, home-permed, the way she'd always worn it, and her jaw-line merged into her neck. One foot was resting on the short stool, and you could see where the sole of her shoe was wearing through.

She must've sensed my presence, because she woke with a start and thinking sharp, as usual.

"You've been gone a long time."

"Lorna took me to this place out in the country called Grasslands."

"Did she, now?"

"Have you heard of it?"

"I've driven past once or twice. Never had cause to go inside. Did you find any shoes?"

I took the lid off the box and passed it to her.

"Hmm. They'll all see you coming in those, won't they?"

I wasn't sure who she meant, but I didn't care.

"The heels are low," I pointed out, by way of making peace.

"Granted. Do you want a cup of tea?"

"I'll make *you* one, shall I?"

She raised an eyebrow, and I smiled as I filled the kettle. When I'd made up the pot, I chatted on about Grasslands, saying she'd *have* to go because it was far superior (Lorna's word) to anywhere else round here. I described the breathtaking view, knowing that would grab her because old people always love a view, and then I told her I had something to show her. I went upstairs to fetch the newspaper article, which I'd hidden in between the leaves of a photo album in the roof cupboard.

It was time.

I folded the paper in four and carried it behind my back into the kitchen. Then I sat at the table, with Mrs Gayle still relaxing in the rocker, blowing her tea.

"You remember when Mark rang and wanted to see me in town that time?" I began. "He'd been looking under the carpets in his house, because they were changing them and his mum had asked him to pull them up. And while he was looking, he came across some old newspapers, scattered about on the floorboards."

I paused, to see if there would be a reaction, but Mrs Gayle was simply looking smiley and interested, the way she always managed to when I had news to tell her.

"What I didn't know that day, was that the article he'd found…it was about me. Well, not exactly me. More about Dad. And Lorna."

Ah now she was looking worried! Her skin had paled and I'd wiped the smile right off.

"Go on," she said.

I opened up the news-cutting carefully and spread it out on the table top, smoothing down the creases. She couldn't have seen it properly from where she was sitting, but the photographs of the two children would have caught anyone's eye. She heaved herself out of the rocker and came over to the table, where she could read the headline.

INFANTS IN FLOOD TRAGEDY

I watched her eyes, how they widened and then narrowed. Her hand went to her mouth briefly, before she remembered herself, and then she slowly lifted the newspaper to a readable height and pushed her glasses up her nose. She took ages reading it all, and I sensed her lifting and turning and considering each phrase, before she went on to the next.

While I was watching and waiting for her to finish, I realised that she'd possibly never seen the article before. There was I thinking, you knew all this, didn't you? But perhaps she didn't – not all the details. I recalled the conversation she'd had with my father, a long time ago. It wasn't hard to remember what they'd said, because Mark and I had discussed it more than a few times. She hadn't seen Lorna, she said. She didn't know what she looked like. But then, Lorna's face was hidden in Dad's coat.

By the time she'd finished, her hand was trembling. She put the paper down and I was wondering whether she might cry, but Mrs Gayle never cried. Then she looked at me and pushed my hair out of my eyes, which she hadn't done for a long time.

"So now you know."

187

That was all she said. So now you know.

"Yes."

"Is your father aware of this?"

"No."

"I see."

She sat down at the table then, shaken. Perhaps it was having the whole tragic story out in the open. Perhaps she'd never known exactly how they died. Eventually she spoke up.

"It was the saddest thing ever to have happened in these parts. Everyone talked about it at the time. There was nobody who didn't know."

No one except me. I asked her why it had never been spoken about in my earshot, not in town, not by any of my friends or their parents, not by my teachers. Well, she said, it was back in 1965 and you were born a good seven years later. Things move on, she said, and people try to forget.

"What are you going to say to your father, Imogen? He'll have to know now, won't he?"

"I can't understand why he never told me. First Lorna, then this. And there's something else I don't get, either."

"Tell me, child."

Mrs Gayle was sitting right by my side, and she'd taken one of my hands in her warm one and was rubbing her thumb over the bone on my wrist, and I could tell she was feeling for me.

"If I'd lost my two children, and then I'd been lucky enough to have another, I'd take care of that child like it was the last child on earth. I'd love it to pieces."

"Exactly that, Imogen. That's exactly what Andrew was afraid of. Loving you to pieces. Loving you to death."

I looked at Mrs Gayle's eyes through the blur of my own, and I tried hard to understand what she was telling me.

"You see, pet, he couldn't allow himself to hurt like that again. Over the years, watching him and how he is with you, I've often thought – he thinks he doesn't deserve you."

"But that's not my fault!" I blurted out, and she cuddled me then and she said I know, Imogen, I know.

I didn't tell Dad about the newspaper article, that day. I didn't need to, because Lorna would tell him about our conversation and about me knowing the whole story. At first I felt angry that she'd stolen my thunder – my great oration. But then I thought, I'd only start yelling and ranting at him, or crying my head off. I would feel stupid afterwards, and it wouldn't have changed a thing between Dad and me.

He found me down on The Beach. I'd taken a walk there by myself, because I wanted space to think everything through. I was sitting on Mark's tree trunk and I heard a crackling sound coming through the wood, so I looked up. Dad slowed down when he saw me and he looked nervous. We must both have been remembering what happened the last time we'd been at Shallow Falls together. I didn't invite him to sit on the log with me. I didn't say hello and he didn't say it to me either. And I thought: I bet Lorna's told you to come. I bet you didn't decide this for yourself.

As usual, he had no idea where to start and was shuffling round and, as usual, I didn't know what to say either.

"Mrs Gayle's had a word, Imogen."

"Oh."

I wasn't going to make it easy for him, was I?

"About the…accident."

"Yes."

I glanced away then, at the river. It was painful watching him.

"You might be wondering why I never told you."

"Not really. It's obvious."

He went quiet for a moment, working out his argument.

"Imogen, the way I see it, it would have wrecked your whole childhood. It would have been terrible for you, a young girl growing up with all that...all that tragedy around you. They were your sister and brother, after all."

Half, I thought. But I didn't say. I waited.

"I took a long, long time getting over it. You never really do, over a thing like that. Can you imagine? It stays with you always."

I nodded but I said nothing, and inside I was thinking, you? Get over it? Chance'd be a fine thing.

"I couldn't speak about them at all, the children. I was responsible, you see. People were all telling me it was an accident, but it was totally my fault. Do you understand?"

"I'm not stupid, Dad. I'm nearly fifteen."

That silenced him awhile, because he could sense my anger, although I was doing my best to bury it.

"No, you're not stupid. I know that." He was almost whispering.

"Why didn't you tell me before? Wouldn't it have been better if...I don't know...if you'd let the story out gently, bit by bit, over the years? If there'd been a photograph somewhere, and you'd explained to me who they were."

After a long pause, he agreed. Yes, that might have been better.

He turned to look at The Slopes.

"I'm not very good at this, Imogen – being a father."

You can say that again, I thought. But I found different words for him.

"You weren't to know it would happen, when you let Rebecca out with you. You probably thought you could keep a better eye on her, rather than leaving her indoors."

Dad came to sit next to me on the log. His hands were rubbing away at the knees of his trousers.

"That was precisely the way I was thinking at the time. I've gone over and over it. If only I could have undone that one, stupid, idiotic decision. If only I'd left her safe and dry in the kitchen."

"She was only two, Dad. That's not very old, is it? I don't think a two-year-old can play for long by herself, without being watched."

I realised I was helping him out and I was even surprising myself.

"But we could have moved upstairs, when the water began flowing in. Not that that's the right way to describe it. It was rushing in, more like – as fast as our river after rain. I should've stayed with the children and taken them upstairs, long before it came to that."

"Easy to say with hindsight," I said, using Mrs Gayle's favourite phrase. "Besides, it's not a man's instinct is it, to leave a situation like that? To let the water flood in. It's certainly not yours."

"No," and Dad allowed himself a little tiny laugh, then, and I did too, because we both knew about his total neurosis.

We watched the river for a while, the glassy surface of the water, the reflection of the hills and clouds against the sky, like an upside-down painting; at the inevitable journey of

191

each stick or leaf, over one ledge after another, on and out to the North Sea.

I felt Dad's arm come round my shoulder and it rested there and we didn't say any more. He didn't say sorry and he didn't say that he loved me. But it was all right. I was glad I hadn't spilled my ranting speech at him, in the end. I didn't think it would help matters.

"Shall we go back then?" he said.

"Yes. I'm hungry."

As we crossed the yard, I looked for the storm drain. I couldn't find it, but there was a rectangular patch where the concrete was different and I knew what he'd done. He'd filled that drain in. I could imagine him, frantically pushing cement down that chute with angry shovelfuls, and tears down his face. Once they'd got her out. Every time I crossed the yard after that, I had to avoid that patch. I asked Mrs Gayle, once, how the water drained away from the backyard, now the storm drain had been filled in, and she said goodness, she didn't know, I'd have to ask my father. But I didn't. I couldn't mention drains ever again.

Lorna moved into Loraligh permanently, once I'd started back at school. They announced one evening, over tea, that they intended getting married again, and Cedric was there too because they'd invited him for the announcement 'specially, and Mrs Gayle. They were both thrilled, they said, and everyone was smiling. Dad opened a bottle of fizzy wine he'd bought for the occasion and even poured a glass for me. It was disgusting, but I didn't let on.

There was a part of me that wanted to be miserable about the wedding, and then there was a part that didn't. I'd got used to Lorna being around, I suppose, and Dad was in a distinctly better mood most of the time. It irritated me, watching them pawing each other, and I said to Mrs Gayle, you'd think they'd got over all that the last time, wouldn't you? Like new lovers, Cedric said, which made me cringe, because they were far too old for that and it didn't bear thinking about. Mrs Gayle said they'd get over it soon enough, and things would settle back to normal, and she was usually the wise one, despite our surname, so I gave her the benefit.

Besides, Lorna was often on my side when anything contentious came up for discussion, so she was a useful person to have around. For example, our form at school had been invited to go on a week's trip to France, but there were only twenty five places and it was first come first served. Dad thought France was a long way to go because after all, it was hours to get to the ferry and I'd never been abroad before, so he wasn't sure I'd cope. But Lorna, who immediately saw how disappointed I was, jumped to my rescue.

"It'll be the perfect opportunity for her. Won't it, Imogen? She never goes on holiday. You haven't taken her away anywhere for ages, have you, Andrew?"

I kept quiet, looking from Lorna to Dad, and letting her do the hard work for me. Dad shrugged and made his helpless face.

"We never had the money. Loraligh isn't a place you can leave easily."

"It's a matter of priorities," she said. "It's high time Imogen went away somewhere – broadened her horizons."

Which I thought was funny, because the only horizon I'd ever seen, more or less, was the moor and our hills, where

193

they cut their wiggly line against the sky to the north, and the grassy bank and trees by our lane out front. Our bus ride gave open views, but more often than not, the windows were covered with condensation, which I spent half the journey doodling on, to pass the time.

"I expect you're right."

"Of course I'm right. And besides, she needs a chance to be with her friends. Don't you Imogen? It's awful being left out of things at her age."

She was certainly right about that. Carrie and Nicola would be sharing a room and talking about me, and then they'd be best of friends when they got back, and I wouldn't get a look in.

"Why are they taking you all to France then?" Dad asked.

"For improving our French," I said, stating the obvious and wondering why he needed to ask. "So we can speak fluently, and learn about the French way of life."

Dad shrugged his shoulders and went on eating (more politely than usual, with his elbows off the table) and I could tell he couldn't see the point, not with France so far away and him not even liking croissants. But the subject was closed as far as Lorna was concerned. She gave me a wink. It was two against one and Dad was never going to win.

The next day there was a fifty pound cheque on the kitchen top, for the deposit, and Lorna made sure it went into my school bag. Mrs Gayle didn't come in the early mornings anymore. She said we wouldn't be needing her now, with Lorna there and me nearly fifteen. I'd argued, because I didn't want her to feel pushed out, and Lorna backed me up and insisted that Mrs Gayle was indispensable. There were so many household chores to be done, running such a large place, and Lorna had a full time job in town, so she wouldn't be able to manage by herself.

Mrs Gayle backed down and agreed to come at twelve every day. She'd get dinner for Cedric and Dad, and sort the laundry and cleaning. But she'd be leaving at five thirty on the dot, because she had a home to go to and a son who needed her. And I thought, he's old enough to leave home and look after himself, your David, and you're using him as an excuse, Mrs Gayle, but I'll keep quiet this time. She was getting older, she said, and was feeling the effects. She couldn't do the long days anymore. Lorna was worried she'd pushed our housekeeper out, and she spoke about that to me once or twice. But the way I saw it, the two of them seemed to rub along all right, and Mrs Gayle gave the impression she was happy enough with the new arrangement, so that's how it panned out.

The wedding was planned for the day after Boxing Day – several months off, but still Mrs Gayle went into a flat spin when she heard, saying however would she manage, with Christmas and a wedding right on top of each other? Lorna patted her shoulder and said the wedding would be a very modest affair: the four of us, Cedric and his wife, Susan and her family, an old school friend of Lorna's, and Dad's sister Vanessa, who'd emigrated to Canada years before I was born. Aunt Vanessa phoned to say she'd love to come over for the wedding, because it had been such a long time since she'd seen her brother.

"Your father and I have been thinking you might like to have a friend your own age at the wedding, Imogen, so you don't get bored. What do you think?" Lorna asked.

I was taken completely by surprise.

195

"Really? You don't mind?"

"Not at all," she said.

"But it wouldn't be family."

"That's all right. There'll be plenty of room."

I had to have a long think, because I had two best friends. If I chose one over the other, I'd never hear the end. I spent a day or two pondering that decision, and asked Mrs Gayle to help me decide.

"It might be simpler if I don't ask anyone," I suggested. "It's going to be more trouble than it's worth."

"Why don't you ask Mark then? He knows your dad, and he worked here for quite a while, didn't he?"

"Mark? He wouldn't want to come."

And I meant it when I said it, because we'd fallen out, hadn't we? Not that Mrs Gayle knew. Added to which, the gap between Mark and I had widened too much since he'd been away. I knew he wouldn't want to be invited.

"You never know unless you ask. He was a very good friend of yours before he went to Sheffield, wasn't he? He might like to come."

She left it at that, but I didn't change my mind. I'd feel an idiot for asking. All the same, it reminded me how I'd left things with Mark, and I didn't feel easy about that. After all was said and done, he *was* the person who'd found out about our family history, who'd trusted me to be grown-up enough to deal with it. I know what Mrs Gayle would say if she knew. She'd say I was letting myself down.

Lorna mentioned the bridesmaid word, but she could tell I wasn't keen. I was in my bedroom at the time, standing in front of the long mirror in my new jeans, and I said look at me, Lorna. I'd look ridiculous in a big fussy dress. It would make me look even fatter, and Lorna said nonsense, I wasn't fat at all and besides, I wouldn't be that sort of bridesmaid because it wasn't going to be that sort of wedding. It would only be registry office, smart suits and such-like, and I noticed our accent was creeping back in when she said that. Even though she didn't pronounce France the same way we did. I could be her flower girl and help out with all sorts of jobs on the day. She'd find me invaluable, and I could choose what to wear. Anything I liked, she said, within reason. And we laughed when she said that, because we were imagining me going off the deep end, like a punk hair-do and ripped jeans and trainers.

"Okay then," I said. "I like the sound of a flower girl."

"Good. That's settled then."

Lorna said we'd have to go somewhere more exciting than our town, when it was time to buy outfits, like Harrogate or York, and we might even make a weekend of it. She said we'd look elegant and sophisticated, and I said fat chance. She made me sit down by the dressing table, picked up my hairbrush and began working it through my hair, which had grown way past my shoulders, over and over until it shone. She twirled it up and round on top and said there – now we can see your neck. See how much older you look? We'll have a proper practice one day soon. It'll look fabulous, you wait and see, she said. And I felt excited, because I had confidence in her that she'd make me look good.

"What am I going to do about this, though?" I asked, pinching my middle.

"There's nothing there, Imogen! To be honest, I don't think you're remotely overweight. It's quite normal for girls your age to have a few curves. You're growing into a woman.

It'll soon settle down. Besides, you'll look perfectly lovely and nobody will notice."

And although I didn't agree with her – because Mandy Sheldon had pointed it out to me in the school toilets, in her usual, spiteful way – it was nice to hear a compliment.

Lorna went to fetch her make-up bag. She had interesting things like foundation and powder, with three shades of peach in a compact. She clipped my hair up out of the way, and then she put blobs of foundation on my nose and cheeks and gradually spread it all in. It felt cold and then warm, and when I opened my eyes, it wasn't me looking back in the mirror.

"There," she said, "you look like a film star."

I had to admit, the effect was amazing – like in a magazine. When she'd finished doing my eyes, she called downstairs for Dad to come and see.

"Oh God, no. Don't get him."

"Why ever not?"

But he'd already started climbing the stairs, because Lorna only had to click her fingers as far as my Dad was concerned. He appeared in the doorway, arms across his chest and his chin jutting out. Lorna was standing right behind me, holding my shoulders and showing me off.

"What do you think of your lovely daughter then?"

He was shaking his head from side to side.

"Cat's got his tongue," Lorna laughed.

"I hardly recognised you."

All three of us were smiling and I realised – that's what we needed all these years. A woman to fill in the spaces between us.

Fourteen

Being Fifteen

Half way through September, I had my fifteenth birthday party. I'd never had a party before, and Lorna said that was outrageous and she asked Dad why he hadn't let Mrs Gayle organise parties for me when I was little. Mrs Gayle looked shame-faced and gave my dad a weighty glance, because she clearly didn't want to speak out of turn, and Dad um'd and ah'd. Mrs Gayle rescued the situation, explaining that she and Cedric and Dad had always made a big fuss of me on my birthday, and made a special tea. And I rescued her back by saying that was true, and it didn't matter because I'd always enjoyed my birthday anyway.

"Nevertheless, a girl should have a party," Lorna insisted, as if it had been written somewhere.

"Would you like one?" she asked.

"I don't know who would come."

"Your school friends, of course. Your whole form could come if you like! We've got space, haven't we Andrew?" But she didn't say it in an asking voice.

Dad's face fell to pieces and we all thought he was funny – even Mrs Gayle.

"There's twenty eight in my form."

"That's fine," Lorna said, "and you can invite that boy you like. The one who used to work here. What's his name?"

"He's not a boy. He's twenty one now. I think he's moved away. He was going to get a job."

"You can find out, can't you? And we'd better invite Philip too, to be fair. Is there anyone else you can think of?"

This was all amazing. A party! Other people had parties, not me. I was scared and excited, all knotted together.

"What if nobody wants to come?"

"They wouldn't have the sense they were born with," Mrs Gayle said. "I'll help you with the invitations."

"What sort of party would you like?" Lorna asked. "Do you want fancy dress, or a disco or something?"

Dad was looking truly horrified.

"I don't want to be the one to put a dampener on things," he said, "but where on earth would we hold a disco? It's too cold to be outside of an evening."

"We could use the shop," Lorna suggested. "We could push all the counters to the edge and set up the party in there. It's perfect."

"We'd have to hire a proper disco," Mrs Gayle said, as if it was the sort of thing she knew about. "If that's what you want, Imogen. And I'll do the food."

I sat back on the rocker, and watched and listened to these two lovely women in my life, making plans and getting so animated, all for me. A big lump was forming in my throat and I felt happy inside, because I'd never had such a fuss made of me. I began to feel like the absent guest – but I wanted it that way. I could tell they wouldn't do anything without my say-so.

After a while, Dad glanced across and caught me far away, and he came over to my chair.

"Is this all okay with you, love?"

"Yes Dad. It's brilliant," I said quietly.

He rested a hand on my shoulder, and I put my hand over his and we didn't say anything else.

Mark didn't come to my party, because he'd already started work in Sheffield by then. Philip told us Mark had started working for an engineering company, designing steel structures or something like that, for doors and windows. His maths must've come in useful, Cedric said and I thought, oh you noticed then, Cedric. Lorna said it was probably better in the end, having people my own age instead.

However, Mark did send me a card with a photograph of a river surrounded by trees and hills and I thought, I know why you chose that one, Mark Wheeler. Inside the card he wrote a message:

Sorry about losing my temper, Immie. Guess we both found things hard to take that day. Hope you've forgiven me. All the best for your fifteenth. Can't believe our Immie's all grown up!
See ya, Love Mark x

It meant a lot to me that he'd put about me growing up, after implying that I hadn't. I felt happier, for him apologising, and I wrote back that I was sorry too. I made a card with a photo of myself all dressed up for the party, stuck on the front. Lorna had put my hair up, the way she'd practised for the wedding, and I had a fabulous dress splashed in multi-coloured flowers, with shoulder-pads like on *Dallas*, and high-heeled shoes, because she said no fifteen year old's wardrobe should be without one pair at least. I got Mark's new address from Philip, and I posted the letter myself in town after school, because we don't have a post-box near Loraligh.

Mrs Gayle had been right about people wanting to come, and we had twenty three in the end. Philip didn't fancy it, and I wasn't disappointed about that because I couldn't see him fitting in. We nearly packed out our shop; you wouldn't have recognised it in there. It was like a real venue in a pub or something, by the time we'd finished getting it ready. Not that we had a bar. Dad relented and let us have cider, because he didn't realise how it can go to your head, but he limited it to ten bottles and plenty of fizzy, so there was no chance of any trouble. Cedric helped move all the shop furniture, and Mrs Gayle hired some extra chairs from her church hall, which Dad collected in the Land Rover. He had to do two trips to get them all in, but he didn't complain once.

Lorna and I concentrated on the decorations. She knew about these coloured lanterns you could use inside and out, and they looked fantastic once it got dark. The DJ said he'd bring one of those glittery balls that hang from the ceiling. And then Mrs Gayle suggested we tie a few balloons to the front gate, so as nobody would miss us, but Lorna said balloons were perhaps for smaller children, so she hung four separate lanterns on tall sticks, either side of the gate, with a floaty banner between that said my name in huge letters. Cedric helped me do the lettering with a fat paintbrush and a tin of blue paint from his cupboard. I think he was chuffed to be asked. When Cedric had left for home, Lorna and I took a walk down the lane, because she said she wanted some fresh air, and I had pins and needles from kneeling so long. When we got to the bend in the lane, I wondered if Lorna knew why it was called Three Boys, since no one else had a clue.

"Oh yes, my mother told me that story. There was this couple, nobody we knew particularly, several years ago. About the time our Susan was born. They'd been on their way to hospital one night, and the woman was about to give birth, but the lane was flooded so badly, they couldn't get through. Anyway, she went into labour and there was nothing they could do to stop it, so she had to give birth there and then, in the car."

"What happened?"

"She had a little boy. That's all there was to it. She had the baby on the back seat, and her husband helped deliver it."

"So why is it called *Three* Boys then?"

"Because they already had two sons, and they were in the car with their parents at the time. They couldn't leave two little lads at home by themselves in the middle of the night. It was on the front page of the local paper."

It was quite an anti-climax, that story. I'd lived in fear of that bend in the road all my childhood. Like spiders, or Father Christmas, or policemen or God. Mind you, I'm still scared of spiders.

Brian Stokes asked me to dance with him when the slow records came on, near the end of the evening. I wondered if he'd only done it because I was the birthday girl, but Nicola said I was being daft, because he'd always fancied me. I replied that Brian fancied anyone in a skirt, and she made a face, but you could hardly hear what anyone was saying over the music. I did quite like dancing with him though, and he was squeezing my side and pulling me in close. My dress was cut low at the back, so he got to my bare skin without trying, and I was worried that he'd notice how sweaty I was. By the time we got to Lady in Red, we'd got right up close and his hand had moved lower down. Carrie and Nicola were making faces and giggling at me, and I was shooing them away.

"I'm glad Mark wasn't there in the end," I said to Mrs Gayle afterwards. "He wouldn't have fitted in, him being that much older."

"Like a sore thumb."

"He'd think we were all beneath him. And he wouldn't have known anybody."

"You could be right."

Mrs Gayle was folding bed-linen and putting it into our plastic basket on the kitchen table.

"Philip's leaving next week," I added.

"Did he say where he's going to next?"

"He's got a job with a carpenter. Mr Moreby, he's called. Got a workshop just off the big roundabout. Says he'll learn the trade from him. He'd never make polytechnic."

"Takes all sorts."

She finished folding the linen and picked up the basket, propping it on one hip like it belonged there.

"Who was that you were dancing with at the party?"

"Were you watching then?"

"Only towards the end. Your dad told me to pop in and check on things."

"Getting you to do his dirty work for him, then?" I smiled. "He's called Brian. He's in my form."

"He's handsome."

"And he knows it."

"Like that is it?"

She huffed in a smiley way and carried on up the stairs, scraping the basket up the walls as she went. Our wallpaper had suffered badly over the years, with the plastic edge of that linen basket. It cut great grooves into the pattern, but the stairway's so dark, it barely showed. Lorna was shocked when she noticed, and said we would need to re-decorate once the wedding was over. But I said I liked it the way it was, and Dad said it added character to the place – charm. And the two of us stood in a line with our housekeeper, like Hadrian's wall, so Lorna agreed to leave it the way it was for now.

The cold in November slipped quickly into that deep, penetrating cold that presses everyone into gloves and vests and an extra layer. They turned the heating on in school, which made it that bit more bearable, but the lessons dragged on as much as ever. I'd chosen my O-levels by then, and was already beginning to wonder if I'd chosen the right ones. Everyone had to do English, Maths and R.E. regardless, but the rest of it was up to us. Except it wasn't, because all the other subjects were put into groups, and you weren't allowed to choose two from the same group. Which was absolutely stupid, Mrs Gayle agreed with me, because I couldn't do Geography *and* History, only one or the other. And they'd always been my favourite subjects, because I was interested in the world, past and present, probably because I saw precious little of it. Mrs Gayle said it was absurd not being able to do both subjects together, because they lent themselves to each other, didn't they? – and she would be up that school to complain, if nobody else did. Cedric agreed with her, and I left them shaking their heads and decrying the modern education system, compared to how it had been in their day. They tried to drag Dad into that argument too, but he couldn't remember a thing about what he could or couldn't do when he was a teenager.

The history of my own family spurred me on, so in the end I chose History over Geography. I picked French from the B list to help me on the school trip, but I had to opt for something on the C list and there wasn't a thing left I fancied. So in the end I went for Art, because at least the time passed quickly.

Watching Mr Usher, my History teacher, write the date on the board one morning, got me to thinking about November, and that got me to remembering that that was the month of the terrible accident at our mill in 1965, and I thought, wouldn't it be nice to do something to commemorate my brother and sister? It might help my Dad, I thought. After all, trying to forget hadn't worked, had it? I'd need to find out the exact date, so I made a mental note to look it up in the newspaper article when I got home that night.

When the rest of the form had gone out of the room, I decided to approach Mr Usher.

"Hello, young Imogen," he said. Teachers always say weird things like that, and then they wonder why we can't relate to them. "What can I do for you?"

"I have a question to ask you."

"Oh yes?"

"Do you remember back in '65, there were some really bad floods around here?"

"Let's think. '65 you say? I'd have been, what? – twenty six or so. I was living in Newcastle."

"Oh, you wouldn't remember, then."

He smiled.

"Newcastle's not *that* far away, you know."

"Isn't it?"

"Didn't you study Geography?" he said. "What on earth do they teach you at school these days?"

If any of the other teachers had said that, I'd have wanted to kick their shins, but because it was Mr Usher I knew he was only joking, because he'd known all about my dilemma over my O-levels, and because he was always good for a laugh.

He fetched an atlas from his top shelf and opened it up on England. He showed me where Newcastle was, and sure enough it wasn't that far, at least on the map.

"Do you remember the floods then?"

"I think I do. You're right though. It wasn't in Tyneside. Further south, I think, and especially bad on the moors. There was a lot of news coverage at the time. Why do you ask?"

"Oh, nothing really. Something happened back then that I found out about recently. Something I want to know about."

Mr Usher was looking pleased, as he replaced the atlas on the shelf.

"Of course, if you're really interested in finding more about it, you can always look in the library. They hold details on local history, possibly even newspaper articles."

"Thanks, Mr Usher. I'll do that."

I left him all fluffed up, because he liked it when one of us demonstrated curiosity about anything. He said curiosity was the key to learning. Without curiosity, we'd never have built an aeroplane, or flown to the moon, or invented the telephone. Without curiosity, where would mankind ever have been? My mind had drifted off when he began that speech, because I could see the wonder of it all, and I'd started to list all the things in my brain that man had invented or discovered, and it was amazing.

I didn't need to read the papers, because Mark had seen to that already, but I did think there might be other facts I could find out about that flood. Or our mill.

That night, I warned Mrs Gayle I'd be late back from school the next day so she wasn't to worry about where I'd got to, because I had some research to do.

"Oh yes? Homework is it?"

"We have to find out facts about local history. Anything from 1815 onwards."

(I wasn't exactly lying, more stretching the truth.)

"By 'eck."

By which I think she meant, that's a heck of a lot of history then. But I could see her glowing, because she and Cedric approved of anyone using the library. She said they'd close it if folk didn't use it. And then I'd asked her how often she went, and she'd flushed up like she does, and I'd think – practise what you preach, Mrs Gayle.

But I didn't mean it nasty.

The librarian was a homely type, with a cotton-wool voice. She wore the same jumper every time you saw her, a home-made pendant with the glue still showing, and elasticated trousers that were baggy at the back. But she was helpful and she certainly knew her way around that place. She showed me where to look for the town records in the Reference section, and then I asked about Loraligh, because that's a few miles out, and she reassured me we'd be included, because it covered the whole parish. She said they didn't have any newspaper articles from those times, because you'd need to go to a much bigger library than ours for that, even London, and I said it didn't matter.

I got so carried away searching through things, I was there right until closing time and I nearly missed the bus. I'd found a book about local history, but it only briefly mentioned the flood in passing, with a couple of black and white photographs of fields under water, and there was no particular reference to Loraligh. I was going to ask the librarian how you could find out who had or hadn't been born around 1963, but I had second thoughts about bothering with that, because it was obvious my sister and brother had been alive once, and it wouldn't have helped me find out anything relevant to me.

I suppose, if I admitted it, I was hoping for information about my mother, more than anything, and she had nothing to do with the tragedy. She came on the scene years later. I closed the book and rested my head on my arms for a moment, thinking it through: Lorna married Dad – 1962. Flood – 1965. My birth – 1972. When did they split up? She said they'd tried getting over it, but it hadn't worked out. I guessed they might've separated about a year or two after their children died, say 1967. I'd ask Lorna when I got the chance. So, somewhere in the gap between Lorna leaving and me being born, Dad met my mother.

Who was she? Who could she have been? He was depressed, angry, lonely – even though he was still quite young. He drew in on himself, Mrs Gayle said, living alone at Loraligh, our great big place, all alone. How could he have met anyone, living like that? There was so much to find out and Dad was the only person to ask. But I couldn't ask him. I wouldn't know how to make the words come out.

209

When December arrived and the wedding was getting close, Mark phoned and Mrs Gayle answered. I didn't know it was him at first, and I was in the sitting room with my homework on my lap, colouring a blue fringe round France.

"Oh hello. It's nice to hear from you. Oh yes…yes…yes that's right. Yes…oh, she'll be thrilled."

I perked up then, because she might be meaning me.

"The twenty seventh, that's right. Yes…any smart trousers. Nothing too fancy. Oh?…lovely…Well, give my best wishes to your mother. I'll be sure to tell her. Ta-ra, then."

I heard the receiver click and Mrs Gayle appeared in the doorway. She was smiling a rainbow across her face.

"Was that Mark?"

"It might have been."

"It was. What did he say?"

"Nothing much."

"Yes he did," I grinned. "Did he say he was coming over?"

"He might have done."

I threw my crayon in her general direction.

"Oh you! *Did* he? Can he come to the wedding?"

She picked the crayon up and passed it back to me politely, with her now that's not-the-way-to-behave-is-it face.

"Nice to be popular, Imogen Wise," she said.

I tried to tell myself it didn't mean anything, Mark saying he'd come. After all, he'd been sent an invitation, hadn't he? – a posh card with a silver border and italic writing. Anyone would accept if they weren't busy. But it was hard not to get excited, because the wedding was going to be a whole lot more fun with him there, instead of a stuffy lot of grown-ups getting all weepy. I'd have to make sure he saw me at my best, and there was a good chance of that, with Lorna taking me shopping and doing up my hair.

Dad couldn't see why I needed yet another outfit, after buying the dress for my party, but Lorna stood up for me.

"She can't possibly wear the same one, Andrew. It's a wedding!"

As if that said it all.

My Dad only stretched his eyebrows, but he never argued back with Lorna. I'd noticed that from the word go, and there were times when it came in useful and times when I'd think – are you ever going to stand up for yourself and be a man? It was always the women wearing the trousers at Loraligh. I wondered if Grandma had been the same, and I asked Mrs Gayle one afternoon, while we were spooning jam into pots, and she said she'd never met my grandmother and I said, oh I'd forgotten. It felt like Mrs Gayle had always been part of our mill.

"How old was I when you started coming here?"

"Oooh, now you're asking. Let me think," she said, and I thought that's not a very hard thing to remember. Anyone would remember that, except Dad possibly, but Mrs Gayle's brain was sharp as a razor.

"Pass those lids over, would you, pet? I think we're just about done here."

I gave her the paper lids and the elastic bands, thinking – you're stalling for time.

"Was I a baby? A toddler? Had I already started at Nursery?"

"You didn't go to Nursery, Imogen. Your father couldn't afford it. Besides, you were perfectly happy at home because I was looking after you by then. I'm trying to remember. I was the one to get you out of nappies, so I suppose you must've been about two."

"So Dad looked after me by himself, all the time I was a small baby?"

I was trying to catch her out, to find out when Mum left.

"No. There was someone else helping out, before I came along."

"Not my mother then? Someone else?"

"He hired another woman to look after you in the day-time, but something wasn't right. He wasn't completely happy with her. I remember him mentioning that, the day he interviewed me for the job."

"Why wasn't he happy with her? What had she done?"

"She was careless, I believe. He needed someone to keep a better eye."

That would make sense, after Rebecca and Jonathan.

We were placing a circle of greaseproof over each jar, and then a larger one made of material we'd cut up from some patchwork remnants, with a paisley pattern in swirls of green and blue. Then we wrapped a band round the top and it was my job to write all the labels, because Mrs Gayle needed new reading glasses. She still hadn't told me about my mother leaving.

"Did Dad ever say why he and my mother broke up?"

"You'll have to ask him. Outsiders can never really understand what goes on in a relationship."

"I sort of understand why he and Lorna might've split up. She said he couldn't get over feeling guilty. I expect she blamed him too. I would have."

"I'm not so sure of that. It was more complicated. Lorna took her share of the blame. She felt bad about not being there

212

that night, you see. Putting someone else before her own children."

"But it was her own grandmother. And she wasn't exactly deserting them."

"No, true. But when tragedy strikes, we all find sticks to beat ourselves with."

Humans are lost souls, I thought.

"Added to which, she blamed herself for them breaking up. She spoke to me about it not long ago. A while before your party, it was. Said she wished she'd tried harder to help him to overcome his problems – your dad, that is. Wished she'd gone to the doctor's. He became impossible. In the end, they weren't getting on at all. Hardly talking."

I'd imagined something like that.

We put all the jars into two shallow cardboard boxes, one for church and one to keep. Mrs Gayle washed up and I took a couple of jars over to the shop for Philip to give to his mother. It was his last day.

He was slipping one of our Loraligh pencils into his pocket when I walked in, but I didn't say anything. I figured he deserved it.

"Thanks," he said, taking the box, and red had spread up from his neck to his chin. "I'll be off in a minute."

"Yes."

I wasn't sure what to say next, how to say goodbye.

"Hope you like your new job."

"Thanks. It'll certainly be different from this one."

"I expect you'll get more money, won't you?"

"Don't know. I hope so. It's got to be for life."

"Dad says apprentices don't get paid so well at first, but it builds up in time. He says it's hard graft."

And then I wished I hadn't said that, because it sounded tactless, but I never could find much to say to Philip.

"'Spect so."

"I'll go and fetch Dad."

I couldn't find him at first, because he was in the sitting room with Lorna, and he was never in the sitting room, my dad. They were watching a matinee together, and Lorna had her feet up on his thighs. He was playing with her toes and she was making out it didn't drive her mad.

"Philip's off now, Dad."

"Is he?"

He didn't show the slightest sign of moving.

"Hadn't you better come and say goodbye? It is his last day."

"Ah. Right then."

"Give him that envelope on the kitchen top," Lorna said. She'd already thought of that. I expect there was a bit extra in there.

Dad and I went out together, and Mrs Gayle untied her apron and followed us. She'd always felt sorry for Philip. We said goodbye, and Dad shook his hand and said thank you for all your sterling work over the years, which was a funny word for him to say, and Mrs Gayle said good luck Philip. And I thought – it wasn't like when Mark left.

Fifteen

Aunt Vanessa

I could never have imagined the flurry of fuss and nonsense before a wedding – and this wasn't even a big one with a church and hundreds of people afterwards – but Lorna and Mrs Gayle never stopped talking about it. In one way, it was a pain in the neck, because there didn't appear to be anything else worth talking about at Loraligh for weeks. But you couldn't help being infected with all the excitement. Nothing much happened year in, year out, at our mill, but suddenly Lorna had moved in and it was non-stop partying. Or at least, that's the way Dad put it, but he was in a good mood, so he clearly didn't mind that much.

Aunt Vanessa phoned long distance, to say she'd be coming to stay for a few days before the wedding, because she'd get jet-lag and be no good on the day otherwise. And that got Mrs Gayle in a fret, because she remembered there'd be one extra for Christmas. Lorna had already invited our housekeeper over to Loraligh, and David could come too, because it would be much jollier with everyone together, but Mrs Gayle said she'd just come for dinner on the day, because her daughter Mattie had invited her over, and Hayley's brood would be there. She'd go to Mattie's for tea, so she could be with her grandchildren on Boxing Day. I asked her about

Karen and little Sonny, whether they were going too, and she said not as far as she knew. Dad said it was all getting far too complicated for him and Lorna said never you mind. You leave it all to us.

I went off to my bedroom to be quiet by myself, and I hid Mum's photo under my jumper so no one would notice I'd taken it again. I talked to her sometimes, even though it was pointless. It was easier with her photo to look at. I told Mum about Christmas, and counted out all the people who would be there. Lorna and Dad, Mrs Gayle and David, Aunt Vanessa and me – so that was six and we'd fill the whole table.

I hoped my auntie was nice. I'd never had a real aunt before, not to talk to. I asked Mum if she minded, what with Lorna moving in and getting married to Dad, and I watched her expression carefully, hoping for some sign, but she kept staring into the distance like she always did. It dawned on me at that very moment: I'd never actually seen my mother make any other face. Never seen her laugh, or frown, or look worried or sad. Never seen her angry. I used to try to imagine her mouth breaking into a smile, or saying something to me, and if I shut my eyes tight and really concentrated, sometimes I could, but it wasn't like the real thing. You didn't know how her voice sounded, or whether her cheeks dimpled when she smiled.

Aunt Vanessa was flying in to Newcastle, and Dad and I went to fetch her in the Land Rover, because I'd broken up for the holidays. Lorna still had to work, so I had Dad to myself all the way there, which meant I could sit in the front.

"How long will it take us?"

"Depends on the traffic."

"More than an hour? Two hours?"

216

"Much more. We're going the country way."

I knew what that meant. It meant avoiding all the main roads and the roundabouts and traffic jams, and driving miles and miles on winding, country lanes that took forever, and getting stuck behind a tractor, feeling sick and getting lost. I didn't bother to argue. Men don't like being told which route to use, or asking for directions, Mrs Gayle says. It's better to let them get on with it. She was stuck in the back with me once, when Dad was driving us the pretty way to Scarborough. It took hours and I was moaning, and Mrs Gayle was seething away quietly, saying nothing, but I could see her frowning in the passenger mirror.

I meant to use the journey as an opportunity to ask Dad a few things. I was staring out of the side window, composing questions, trying to work out the best way of putting things, so as not to upset him. When did you meet my mother? What was she like? When did she leave you? Why didn't she love you anymore? Was it because of Rebecca and Jonathan? Why didn't she take me with her? You can see my point. They weren't easy questions to ask.

In fact, I dropped off to sleep and didn't notice the time passing, so we arrived quicker than I expected. It wasn't a big airport, Dad said, but it was the first one I'd ever been to, so it looked fairly impressive to me. The plane was due to arrive twenty minutes earlier, but Dad said it didn't matter because she'd be ages in Customs. We'd probably even have time for a cuppa.

It was really noisy and windy when I opened the car door, and I was glad I'd brought my wool coat and scarf. You could hear planes in the distance, and smell petrol or something. I was excited, being at an airport – and about meeting my aunt.

217

"What's she like, your sister?"

Dad was pushing coins into the machine in the car park, and it was gulping them down.

"Vanessa? I haven't seen her for…what would it be now? – not since you were a baby."

"Fifteen years?"

"She was built like a London bus, back then."

"*Dad*!"

We laughed.

"Well. She was."

"That's odd. You being skinny."

"I am *not* skinny. I just look after myself."

He ran his hands down his ribs, sucking in his stomach and grinning, and I thought, you never looked after yourself once, you. It's all the women around who look after you. But then I supposed, that's not quite true, because he did have to live by himself for a few years after Lorna left. Before he fell in love with my mother.

We had to go back to the car for Dad's jacket, because he'd said he wouldn't need it, but halfway through the car park, he changed his mind. We found Arrivals, and a stream of people flooding into the hall with their luggage piled onto trolleys. Somebody was giving announcements over the loudspeaker, but you couldn't make out a word. There were several pushchairs with tired-looking tots in them and I thought, that's a long way to go with such young ones. I bet they were a nuisance.

"That won't be her plane yet," Dad said.

But it was, and he caught a glimpse of Vanessa near the back of the group. He was right – she was enormous. Tall as well as wide, and wearing a bright red coat, which made us

both laugh because Dad nudged my elbow and said see? –
London bus.

She recognised him even from that distance, and held her
handbag high in the air. I'd imagined a movie star, with a
name like Vanessa. You would, wouldn't you? A beautiful
lady in a fur coat, with matching luggage and long, perfect
hair. But my aunt had a ball of curls speckled with ash blonde
highlights, and she was anything but glamorous. She was
smiling from ear to ear.

She threw her arms around Dad, squealing, and wouldn't
let go. He was looking over his shoulder at me and making a
face, and I was giggling.

"Andrew, Andrew, my baby brother!"

We all laughed then, because anyone could see how daft
that was.

"And look at you, little Imogen, all grown up. Your daddy
told me all about you. Call me Nessa. Everybody does." And I
thought – that's the first I'd heard of it.

Her accent was so strong, you couldn't help noticing, and
it took me all the way home to get used to it. She talked
virtually the whole journey back, filling us in on where she
lived and what she'd done when her husband Tom died; how
she'd moved house twice in an effort to come to terms, and
then ended up right back where she'd started, because she
realised what a godsend her friends had been.

She told us about the business she ran – something to do
with printing cards and orders of service and invitations and
such-like. Then she took our wedding invitation out of her
bag, and strained her neck round to show me in the back seat,
describing the different type-faces you can get, and how to
balance up the design with the headings and footnotes and

suitable colour schemes. She made me see a whole lot more in that invitation card than I'd ever noticed before, and I'm certain than Dad or Lorna had ever intended.

Dad didn't speak much, partly because he was driving at a fair lick, but also because Aunt Nessa didn't let either of us get a word in edgeways. She's going to be hard to stomach for five days, I thought, and I bet Dad was thinking the same thing, but I had to admit she had a knack of entertaining you, with all her interesting stories.

When we were almost home, she'd exhausted all her news and began on me instead.

"How old did you say you were, dear?"

"Fifteen."

"Practically a *laydee*."

Dad winked at me in his mirror.

"You should've seen her all dressed up for her party."

I was glowing inside when Dad said that, and I wondered about digging out a photo to show her, when we got back.

"Can you imagine? It's been all those years since I came over, and I missed your little Imogen growing up. Why *did* we leave it so long, Andrew?"

I knew exactly why.

"If you will move the other side of the Atlantic, what do you expect? And you can't leave a business. You know that."

Aunt Nessa sighed, but it was a happy sigh. She had a face that beamed from east to west, with her red handbag sitting upright on her lap, and her holding onto it like a little dog that always did as it was told.

"Never mind, I'm here now, and we're going to have a ball."

She reached across and jiggled his hand. They didn't look one bit like brother and sister – more like Jack Sprat and his wife.

"Here we are then," Dad said as we drove up to the gate. I jumped out to let us in.

Only Lorna was home, and she came hurrying out to greet us.

"Darling!" Aunt Nessa said, smothering her in red.

"Nessa, how lovely to see you," and I thought, how come Dad hadn't remembered her nickname and Lorna had? She kissed my aunt on both cheeks, which must've been a bad habit she'd picked up in London, and led Nessa into the kitchen, asking how the flight had been, and had Andrew got her lost on the way back? And my aunt laughed and said goodness no, they'd had a lovely chat and a catch-up. I wondered how these two women knew each other. They must have met when Dad and Lorna were married before. Perhaps Nessa knew Rebecca and the baby. I'd find a moment to ask her later on, when she'd settled in.

Dad followed his sister into the house, carrying her luggage, and you could see her coat either side of him. I helped him with one of the smaller cases, because he was making pretend faces to me about how heavy it all was.

"This is going to be quite an experience," he whispered, and I stifled a laugh. It was strange, being the one to share in the knowing looks, instead of standing on the outside.

If I'd thought Aunt Nessa would run out of things to say after her non-stop narration in the car, I was wrong. She carried on right through tea and for another hour or so after that. When she finally went up to her room to recover from jet-lag, which she kept talking about but didn't show any sign

221

of, and she'd shut the door to the spare bedroom, Lorna and I started giggling, because Dad was grabbing his hands round his throat and pretending to die a slow and painful death, crumpling himself onto the sitting-room carpet.

"Forty days and nights!" Lorna said. "She was like a complete *deluge*. Doesn't the woman ever stop?"

"Shush, she might hear you," I whispered, but I was laughing.

"I'll never survive it," Dad said. But I knew he would. He'd have to.

"I don't remember her being so bad, the last time I saw her," Lorna said.

"She's making up for lost time."

"Well *I* thought she was interesting," I said. "I didn't know all that stuff about Elvis Presley."

"Aye, she can certainly be entertaining," Dad said. "In a sadistic way."

"Did you remember to put those towels on her bed, Imogen?"

I said I had. And the matching tissues, and the fresh bar of soap and the *Daily Mail,* because apparently she'd taken it every day, the last time she'd stayed here.

"When was she over here last?" I asked.

"I wasn't here then. When would you say it was, Andrew?"

"I think it was 1972 or...no, it must've been '73, because she said Imogen was a tot. She came over with M..."

Suddenly my Dad stopped speaking and he looked flustered.

"Who?" I asked. "Who did she come with?"

"Oh nobody. I forget. Just a friend of hers. Can't remember her name."

But I caught the look on his face, and I knew that look. It was fear. He disappeared into the kitchen, and then he came back in and guided Lorna out by the elbow. It was obvious he wanted to talk to her, and I wasn't invited. I felt deflated, because I'd been thinking all the secrets were out in the open and I was considered old enough to be included.

I left it only a moment and followed them into the kitchen, but they'd both vanished. Then I heard Lorna's voice upstairs. She sounded stern.

"You know I don't approve of this, don't you?"

"But where could it possibly have gone? Where would she have put it?"

"It's usually by the side of her bed, when it's not on the mantelpiece."

"I told her she could keep it in her room if she liked. Out of respect for you."

It went quiet then. I'd made it to the bottom of the stairs, listening hard.

"Why don't you ring Mrs Gayle? She usually knows what Imogen does with her things."

I'd already cottoned on. They meant the photograph of Mum and me. I'd hidden it under my mattress, so I could take it out at night. Dad had advised me to keep it upstairs, now Lorna was around most of the time. I could see why. It wasn't very tactful, having a picture of Dad's other wife staring her in the face, day in day out.

If I left it much longer, they'd discover its whereabouts. I decided to climb the stairs to put a stop to it. I made sure they heard me coming, so they'd both scarpered by the time I reached my room, and I could hear muffled voices getting tetchy in Dad's room. I lay on my bed and slid my hand under, to check it was still there. I could feel its cold, hard edge, so that was a relief. I'd have to think of a better hiding place before morning, because everyone looks under a mattress.

I couldn't get to sleep that night, for puzzling what it was all about. Why did Dad suddenly want my photograph? Who had come to stay with Aunt Nessa, all those years ago when I was a baby? He was about to say a name, and the name began with M – Margaret, Mandy, Maureen, Marianne. Who *was* she?

The next morning, I could hear Aunt Nessa clattering about in the bathroom. She was humming *Oh When the Saints*, and Lorna never did that so it couldn't have been anyone else. She was ages in there and I was dying to go, by the time she came out. She was still wearing a shower cap, which was smattered with red and green flowers, to match her wash bag.

"Good morning, Imogen," she sang. "And how are we today?"

I said good morning, and dived into the bathroom behind her, too desperate to be polite.

"Sorry, my angel. Was I hogging the bathroom?"

"It's all right," I shouted through the door, because she didn't understand about the other lav' being a mile away downstairs, next to the boiler house, and too cold for comfort.

When I'd finished getting dressed, I decided to make Aunt Nessa a cup of tea and bring it up to her room. That way, I could do a bit of research before Dad and Lorna woke up. I took it up on a tray, with a separate jug for the milk, in case they had standards in Canada. Mrs Gayle went on about standards and how you have to keep them up. It's about personal pride and has nothing to do with the Joneses.

"You're such a poppet," my aunt said. "You must come out and stay with me in Vancouver. I could do with a sweet girl like you at home. We'd get along famously, wouldn't we?"

I smiled and nodded and I thought – wow! Canada. But then I thought – I'm not sure how much of you I could take, Aunt Nessa.

She'd removed her shower cap by then, and it left a sharp groove where the elastic had cut into her forehead. Her hair was sticking up at the front and she looked hilarious, but I tried not to make it too obvious.

"When are you going to show me your room?"

I thought it was odd, her being interested in a teenager's bedroom.

"It's not that tidy."

"Mum's the word," she replied. "You young things like your own space, I know that."

"Have you got any children, Aunt Nessa?"

"Me? Heavens no. Can't think how I could've run a business with a brood of kiddies around my feet."

And then I could've bitten my lip, because I remembered Dad telling me about her having several miscarriages, back in her thirties, and eventually giving up.

I led Aunt Nessa into my bedroom, grabbing a few things off the bed and shoving them into a corner. Then I realised, too late, that I'd left my mother's photograph propped up on my bedside cupboard. I'd meant to find a good place for it before I got up, but needing the bathroom so badly had completely distracted me.

My aunt paid me a compliment about the posters on my walls and on the ceiling that slopes down to the window. That was a good place for them, she said, with the light. Then she went to look at the view. You can see right over the roofs of the outhouses to Deer Meadow from my room, and then out to the hills in the distance. They look a different colour, the further away they are – almost blue – and when the clouds are racing, the shadows chase across like they're playing Tag.

"Gee, that's fantastic, isn't it?" she exclaimed. "What a lucky girl you are! I'd give anything for a view like that from my room back home."

"Auntie, could I ask you a question?"

"Fire away, sweetie."

"Did you ever meet my mother? Do you know who she was?"

I was standing right in front of the photograph, deliberately hiding it from view.

"No Imogen, I'm sorry, I didn't. I think she and your father had already separated before I came over. You were…let's think, you were sitting up, by the time I came to England. Not walking yet. And you could say a few words. You could say Dada; I remember that. You must've been about one, I should guess."

"So my mother had already left?"

"That's right."

She patted my arm and made a sympathetic smile. I reached behind my back and took hold of the frame. Then I pulled it round in front and showed her.

"I'll be darned! If that isn't Molly. My old friend, Molly Brummel. I'd completely forgotten about that photograph."

She took the picture from me, her eyes dancing.

"Dear Molly. See how lovely she was."

She didn't notice me at first – the way my mouth had fallen open, the way the blood must have drained from my face, or how my limbs had frozen. My mother had a name. Her name was Molly. She was one of Aunt Nessa's friends.

My aunt looked alarmed. She immediately stopped smiling and gripped my arm.

"Imogen? What's the matter? Whatever is it, honey?"

I needed to sit down. I looked at the photo, and back at my aunt.

"What did you say her name was?"

"Molly. Molly Brummel. Why?"

I barely made a whisper.

"She is my mother."

Nessa came to sit her great bulk on the mattress beside me, and it sank beneath us. Her eyes softened.

"Your mother? Molly? No, you must be mistaken, my treasure. Molly never had any children either. I knew her all her life, since school days. She came out to Vancouver with her husband, at about the same time as I emigrated and married Tom. She and her husband were friends of ours, right up until she died."

"She died?"

"Yes, it was very sad. She'd struggled with leukaemia on and off for years, and eventually succumbed about a year before my Tom went. Dreadful disease. I lost my best friend and then my husband, both within a year or so of each other."

227

"Are...are you sure this was her? Are you absolutely sure this was...your friend Molly?"

Aunt Nessa looked again at the photograph and then back at me.

"Yes, dear. This is definitely Molly. She came over with me to England, when you were small. She must've put you on her knee for this picture to be taken. She really took to you; she was always picking you up. We were only over here for a few days."

At that very moment, Lorna appeared at my bedroom door, and Dad the second after her.

I grabbed the frame from Aunt Nessa's hands and slammed it as hard as I could against the table top, shattering the glass into pieces, and then I smashed it onto the floor. It landed face up, with my mother staring up at me with that damned expression of hers that never changed, never once in fifteen years. I rammed my foot down onto her face so many times, you couldn't recognise her. The glass had turned to a spider's web, and the picture of me in my topknot and ladybirds was completely ruined.

And then the screaming started. Screaming that poured from my mouth in strings of angry, poisonous words. And the words were frightening, even to me. I felt possessed by some outer force, compelling me to yell and condemn and blame.

Because my dream was broken, and my father had been the one to destroy it.

I ran screaming and crying towards my dad, and I beat him with my fists, hard, three times on his chest, once for each time he'd struck me, and then I pushed past him and fled from the room, leaving the whole group of adults utterly shocked.

How I didn't fall down the stairs I don't know, because they rushed past me in a blur. I pushed over kitchen chairs, and swiped every ornament from the mantelpiece, shouting you liar, you liar! I pulled a pile of plates from the dresser and crashed them onto the flags. I ran out into the back yard and upended the wheelbarrow, and ran and ran, across the meadow, through the wood to the beach and the river. It was freezing in the water, leg-numbingly cold, but I didn't care. I didn't care if the water gripped me and pulled me down and took me far away, where no one could ever hurt me or lie to me again. I tripped over and fell. I gasped with the cold, as it clawed its way through my clothing and over my face, and I lay down until the water covered my head. It was December and I didn't care, because that was the way Rebecca and Jonathan had gone. I would be with them – my brother and sister, who would never be able to tell me one lie. Ever.

Sixteen

Loss and Gain

It was Dad who pulled me out. I didn't remember. Not then and not afterwards. Lorna said he'd chased me the whole way down the field, faster than she'd ever seen him run, because I was sprinting like a deer in flight. She'd been running on behind, and Aunt Nessa had phoned Mrs Gayle, because Lorna had thrust the number in her hand and said get her quick. Tell her it's Imogen. Tell her it's urgent.

He waded straight in after me, she said, and lifted me up in one huge swish, with water pouring from my clothes, and there was triumph on his face. Triumph, she said, because this time, he'd been able to. He carried me high to his chest, even though I'm no small package, and wrapped me in his pullover, clutching me to him and saying I'm sorry Imogen, I'm so sorry, over and over.

I do remember Aunt Nessa arriving at The Beach, all in a puff, with a couple of blankets, and then Mrs Gayle turning up in our kitchen, and Lorna making an enormous pan of hot porridge for everyone. I was put in the rocker, with my wet clothes peeled off and my dressing gown wrapped round me, the extra blankets over my knees. My whole body was shuddering and I was wheezing furiously, because the cold had taken my breath away. Mrs Gayle made tea, and I remember the noise the kettle made, because it was wobbling on the kitchen top where it had warped.

They were all talking in hushed voices. Mrs Gayle was trying to explain things to my aunt, who was prone to breaking into snivels every now and then, because she hadn't the faintest idea what was going on and felt it was all her fault. Dad was sitting at the table, rubbing the back of his head with a towel.

"Right!" Lorna said in her determined way, when she'd finished drizzling syrup all over the porridge and passing a bowl to each of us:

"Time for a family conference."

Dad looked up and Mrs Gayle said yes, she quite agreed. High time.

"Nessa," Lorna said, "we quite understand if you don't want to be in on this. It's all been most upsetting for you, so if you'd rather find a quiet place to sit by yourself for a while, we wouldn't be at all offended."

"Perhaps that would be best. I'll take the paper through to the sitting room, shall I?"

I could sense everyone's relief and I thought, you see? – she's brighter than you give her credit for.

"But I would like to know…eventually…what this is all about."

"Yes, naturally," Lorna said. "We'll fill you in later, when we've set it all straight."

So my aunt took her bowl and mug on a tray, and shut the door behind her with her backside, leaving the four of us all looking at the floor and nobody knowing where to begin, or what setting-it-straight might mean, so we slowly ate our porridge, each one of us playing through our thoughts.

231

Mrs Gayle kicked off first, even though she hadn't been in on the drama up in my bedroom. Or at Shallow Falls.

"Imogen, you've had a lot of shocks lately, a lot of surprises, and some of them haven't been at all pleasant, have they lass?"

She waited for me to speak, but I was still thawing out and hadn't made it as far as words.

"But you have to know, my pet, that nobody – not one person in this room – would ever have set out to do anything to deliberately hurt you. Now you know that, really, don't you?"

"She's right, Imogen," Lorna chipped in. "You know all about our children now. You're a clever girl. You must realise how difficult it has always been for your father to know what's best for you. He never wanted to drag you down."

An interesting expression to use.

I looked at Dad, whose head was beginning to rise up out of his hands, and who turned now towards me. I wanted him to speak to me. I wanted it to be *him* who would explain this one. He couldn't hide in the capable words of these women any longer.

Our eyes met, only a glance, and I looked away. I know it must've hurt, but I didn't care.

"I think we need to give Imogen a chance to speak for herself," Mrs Gayle said. "After all, if it's a conference, like, then each person should have their say-so."

"I agree," Lorna said.

All three of them were waiting for me. I could feel their eyes bearing down on me, even though my gaze was fixed firmly on the front window, where the light was catching the

232

steam from the clothes airer, and it was swirling up to the ceiling and then spreading out flat on top, like a storm cloud.

Then I looked at Dad. Straight at him.

"All I want to know is...*who my mother is*. If that woman in the photograph, who I have believed every day of my life is my mother, who I have dreamt about, and wished and hoped for, and talked to, night after night, if that isn't her, then who the hell is my mother?"

Dad looked across at Mrs Gayle and she nodded. Lorna was gazing down at her hands; she couldn't look me in the face.

"Dad?"

He began slowly. His words were faltering and he only caught my eyes now and again, but I was staring right at him, and I wasn't about to make it any easier for him. Why should I?

"When Lorna left," he started, "I was very lonely. I'm not blaming her. I wouldn't have stayed either. I wasn't any good to anyone. She tried, Lorna, she really did, but I couldn't forgive myself."

"I panicked, you see. When I saw the carrycot tip over...I left it for as long as I dared, but it was dark in the kitchen, from out in the yard. I couldn't see properly what was happening inside the house. It was still belting down. I could see the blanket floating on the water, caught around the table leg, and then I panicked and let go. I was too late. It was nobody's fault but mine, Imogen."

"My mother?"

"I was left alone, here at Loraligh. I'm not blaming anyone for that, but they were the worst days of my life."

Lorna rubbed his shoulder while he was speaking, and Mrs Gayle was sitting opposite, playing with her spoon, her eyes reddening.

"I won't make any excuses," he went on. "I couldn't keep up with all the housework, trying to cope with the farm as well, so in the end I hired a girl. Someone to take care of the cleaning and laundry. Not every day. She came three times a week."

He stopped and waited, checking I had absorbed what he was saying, but I still hadn't twigged.

"Go on," Lorna said quietly.

"She was the only person I spoke to. For ages. The only one. She was kind. She listened."

"A girl. You said a girl."

"She was too young, but I didn't notice. I wasn't even thinking about that."

"How old?"

"I can't remember exactly."

Mrs Gayle interrupted him: "She was just sixteen."

My age, good as.

I felt sick. What was he saying? That he slept with her?

"We began a...a sort of relationship, I suppose you'd call it. Except it wasn't, because we never went anywhere together. Never did anything. She fell pregnant very quickly...with you."

My father stopped talking.

Nothing else could surprise me. I was beyond shock. I stared at him and then looked away, and all I felt was a despising. My dad with a teenager. It was revolting.

"You have to remember," Lorna added, "your dad was much younger then. He'd only just turned thirty. That might

234

sound old to you, but it isn't. She didn't seem so young to him then. And he'd been by himself for almost five years."

"What was her name?"

Mrs Gayle was about to speak, but Dad put out his hand. He spoke slowly.

"Her name was Karen," he said. "Karen Stockington."

Mrs Gayle was directing her gaze right at me and waiting.

"Then…then *you*…you're…my grandmother?"

"Yes, Imogen."

She came over to me and she pulled me close-in to her, and held onto me for a long, long time. My grandmother, Mrs Gayle. I clung on to her, because the world had given way beneath me, like a trap-door opening. I was falling down and down without end. My eyes were shut and I didn't notice my dad leave the room.

Eventually, after a very long time, she let go and sat back on the chair in front of me.

"So that's why you came to work here," I said slowly.

"That's right. Karen was far too young. She couldn't cope. Didn't *want* to cope's more the truth of it. They never intended, you see, to make a go of things. Your father knew from day one – that was never on the cards. Once my Karen knew she was expecting, it terrified the life out of her."

"Where was I born then?"

"At the District. Like any other baby round here."

"So why didn't I stay with…Karen?"

I couldn't say the word *mother*. I couldn't get to grips with the fact that my mother wasn't the woman in the photograph. That she was actually Mrs Gayle's youngest daughter, the one

235

with the cleavage and the bewitching eyes. My Dad didn't stand a chance, did he?

"Like I said, she was too young, but your father wanted to stand up to his responsibilities."

"But *you* could have looked after me."

"I already had four of my own, and they were all grown up. I was too old. All those sleepless nights. I didn't have the strength. And besides, your father wanted you. I suppose he saw it as a chance to make amends. To have a fresh start. And at any rate, I felt sorry for him."

That surprised me. I thought she'd have been gunning for him, getting her youngest pregnant. But she knew what Karen was like, did Mrs Gayle. You couldn't pull the wool over her eyes, Cedric always said.

We all held our tongues for a while, and then Lorna said it's a lot to take in isn't it? And Mrs Gayle said give her time, give her time. Dad was nowhere to be seen. He was the one who couldn't cope.

I don't remember much after that. Looking back, it's a wonder I didn't try to run away again, after finding out all that about my father, and the photograph, and Molly Brummel, and Karen being my mother. But I was tired of running, and numb with cold and shock. It was strange; a sort of peace washed over me. It was because all the secrets were out and I knew. I knew who my mother was and who my grandmother was. My great dream had been destroyed, but at last I was rooted somewhere.

In bed that night, I drew my first family tree in my notebook, and it was strangely comforting, being able to put in all the names. Mrs Gayle told me that Mr Stockington's name was Bernard, and so I had a grandfather too, somewhere in the north of England, but God knows where, she said. How do you know he's still up north? – I asked, and she said because Bernie wouldn't be seen for love nor money down south.

I told Mrs Gayle I couldn't imagine calling her grandmother, and she said that was all right. She couldn't imagine it either. So I carried on calling her Mrs Gayle and I still do.

The next day was Christmas Eve and Cedric came over for a sherry at twelve, because he didn't open the shop that day. He'd been working full time for us since Philip left, and he'd become part of the furniture, as Mrs Gayle put it. Cedric didn't know about the revelations of the previous day, so I had a whole saga to tell him. It was my story, and nobody was going to steal it from me. I took him out to the garden, even though it was below zero, and we sat in our big coats on those two chairs, with a glass each – although I had lemonade in mine because sherry's only for old people – and we looked at the bare trees in a sad line across our meadow. The old rooks' nests had all but disintegrated. When I revealed the part about Mrs Gayle being my grandmother, he smiled.

"You don't even look surprised," I said. "You knew, didn't you?"

"Not in so many words, but it wasn't hard to guess. I'd seen the way she was with you as a little'un. She'd no more abandon you than one of her own. I could tell there was something more to it."

And I thought, you're right Cedric. I'd always taken her devotion to us for granted. Part of her job. There had been a

237

reason all along. Cedric gave my shoulder a squeeze, and said three cheers and down the hatch.

Lorna was worried about the effect all this was going to have on the wedding. She didn't want to put their celebrations ahead of me, she said. If I wanted them to delay things, they would. She and Dad agreed.

"You come first, Imogen," she said. "This has all been dreadful for you. You must be angry and upset. Your father and I have had a chat about things, and we're both adamant – if you can't cope with the wedding going ahead, then we can postpone it. It's not out of the question."

But Mark was coming, wasn't he? And Dad had bought me a fantastic dress and shoes. And Aunt Nessa had flown all the way over the Atlantic to be there. So I wasn't about to spoil their day. Or mine.

It was strange, her saying I came first. Never in my childhood had I felt that important. Yet Lorna had moved in, and now I seemed to matter more than anyone. There was Mrs Gayle, my grandmother, making a fuss of me. And Lorna taking me shopping and arranging my party, and even Dad, trying much harder to talk properly to me, although he was pretty hopeless at it.

"It's okay," I said. "Everything's booked, and besides, I've been looking forward to it."

"Good. So have I," she smiled. "You know what I think? The way you've coped with all of this, it goes to show how mature you've become. I'm really proud of you."

I'd surprised myself too. I felt like I was floating on my back in a quiet river. I was trying to analyse how I felt about my dad now. I couldn't imagine him with Karen, not for a minute. He had silvery hair, thin on top, deep creases running round his mouth to his chin – but Karen? She still looked like a young woman to me. A part of me had lost respect for him. He seemed smaller somehow. I realised, when you feel sorry for someone, it makes you feel strong inside. Lorna had been making excuses for him, but I knew she was right; he couldn't be perfect, and I was past expecting it of him.

"There's something else that's bothering me about all this. Something I don't get at all," I said to Lorna, when we were on our own together upstairs, folding things for their going-away cases. I'd said Dad was no good at packing, and she'd said, well in that case you can give me a hand, Imogen, because I need someone who's good at organising things.

"Go on," Lorna said.

"You finding out about Karen and Dad. Didn't it screw you up? I mean, her being so young. How did you accept him again, after that?"

"I didn't. Not for ages. When I first found out, I thought he was sick."

"Who told you?"

"Susan, my sister. She and her family never moved away from this area. She said it was common knowledge."

"Not to me, it wasn't. Nobody thought to tell me."

"No. I expect they thought it was for your own good, but in the end, it did more damage than good. Easy to say with hindsight."

I joined in the end of that phrase with her.

"Have you put Dad's reading glasses in?"

"Oh no. He'll need those. Good thing you're here."

"And the Ralgex for his back. He won't take tablets."

"He's his own worst enemy, your father."

"So when did you change your mind?" I asked, climbing up onto the bed for a rest. I leant back against the pillows, and I liked it, relaxing on the bed and chatting to Lorna.

"Mrs Gayle wrote me a letter. She sent it to my parents, so it found its way to me eventually."

"What did it say?"

"She must've sent it after that first time I visited. You remember."

"When you wouldn't stay."

"That's right. She told me how much your dad loved me; how he never got over me; how he wished he could turn back the clock."

Didn't we all? I suppose Lorna must've given in. Time, the great healer.

When she went downstairs, I dug around in Dad's bedroom cupboard, because Lorna had brought back their old photo albums and I wanted another look. She'd let me leaf through them several weeks before, and I couldn't believe it – all those pictures of her with Dad. He looked so young. So much hair. I should have expected that, but there's nothing quite like the evidence staring you in the face. Lorna didn't look that different. It was hard to believe she was in her forties now.

There was an entire album devoted to Rebecca, right through from when she was born, to her first teeth, and sitting up in a highchair, or pushing her own pushchair along, even though it was twice as tall as she was. There was a funny photo of her having a paddy in her playpen, face bright red and eyes screwed up tight. Lorna said she'd never liked being in there. They'd given the playpen away in the end. That

240

made me sad, because they'd had to give everything away after the children had gone.

I wondered about that – if they'd kept anything belonging to Rebecca or Jonathan. There hadn't been one scrap of evidence all through my childhood. I asked Lorna, the day she showed me Rebecca's album. Oh yes, she said, a whole box of things. She'd taken it with her when she left Loraligh, because Dad didn't want anything left behind.

"There's something else I don't understand about all that, Lorna."

"How do you mean?"

"Why it was that you could…deal with things, you know, when my dad couldn't. I mean, you were their mother. It must've hurt you just as much as him. More, even. How come you didn't cave in?"

"I did. The day they died…I don't know, it's stating the obvious to say my world came to an end, but it did. There didn't seem any point going on, not for either of us. We didn't feel we had the right to laugh or enjoy anything ever again. To go on living, when they couldn't. I would imagine the children's future, what they might have looked like as they grew up. You can't help it. From the moment they're born."

She was running her finger over the cellophane, tracing Rebecca's outline. I could detect the well of sadness she was holding in, and that's when I realised: it wasn't that Lorna didn't feel the same despair as my father – it was that she'd found a way to fence it in.

"Andrew and I couldn't stay together, because we felt we didn't have the right. That's the way I see it now. We didn't realise it at the time – I think we were both too devastated to

241

see anything straight – but all those years away from him I began to realise, he'd been my greatest friend."

She looked at me and smiled then. It was amazing how she could be that strong.

"My one true love," she said in a silly voice, because she was trying to lighten things.

She snapped the album shut. I don't think she could cope with it anymore that day, but I looked at it often, when I got a chance. And I looked at the objects she'd saved in the box. There were two tiny pairs of shoes, one slightly larger than the other, made of soft pink leather. There was a rattle, a furry penguin with a wonky beak and a button-eyed teddy. The saddest thing of all was the baby's little hospital bracelet – Wise Jonathan Andrew, seven pounds ten ounces. He'd hardly had a life, had he? I could see why Dad had given Lorna the box.

There weren't so many photos of Jonathan, but that was hardly surprising. There was one framed picture though, taken in a proper studio, of the four of them together, the baby on Lorna's lap and Rebecca on Dad's. It was a lovely photo and I wished they'd put it on the mantelpiece, but I guess it was too painful.

We'd had our little ceremony, that day in November, to remember them. It was a cold, still day, with a mist hanging over the meadow. Droplets of water were clinging to the grass and bushes, like rows of tiny pearls. Mrs Gayle helped me cut armfuls of evergreen from the woods, and Lorna had bought some fresh-cut flowers from the stall by the bus station.

Then we'd made a lovely arrangement and tied it to the fence by the back yard. I found some pink and blue ribbon from my old dolls' trunk, and tied on two of my cuddly toys, from when I was small. I hadn't let Mrs Gayle take them to the jumble sale, and I was glad. Lorna went to fetch Dad, even though he didn't really want to be there at first. Even Cedric said he'd come too, so he poured us each a drink, and we all stood round our little arrangement, which was set right away from the funny concrete patch, because there didn't seem to be any point making it worse.

I asked Mrs Gayle if I should prepare a speech or something, but she said perhaps that would be a bit much. She said that a few moments silence, to remember them, was probably best. And when we'd done that, we raised our glasses and Lorna and Dad couldn't speak, so I said 'To Rebecca and Jonathan, for all the happy days.' And afterwards Dad said thank you, Imogen. That was nice. That helped.

I was in my bedroom, when Lorna came in to ask me which shoes for the going-away dress, but as she glanced down, she spotted the broken frame in the bin.

"Do you want me to try and save that?"

"Not really. It doesn't mean anything now, does it?"

"But it's something you've always treasured. It's a record of how you were at that age, too. And it's the only photograph we've got of you and Molly together."

I went over to the bin and pulled it out.

"Careful. The glass might cut you. We'll give it to your dad. He can get the pieces out safely."

I looked at our two faces, Molly's and mine, contorted by the heel of my trainer. My little mouth wasn't smiling back, and one of the ladybirds had disappeared.

"No, it's all right. I don't want it. Those days have gone now."

Lorna was looking concerned, but I was sure.

"I don't mind," I said. "I've got to get used to the truth. And I'm glad. It's what I always wanted, the truth, and now I have it. I just don't get why Dad didn't tell me everything straight in the first place."

"I know. He made a bloody mess of it, didn't he?"

She shocked me, swearing like that. But I thought, she'd never say that to a child.

"Men are hopeless, aren't they?" I said.

"You can say that again. So what are we going to do about things? What do you want to happen now?"

"You mean about my mother?"

"Do you want to meet her? I expect Mrs Gayle will tell Karen that you know."

I dropped the frame back in the bin and shoved my hands deep into my jeans pockets – must've got that habit from Dad. I walked over to the window and looked out at the hills. There'd been a thick frost in the night, and the ground was dusted in white. It was beautiful, the best place to live in the world.

I wasn't sure what to say.

"Do you think she even wants to see me? She gave me up years ago, didn't she? She didn't want me, back then."

"No. That's true."

I loved the way Lorna levelled with me. She didn't try to dress things up, the way the others did.

"But she'll have changed, Imogen. She's in her thirties now. She'll have grown up, and maybe she's had second thoughts."

"Then why hasn't she tried to contact me?"

"Because her mother wouldn't let her. Karen's had to keep up the pretence all these years, to preserve your father's ridiculous story."

"It was crazy, wasn't it? What did he expect to do with that lie, once I'd grown up? Once I'd got a family of my own. What if I'd ever needed to know something...I don't know...like something medical that would affect my health, or my children's? It was nuts, him pretending Molly was my mother. He barely knew her."

"I know. I told him that. He said the trouble was, you'd been holding that photograph once, when you were a little girl, and you'd been wondering why you didn't have a mummy like other children, and your father thought that at least having a notion of a mother, with a picture to look at, would help. So when you asked if that was your mother, he said yes, and then the whole idea escalated. He regretted it almost at once, but it was too late. He didn't have the heart to take it all away from you. Mrs Gayle kept the story up too, because she could see Karen wasn't going to show much of an interest. She was quite a handful at that age, a tearaway. It was a marvel she'd kept up a job of any sorts."

It made sense, what Lorna was saying.

"Funny," I said, "that time I saw her at the beach with her little boy, something in me was...I don't know...drawing me to her, like a magnet. I didn't realise what, at the time."

"Shall we wait until after Christmas?"

I nodded. It was the best option.

But Mrs Gayle had other ideas and when Christmas day arrived, she said she had a surprise for me and it wasn't the sort you wrapped up.

245

"I hope you don't mind," she said. "I've spoken to Karen about you knowing. She said she'd like to see you, if that's what you want."

"Did she?"

I felt strangely excited about that, but terrified at the same time. What if she didn't like me? Or vice-versa.

"Did she look pleased or not?" I asked. "I only want to see her if she's keen on the idea."

I wasn't about to face another rejection.

"She's coming over to Mattie's for tea later, with Sonny. If you're willing, you can come over with me after our Christmas dinner and join us for a bit of cake. I'm dropping David back home anyway. He wants to go round his girlfriend's house for the afternoon."

That surprised me. I couldn't imagine David having a girlfriend.

Lorna was smiling and looking hopeful, and Mrs Gayle was being sensible, as usual. Dad was peeling parsnips and I couldn't get over how weird that looked. He didn't know a thing about preparing vegetables.

It all felt too soon. I'd hardly had time to get used to the idea of it – Karen being my mother. I was trying to let go of that other image, that woman in the white dress blowing in the breeze. That woman who was never going to appear at the gate.

"Do you mind if I go out on Christmas day?"

"Course we don't," Lorna said. "You spend as long as you like."

"Dad?"

"It's your choice. We're happy either way."

"I don't know," I said.

I wasn't sure it was the best way to do things. There would be so many other people there, and all those children.

"We can wait, if you'd rather," my grandmother said. "There's no rush. We can wait until you're good and ready."

But then the thought of being part of her big family celebration sounded interesting. There'd be other children there, and they would be my cousins. Mattie's boys weren't much younger than me. Perhaps it would be easier, with other people around. Plenty going on. No awkward silences.

"I'll come."

"Good," Mrs Gayle said. "She'll be thrilled."

"And so are we," Dad said.

"Really?"

He wiped his wet hands on his pinny, came over and put one arm round my shoulder, right in front of everyone. It was the first time he'd done that, since I'd found out the truth of things.

"I'll be over to fetch you later. You can ring when you're ready."

So Christmas wasn't going to be quite like any other. And neither was Boxing day, with a wedding to prepare for, the day after.

Seventeen

Karen

I was a bag of nerves. It wasn't as if I didn't know what Karen looked like, or about her having another child now. The worst of it was wondering what she would think of me. Of noticing her reaction and being disappointed.

Imagination and reality: one for a child and the other for an adult. Time to face the way things were.

We pulled up in the road outside Mattie's house and I was surprised, because I thought it would be council, like Mark's, or the same size as Mrs Gayle's. But this house was a big semi-detached, thirties, because of the bay window and the pattern over the door. I knew that from History. It had a fair garden out front and a tub of winter pansies by the porch, which were still struggling on, despite the frost.

Mrs Gayle looked at me. "Her husband's a policeman."

She always knew what I was thinking.

"Have you got that bag of presents, Imogen?"

"Yes. Will it matter that I haven't got anything for Karen?"

"You've got the best gift there is."

I thought Karen might be the one to open the door, but she wasn't. The hallway was full of shoes. There were coats piled over the banister and three small children playing on the floor with a remote-control toy. I recognised Sonny, but the other two were girls. I guessed they must be Hayley's, from the age of them.

The man who let us in was Mattie's husband, Dave – so there were two Davids in one family, and that could be confusing. But this Dave was clearly brighter than the other one, and he certainly had more to say for himself. He was wearing a patterned waistcoat, with a shiny gold back pulled in by a buckle, and his shirt sleeves were rolled to his elbows. The hair on his head was as thick and black as a shoe-brush, and I noticed one of his fillings because it flashed gold, to match his waistcoat. He didn't look much like a policeman to me.

Dave grinned and kissed my grandmother on the cheek and said Happy Christmas Mum and you must be Imogen. Welcome to the mad-house. He kissed me too, which I wasn't expecting, and I smiled shyly and let him take my jacket. Sonny, who was flat on his stomach, stopped playing and looked up at me with serious, big eyes. I tried to smile at him too, but I was fighting my nerves.

Dave led us through to the sitting room and it was cram-packed with people. Karen wasn't in there, I could tell straight away. It was all prolonging the agony.

There were people all over us, saying Happy Christmas and lovely to see you and glad you could come, Imogen. Dave went round the room pointing, and telling me their names, and all these strangers were smiling and saying you'll never remember, will you? Mattie was holding the baby and playing peek-a-boo, and the baby kept smacking her on the nose and chuckling, so Mattie grabbed hold of the baby's fist and put it in her mouth – whole. Her two boys stayed on the sofa, looking shy and suspicious, but Mrs Gayle said it was because of their age and they'd soon warm up.

Then she said she'd take me through to the kitchen, because there was someone special I needed to meet, and perhaps I'd like to do that without an audience. You could sense the excitement in the air right around that little party. Weird, I thought. This had to be the strangest mother-daughter reconciliation ever, in the history of the universe.

Karen was drying up glasses when I went in. She smiled a great big smile and said would you just look at this lot! I'll be here 'til Boxing Day. Then she wiped her hands on the tea-towel and put it over the radiator.

"I'm glad you decided to come," she said, hands on hips, flashing her nail varnish. "You can't believe how pleased I was when Mum told me."

"I nearly didn't." I broke into a nervous laugh.

Karen pulled out a chair for me. She was wearing a shiny tracksuit, and I wasn't sure it was suitable for Christmas day.

"I can understand that. It's a big decision."

It was better sitting down.

"Would you like a drink? Wine or something?"

"No thanks. Well, yes maybe, if you are."

She poured us each a glass of white from the bottle on the table.

"To the best Christmas ever," she said, lifting her glass.

I wasn't so sure about that. It was certainly different.

"Do you really feel like that? Glad, I mean, that I've come?"

"Course I do. Did you think I wouldn't?"

"I don't know. I didn't know what to think. I haven't had much time, to be honest."

250

"No, I realise that. It took him long enough to tell you, didn't it?"

She smiled out of the side of her glass and took a huge gulp of wine and I thought, you're as nervous as I am, Karen Stockington.

"I don't know if he would ever've told me, if it hadn't been for Lorna."

"That was surprising, her coming back like that, wasn't it? I'd have put money on him never seeing her for dust."

She knocked back another mouthful and wiped her lips with the back of her hand. I know what Mrs Gayle would've said about that.

"It was years before she came back, though, wasn't it?" I said. "Your mother always says love will find a way. If it's meant to be, it's meant to be."

"Oh, that sounds like my mother. Do you know what we say about her in our family? We say there's a section in Mum's brain which stores virtually every saying, every proverb that was ever created, waiting for the right moment to bring it out. We say the English language won't be the same, once Mum's gone."

Mrs Gayle and Cedric both, I thought. A double act.

"So," Karen said, looking a bit more serious, "how did you feel when you found out? What did you think?"

She was watching me carefully and I tried not to blunder straight in. I knew it mattered.

"I don't know. Sort of…shocked and surprised. It wasn't what I expected."

"No."

"I suppose the best thing was – knowing."

"Mum tells me you'd pinned your hopes on someone else, from a photo."

"It turned out she was nothing to do with me. A friend of my aunt's. A complete red herring."

"Were you disappointed that it wasn't her?"

"At first."

Karen took a lighter out of her pocket and lit a cigarette. I watched the end flare up as she drew in hard to get it going. She wouldn't be allowed to do that in our kitchen.

"I can understand that," she said. "It takes time to get used to things, doesn't it? Changes an' that."

She offered the packet to me but I shook my head and said no thanks. I don't.

"Did your dad explain things – the way it was back then? About why you stayed with him instead of me?"

"He didn't say that much. It was Lorna who explained everything, really. And Mrs...your mum."

"I doubt if she had much good to say about me. She never approved of me, my mother."

"She only said you were too young. Too scared to bring up a baby."

Karen smiled, and her teeth weren't as white as you'd expect. She was still wearing those enormous earrings she had on the last time I saw her. They didn't look right, at her age.

"That was true enough. I was only sixteen. You were better off without me," she said.

I was already coming to the same conclusion myself. I was curious, though. How had she felt about giving up her baby? Didn't she feel any love for me at all? I decided to save those questions for another time. I wasn't about to ruin the atmosphere so early on. Especially on Christmas day and in Mattie's house.

At that moment, the door burst open and Sonny ran over to his mother and cuddled up to her, resting his head on her thigh. He looked up at me, rolling his tongue, and Karen ran her hand through his curls.

"Hello, buster," she said. "What have you been up to?"

Nothing, Sonny said, and she laughed and said, you? You're never up to nothing. And I wondered about whether or not that was a double negative and what my English teacher would say.

"Do you know who this is?" she asked him.

Sonny nodded slowly, because his grandmother must have been explaining things to him. He was peering out from under his fringe, and his lower lip had disappeared.

"This is your big sister. This is Imogen."

He managed a hint of a smile, peering up at me.

"Hello, Sonny." I wasn't sure what came next. "How old are you?"

"Four," he said, and Karen laughed and said no you're not. You're only three. He looked up at her confused, and held up four fingers, and she laughed again and tucked one of them away.

"You'll be four next birthday. That's what I said. *Nearly* four." And Sonny said oh, *nearly* four.

"I'm fifteen," I told him. "I'm a lot older than you, aren't I?"

He held up all his fingers.

"Do fifteen," he said, and it was all I could do not to laugh.

"Well," said his mother, "you can't exactly do fifteen, because it's more than you've got fingers for, but you can do it like this."

She gave him a five with one hand, and then another five, and another, and I thought – that was a good idea, Karen. Sonny took off then, back to the other room, and how he didn't trip over his trousers I don't know, because the elastic was too loose around the waist.

Karen kept pulling at a chain at the back of her neck, where her hair was caught up.

"What else do you want to ask me?" she said. "Anything you want to know?"

I ran my finger round the rim of my glass, thinking.

"There's so many questions. I'm not sure."

"We've got plenty of time haven't we? And it's Christmas, so p'rhaps it can wait for another day. Do you want some cake?"

I'd been admiring that cake on the kitchen top. It was one of those enormous chocolate logs, with little ornaments buried in the frosting and a silver label in fancy writing. The chocolate butter-cream was glossy under the light and it looked delicious. I couldn't believe I was still hungry. She said there'd be another day for talking, and that was all right with me. It meant this wasn't a one-off.

Karen gave me the knife and candles to take through to the sitting room, and she carried the cake. Everybody cheered when we walked in and Karen said give over, it's only a cake, and Mrs Gayle said you can share my chair if you like, Imogen; we're running out of room in here. So I squashed up next to her on the armchair, and Dave passed round all the plates and napkins. The baby was sitting on the floor by herself, in woolly tights with grubby feet. She was banging a toy with her teething ring and making a racket, which she thought was funny. Nobody was paying her the blindest bit of attention.

Mattie's two boys were eyeing me suspiciously. They looked like wooden soldiers, sitting there all still and awkward. Eventually the taller one looked over and said we go to St. Simon's too. We've seen you there before. That surprised me, because I didn't recognise them at all, but then there's hundreds of kids at our school. And then he said my name's Steven and he's Gary. I'm the oldest.

"I can tell," I said.

He liked that.

Then Hayley, who was sitting on the carpet because it was such a squash, piped up that I hadn't been introduced to her girls yet.

"This is Amethyst and the little one's Ruby," she said, pulling the younger one towards her and straightening her frock.

They both looked little to me and I'd thought at first they might be twins, but they weren't. Both girls had wavy hair the colour of sand after the tide's turned, and a smattering of freckles like their mother. Neither of them would've won a beauty competition, and I thought – if I'd been their mother, I'd have saved those names for another day. They never sat still, not for a moment, and you felt exhausted watching them. The older one kept taking things off her sister, and saying she wasn't to have them, and the younger one, Ruby, kept saying that's not fair, I had it first. Then she'd look at her mother with wide eyes, like a koala, but Hayley wouldn't notice because she was talking, so Ruby would give her sister a pinch or a clout.

"They never stop squabbling," Hayley said, and my grandmother said you lot were just as bad, and Dave said they still are. Then all the women laughed and Karen sat down on the bean-bag, with Sonny in between her legs.

I watched her across the room for a while, talking to her older sisters and letting little Ruby fiddle with her hair and put it into plaits. She didn't look like anyone I could call my mother. She didn't feel like one either. I tried to work out what I'd inherited from her genes, rather than from my father's, but I thought – other than her curves and her brown hair – there wasn't much resemblance. Mrs Gayle told me later that I had my mother's eyes. I wasn't sure whether or not to be glad about that, seeing as they'd got her into a bag of trouble, and I spent ages that night looking in the magnifying mirror in our bathroom, to assess the truth of that opinion. I tried to make alluring faces into the mirror, but it made me burst out laughing. It wasn't me at all.

The morning of the wedding we got up dead early. I set my alarm clock because Lorna had promised she'd do my hair, even though it was her wedding day and, strictly speaking, it was her hair-do that mattered. Nobody else had woken up, so I decided to bagsy the bathroom before Aunt Nessa got in there. We all had sinks in our bedrooms, but my aunt wanted a bath every single morning. Mrs Gayle couldn't believe it. They must be squeaky clean in Canada, she said. Dad laughed and said he hoped they had big hot water tanks, because ours certainly wasn't up to the job.

256

A spot had appeared on my left cheek and I couldn't believe my bad luck. The steam made it flare up and go an angry red colour. Mark would be sure to notice. I'd been a state of nerves all Boxing Day, wondering if he was going to turn up, and Lorna asked me if I wanted to ring and check, but I said no way.

I only ran a shallow bath, because Lorna needed the water more than I did, but it felt good. I put in a few dollops of the bubble-bath Nicola had given me last birthday, which made the bathroom smell of lavender. I lay in that water for ages, twenty minutes or more, until I heard a tapping on the door and Aunt Nessa loud-whispering was I going to be much longer?

"Sorry Auntie. I'll be out in a flash."

When I opened the door, there she was, standing strangely with her thighs crossed over, and I thought – got my own back.

Lorna, true to her word, brought her cuppa into my bedroom and started work. She held the pins in her mouth while she was talking, and you couldn't help watching her in the mirror and hoping she wouldn't choke. She brushed and brushed, getting right through and underneath my hair until it shone. By the time she'd finished, it looked like I had twice the amount. Then she twisted it round and up, rolling the back somehow and pinning it as she went.

"That's fantastic," I said when she'd finished, and was holding a hand-mirror up behind me.

"It's come out even better than last time," she smiled.

"What time's the hairdresser coming for yours?"

"Half nine. We've got time for breakfast."

"Is that woman out of the bath yet?" I whispered.

Lorna laughed. "She'll turn into a prune."

We got the giggles then, and Lorna was trying not to lose her tea all down her dressing gown.

"Is Dad up?"

"He's coming round, slowly."

"Do you think he's happy?" I asked. I didn't say it to be unkind. I wanted to know.

Lorna's face straightened up and she said, do you know, Imogen? – I really believe he is, in spite of everything, and I said good. I'm glad.

My dress was made of stiff turquoise silk, just above the knee and quite straight all the way down, with short sleeves and an open collar. Cedric said it made me look like a grown woman, and Mrs Gayle said that was quite a dress for a fifteen year old. Her eyebrow went like a boomerang when she said that. Lorna assured me later, behind her back, I wasn't to mind because a grandmother never likes to be reminded how old she is.

I felt like the bee's knees, what with my hair piled up, strewn with diamond clips. I wore the same shoes we'd got for my party, because they did the job, and I borrowed Aunt Nessa to paint my nails for me, because Lorna was busy by then. We chose a colour out of my aunt's cosmetic purse. Mississippi Rose it was called, even though that was nowhere near Canada – because it didn't fight with my dress.

We were sitting at the kitchen table, looking like the dog's dinner, and my father was pacing up and down because it didn't take him long to get ready, and I figured he was nervous. Aunt Nessa's hand was as steady as a bomb disposal expert, she said, and Dad said he hoped we wouldn't be needing one of those on his wedding day.

"Have you got a minute?" Dad asked me, which was a daft thing to say, with us all sitting there like patients at the dentist. "Only I've got something to give you. Come through to my office, would you?"

More like a headmaster. I followed him through, thinking, I never get invited into Dad's office, me. I must be in trouble. But I wasn't. He reached up to one of his bookshelves and there, resting on top, was a small box wrapped in pink paper. He passed it across to me, looking shy.

"I was going to give this to you after the wedding, but perhaps it's better to do it here, just the two of us."

I pulled the bow and slid my finger under the paper. Inside was a leather box embossed with gold. I looked up at Dad and he nodded, so I opened the lid. Draped over the blue velvet was a silver locket on a delicate chain. The locket wasn't a heart shape; it was oval, and engraved with tiny leaf patterns on the front. I turned it over and saw this minute writing.

"Read it out," he said.

"To my daughter Imogen, love Dad."

The locket had a hinge along one edge, so I knew it would open. Inside the locket were two tiny photographs, one either side. One was of me, taken at my last birthday party, and the other was of Karen. She looked really smart in the picture, as if she was about to go somewhere special.

Dad was looking expectant and worried at the same time. The door pushed open, and Mrs Gayle was waiting in the doorway with one of her satisfied expressions, and I knew she wasn't one bit surprised about the contents of that locket.

I turned round, holding the chain so he could do it up for me.

"Thanks, Dad."

I kissed him on the cheek and he said I hope you like it, Imogen. I hope it's all right.

"It's grand, Dad."

And it was, because I knew straight away why he'd done it. I knew he didn't expect me to love her or anything.

We went back into the sitting room and waited for Lorna to come down.

"I thought the groom wasn't supposed to see the bride before the wedding," I said. "I thought it was bad luck."

"Well, seeing as we're all going in the same car, there's not much chance of that, Dad said. "Besides, we've had our dose of bad luck. Nothing else can go wrong."

"Have you got your flowers, Imogen?" Mrs Gayle asked, and I gasped and said oh bugger, and she said a bridesmaid doesn't swear. I reminded her I was a flower girl, not a bridesmaid, and Dad said fat lot of use I'd be without my flowers then, and we all creased up.

The road to Grasslands was all bends and curves. Luckily, it had turned milder and the frost had melted, which solved the problem of which coat to wear over my dress. I didn't want an old coat spoiling things. All the way I was worrying about Mark. I needn't have wasted my nerves, because when we turned into the drive, he was already standing outside his car, smiling. He'd had his hair cut, and was wearing a dark grey suit, and he took your breath away.

Mark walked over to us and held the door open for me.

"You look lovely, Immie," he said. "Like a movie star."

If I'd written the script, I couldn't have done it better.

He leant down and kissed my cheek, and I held my flowers to one side, so he wouldn't squash them.

"So do you," I said. "I'm glad you made it."

Cedric had arrived too, with his wife April in her fancy hat which made her taller than him. She was dressed all in green, and Cedric had a tie to match, and a smart grey suit. He looked odd, standing there with a woman by his side. I never could work out how she let him out every day of the week without complaining. But Cedric said she was glad to have the house to herself, and they had evenings, after all.

"Don't we scrub up well?" he said.

Then we all chatted about the weather, like you do, because the clouds looked thin and there was a chance the sun might put in an appearance, although it wasn't trying very hard. After we'd gone inside, Dad said I should sit with Mark once I'd finished on flower duty, and he winked at me.

"Are you sure? Am I allowed?"

"Tell him to save you a seat." Which was a funny thing to say, because we weren't exactly a crowd in the first place.

Mark and the others went into the back-room, where the ceremony was going to take place, leaving the three of us behind. I passed Lorna her bouquet and looked at her.

"You're the most beautiful bride in the whole world," I said. It didn't matter that she wasn't wearing a long white dress. I meant – for a middle-aged woman – but I kept that to myself.

"You've stolen my line," Dad said, and he leant down and kissed her neck a bit too roughly, in public, and I slapped him on the arm and said Dad stop it. And Lorna squealed and said yes, stop it Andrew. You'll spoil my hair. Honestly, Imogen, your father can be so embarrassing.

And some onlookers, who had nothing to do with our wedding, had disapproval written all over their faces, but we didn't care.

"Are you all right about this?" Lorna asked me.

And I said yes. Because I really was.